the
Possessions
of
Bartholomew
Ka

SUNSHINE KNIGHT

KNIGHT
INDIEPUB

For my readers, who believed in me when there were days I struggled to believe in myself. Especially my biggest fan, my husband, Steve.

AUTHOR'S NOTE

Each book teaches me something about the world and my perspective on it. This one had a profound change for many reasons. The first was the gut wrenching experience I had in writing the ending. Then the realization that the pain I felt, and the fear I had of facing that pain, had been making me sick for so many years. I'd been terrified to write this book because I had to focus on the very difficult issue of depression and addiction, both things unfortunately/fortunately have overshadowed my entire life. I carry my stress, my pain in my core. After two surgeries in two years to resolve the medical issues my stress caused, I still did not feel better. Until I finished the ending of this book. Then the healing began.

The second change came during re-writes when, Kelsey, one of my sensitivity readers said (in a very kind way) the draft she read had racist elements. In the book, I wanted to delve into the subject of racism, but I did not want to be racist as the author. So, began my spiral into getting uncomfortable and understanding my own racist biases. It's a hard pill for me to swallow, but it's getting easier. Now that I understand how I am and have been racist, I can truly work to change how I see myself and the impact I have on those around me. This book is the first anything where I wrote people of color and I am sure I did not get it completely right as I am writing from a white perspective. I cannot truly understand what it means to experience racism. I now know, I can (and have) experienced prejudice and discrimination. But I cannot experience racism.

The setting for The Possessions is 1984, a very different time than what we live in now. It was a time where dealing with race in a positive way was being "color-blind". Language was different, interactions were different. However, I hope the characters I created in this book are as true as I could possibly make them.

For those of you who want to explore your own relationship with racism, I highly recommend "White Fragility: Why It's So Hard For White People to Talk About Racism" by Robin DiAngelo. I have a lot of work to do, but finally I feel I am on the right path.

I engaged the assistance of several sensitivity readers as I did not want to publish a book without their help. I am grateful for Kelsey Kuehn for having such an uncomfortable conversation with me to begin with. Thank you to Carter Keegan for ensuring I did justice to Max. Thank you to Veronica Calisto, Mariah Evans and Merrily Talbott for teaching me more about how not to be racist and doing a final read to ensure I didn't misrepresent my characters of color. And a huge thank you to Jesús Arroyo -Moosey- for your willingness to always have the hard, uncomfortable conversations with me, even when we go years without talking. Thank you for laughing, teaching, and not judging (too harshly) this able-bodied white girl who has much to learn about the world.

POSSESSION
By Felicia Sabartinelli

You own the right to take me
use me, mold me until nothing exists but
fragments of bone and plaster.
A sculpted prize for your mantel. Just
something to leave behind for the next owner.

BARTHOLOMEW

Love ended in betrayal. Every time. I unconditionally devoted myself to Samantha and I believed she felt the same way. We were compatible! Except she was living and I was not. But when I found a way around our predicament, she rejected me. All I desired was for us to be together; for her to share eternity with me. Why could she not understand?!

Instead of accepting my proposal to share death with me, Samantha abandoned me, leaving me exiled and alone. It had been years since she and her two ninnies created some invisible shield. All because I beseeched her to love me as I deserved. Something my dead wife, Abigail, could also not bestow upon me. I fed her a hemlock salad on our twenty-fifth wedding anniversary. Samantha, however, slipped through my grasp.

Women were whores.

Before *Sam*, I believed the best thing about being dead was the mobility. I hid in daytime shadows and manipulated the minds of the living imbeciles who occupied my beloved Victorian home. They were my brainless playthings, doing my bidding.

Until her!

Over the almost one hundred years since my suicide, I remained imprisoned on this earthly plane for reasons I could not comprehend. Many of those years were spent inside my home in Stafford, Colorado.

It took me some time to educate myself about death, as there are no rulebooks for the afterlife. I could not walk through walls, or solid objects. But I could pass through the human body. My only explanation? The body is porous so my soul inherently understands how to inhabit one. I still could not comprehend why I glimpsed no other ghosts. I did watch for others. I supposed I could go into another house, one without impassable barriers. But then I might miss an opportunity if the whore let her guard down.

I wanted *my* house!

Rosemary Jensen, the horrid woman who lived across from my home, became an obvious—or more accurately, an *oblivious*—target and I used her body to regain some strength several times over the years after angry tirades drained me. After getting snagged the last time and being temporarily stuck while her thoughts rambled on about the latest piece of gossip, I avoided her altogether.

Crystals have an odd power. The right combination created a hidden barricade I could not penetrate. Those crystals prevented me from returning to the home I built with my own two hands. Crystals placed there by Samantha, her lover and the imbecile who helped maintain her gardens.

I had many regrets; not killing Sam remained high on my list. She would not listen to reason. If only she had accepted how important I was to her, then she and I could have returned to our home together. Instead, she survived my attack in the woods and after months adrift around Stafford, I finally found my beloved home. Not only had she not been pining away for me, she prevented me from even entering my yard. My love turned to hate. I now fantasize about wrapping my hands around her delicate throat, feeling the bones crunch under my fingertips, while she gasps for her last breath. Maybe I would loosen my grip enough so she could beg me to let her live, and promise me with her forked tongue she would love me and only me. Then I would choke the life out of her.

One day, I will get my wish. But only after I get back inside my home.

When I lived, I believed no matter how horrible the sin I committed in life, God would accept me and I would be forgiven if I prayed. This was false. Instead, rejection greeted me after my suicide. Sure, I poisoned Abigail and watched her claw at her own throat trying to breathe. A righteous killing. I should have been forgiven! God never sent me a chariot to reward me for my piousness in life, or even an angel to lead me home. Instead, He abandoned me, so I had to find alternative entertainment for my earthbound existence. Now I haunt the sidewalk outside my picket fence, watching the home I built and its intruders.

Sam made me a Beelzebub.

THE POSSESSION
OF LANIE SCHNELL

September 1984

BARTHOLOMEW

One afternoon when the sun burned bright and a few of the cottonwood leaves had begun to change from vibrant green to sallow yellow, two teen girls approached. They screeched at the top of their lungs, garishly enough to get my attention. Mostly, I paid no attention to those on the street—the living were a waste. I focused on the trespassers in my home. No one entered my yard with the exception of the whore and her two men. I never even saw mail delivered.

These girls would not shut up! Their singing sounded like cats being devoured by rabid dogs. Nothing in life was worth singing about.

One of the girls wore a tattered shirt and shredded jeans which showed more skin than was proper. Her long black hair hung down, greasy and tangled. Dark eyes looked like holes in her stark white face. The other girl, with curly, dark red hair and a purple skirt with a pink and white floral blouse, clashed with everything she passed. Her nose and mouth were disproportionately grotesque, and her light brown skin indicated she spent too much time in the sun. What kind of parent would let their child out of the house in either of those outfits? The girls would no doubt end up as street-walkers.

I turned my attention back to my home. The whore had returned from work a few minutes before and entered my house. Occasionally, I would get a glimpse of her shadow walking past a closed curtain. I sent her as much hate as I could muster in those moments, hoping she felt it, like tiny hammers pounding her flesh. I could not pass through the openings in the fence no matter how I tried, so hating her provided my only solace. Crystals, at least two feet tall, had been placed in each corner and the imbecile who instructed Sam on gardening and crystals came once a week to clear them of any debris. They had installed a gate across the driveway to match the picket fence. Holes had been drilled into each picket and small purple and black crystals were glued into them. The same stones hung from strands running the length of the porch railing. In the winter, the crystals were often the only things not covered in snow.

The weather was changing. In the mornings I could see the breath of the inhabitants of my house when they warmed up their cars. I often wondered if they thought of me. I hope she missed me, filled with regret for banishing me into the cold, alone and friendless. Lost in a world of isolation. Did the whore still dream of me? When she bedded her carpenter did she remember how *I* made her moan?

The two girls were now within a few feet of me. Their screeching had reached power-saw levels, reminiscent of the days when Samantha's carpenter drove me out of my home during their remodel. I stepped into their path to shut them up.

I collided with the girl with black eyes.

We fell to the ground.

The girls eyes were closed, so I could see nothing, only hear and smell. What curious sensations! It had been so long since I experienced life. The friend stood near us; I could smell her nauseating chemical perfume. I wished she would move.

I had passed through the living many times before, occasionally becoming snagged if they were angry or bitter. But now, after trying to pass through the girl with the black eye makeup, I could not get back out. I pushed against her human confinements with no success.

Torn between the sensations of living and wanting my freedom, I lay on the ground attempting to escape. The girl I occupied felt disoriented. I could hear her thoughts.

Why am I lying on the sidewalk? What was in the weed Mark gave me? Her confusion matched my own. Since I could hear her thoughts, did it also mean she could hear mine? I would have to remain cautious until I knew for certain.

After being and feeling nothing for so long, physical sensations felt so very strange. I could not hear what the red-haired girl said over the pounding of the heart, over the whooshing of air through the lungs. Pain pulsed through the arm from the scraped skin where the girl's elbow smacked the asphalt. I fought to leave the body, but I could not escape. I remained trapped. How did this happen?

I could see The Light of her soul attached to the muscles and tendons inside her body, from her lips, through her fingers, and down to each toe. There were multiple dark fractures around her heart, her stomach and in her skull, the opposite of lightning streaks in the sky. The cracks were not uniform in size. Some were several inches wide; one straight down her middle cleaved The Light in half. These were the areas I inhabited, almost as if my soul had split into pieces. I moved about freely between The Darkness, but I could not access the space where her light shone strongest—the left side of her brain, her right cheek, her fingertips, and her belly. None of this corresponded with any experience I had before. None of the bodies I passed through had cracks like this; I only saw The Light of their souls. Were these vacancies there for me to inhabit? Did they prevent me from leaving her body?

The girl's thoughts and emotions were amplified, almost like they were my own. I still had a sense of my own self, but she felt crowded, confined. No matter how hard she stretched her arms, her legs, she could not get the sensation of release. Comprehension escaped her and she wondered why a moment before she had been walking along enjoying her green cloud and now she had an ache in her rear and a scrape on her elbow.

Her friend shook us saying, "Lanie, Lanie are you okay?"

Lanie opened her eyes. The sun blinded us. I tried to close her eyes, but she blinked instead, forcing them open. The red-haired girl stood over us, her bright clothes an even more horrible contrast to her hair up close. She stooped down and her sickly-sweet smell overpowered us. We sneezed. What a strange and gratifying reaction. The tickling of the nose, then the relief.

"Do you need an ambulance?"

The girl closed her eyes against the brightness.

"Lanie!"

"No fucking ambulance," Lanie said. "They'll make me pee in a cup and I'll get busted. Give me a minute."

We scooted back to the fence and leaned against the white boards, head tilted back. I tried to keep our eyes open, but the brightness of the sun blinded us. We used our hands to shield our eyes. The friend picked up Lanie's purse and moved closer to provide shade. The sun created blood-red streaks in the friend's copious hair.

We sneezed again.

We, our, us? It had been a hundred years since I had referenced a body as my own. How easy to slip back into such vernacular. I poked around in the girl's brain, looking for memories like I had done when I briefly passed through Samantha all those years ago. The girl recently turned fifteen. Her father died in a car accident. Her mother...

I hate her, Lanie thought as I found an image of the mother at the edge of her mind. Her stomach clenched at the thought.

"Your perfume reeks, it's making me sneeze," Lanie said to the friend, motioning for her to move away from us.

"Are you okay? You gave me the perfume for my last birthday, because you liked it so much. I think I should get some help. You're scaring me." The friend shuffled her feet, scraping her rubber shoes on the concrete. A rock caught under her shoe and she moved it back and forth across the sidewalk. The noise grated on our ears.

If only we could sneeze out *that* irritation.

"I said give me a minute!" Lanie yelled.

"A minute? You've been out for at least ten," the friend said.

"What...what happened?"

"No idea. You stopped like you ran into a brick wall and fell to the ground. Do you know what you smoked?"

"The joint was clean. Mark gave it to me. He wouldn't give me anything laced," Lanie said.

The conversation disturbed me. Who in God's name did I occupy? A drug addict?

Mark wouldn't have laced the weed, would he? No, it's the same bag I smoked out of yesterday, it's fine. What the fuck happened then? Lanie thought.

Her vulgarity appalled me. Did all females speak this way now?

"Shit, I feel weird! My head is spinning like I drank ten shots of vodka," Lanie said, putting our hands on either side of our head to try to stop the spins. Lanie looked up and down the street. *Have I attracted attention? If I'd been out for nearly ten minutes, someone would notice.*

We looked across the street and caught Rosemary's eye. She held a broom in one hand. I wondered if she attempted to fly. The witch.

"Help me up," Lanie said, reaching for her friend.

The friend came over and grabbed both of our hands to pull us up. As we stood, I spun and we crashed to the ground again; this time we landed on our knees. The sting, the dull smack of bone on concrete jarred us both. The pain burst through our knees down to our toes. She broke us!

"Shit," Lanie said, looking down at our knees.

We had one small cut on our left knee and a white scrape on the right. I writhed with pain. How could Lanie be so calm?! She brushed the dirt off her skin and examined the cut. Tiny droplets of blood dotted the surface.

It isn't broken, only a little scrape, she thought.

I was not convinced.

Get up and walk if it's not broken, I told her, testing to see if she could hear my thoughts.

"Okay, okay, I can do this," she said.

Her response did little to clear up whether she could hear me. She could have been attempting to convince herself she could move, instead of answering me. Once again the friend reached down and grasped our hands. This time I held still and focused on keeping us up right. We staggered a few feet to the gate and I desperately wanted to see if I could walk through it in this new body.

Because of my hesitation, Lanie stopped. The pink and blue butterfly bushes Sam had planted soon after she kicked me out fluttered in the light breeze. Bees and hummingbirds darted around the flowers. If the friend would move away from us, I could smell the blossoms instead of her overpowering perfume. How much time had passed since the whore and her friends barred me from my home?

I filled all the vacant cracks Lanie's soul did not occupy, forcing them wider, shoving my soul down through her middle into her legs, out through her arms.

"Come on, let's go," the friend said, tugging at the back of our shirt.

I opened the gate.

"Lanie, what are you doing?"

I walked up the sidewalk, leaving the friend behind to gape at us.

"You are seriously freaking me out," the friend said.

I ambled past the tourmaline and amethyst, smelling the sage and juniper bushes as I passed. Smells were everywhere—some assaulting marigolds, others subtle butterfly bushes and fragrant sweet peas.

I walked right up the stairs of the front porch.

The now solid porch, stained dark brown to match the trim of the house, no longer splintered with rotting wood. The strands of crystals hanging from the porch roof were useless. I reached up and flicked one so it swayed in the sun, sprinkling light across the dark stain. The two rocking chairs were still in place, straddling the living room window with a small spindly table between them.

The friend ran up the sidewalk to us and whispered, "What are you doing? Come on!"

She tugged at the back of our shirt, but I shrugged it off and knocked on the door. A few moments later Sam answered. Her long brown hair was pulled up, emphasizing her neck. Leather sandals with ties circled up her ankle to hide beneath her long skirt. The blouse she wore covered half of her arms and showed very little of her decolletage. She stood inside the wooden screen door, a look of confusion on her face, then joy lit up her eyes. Did my appearance somehow show in the young girl's? She seemed happy to see me. I ached to caress her cheek, to squeeze her throat.

"Lanie, Stephanie, what a surprise! What can I do for you?" Samantha pushed the screen door open, and I noticed simple gold wedding rings on her left hand. She married the disgusting carpenter. Her mother's rings had been moved to her right.

"Um, hi Ms. Blaine," Stephanie said, shifting her gaze back and forth from Lanie to Samantha.

I showed her the skinned elbow and knee, but I could not form the words to ask her for aid. I forced my way up to Lanie's mouth, but realized I had not spoken for almost a hundred years. I did not know how to control the tongue, the lips. I had "walked" the entire time I had been dead, so the motion seemed to come more naturally now. Speaking felt much more intricate.

"Do you need a band-aid?"

I nodded. I now had the perfect excuse to get inside my home.

"Sure, come on in." Sam held the door open. Then she hollered, "Hello, Rosemary! Everything's fine. She just has a scrape." Sam waved to her, then motioned us inside.

Ecstasy mixed with regret filled me as I walked across the polished pine wood floors. My fireplace had been restored; the pink and white tiles were no longer tinged yellow from the cigarette smoke of a previous tenant. Her carpenter had stained the banister, all remnants of paint removed. I turned to the right and went straight to the kitchen, sitting down at a new butcher block table, with a bench lining the wall and two chairs opposite. The ceramic tiles made a checkerboard pattern on the floor and the countertops were polished black granite. Sam kept the original cupboards I had crafted, but they were painted glossy white. The memory of being here when they remodeled the kitchen came back to me. Brian had helped Sam while the carpenter moped, until Brian had an *accident*. If I had known what would transpire after killing Brian, would I have gone through with it?

"Have you been here before, Lanie?" Sam asked, interrupting my thoughts. I shook my head.

"Hmm...you sure know your way around," she said.

I sat at the kitchen table. Stephanie stood next to us shuffling her feet, refusing to sit. Lanie felt confused. She could not remember how she got to the kitchen. Her soul fought mine for control, forcing me out of her head, down into her throat. I watched Sam pour us glasses of water, then she disappeared up the stairs, her footsteps fading as she climbed.

"What are we doing here?" Stephanie whispered. "You're going to get us in trouble."

"I don't fucking know," Lanie snapped. "I'm going home."

She tried to stand, but she could not move her legs as I still controlled them.

Lanie's confusion and fear allowed me to gain control once again. I forced my way back up into her head.

Sam walked in with a first aid kit and tended to our cuts. Her pure white fingers felt like the petals of a peony flower, cool and soft and silky. I grasped one of Sam's hands in our own. I slid our fingertips up and down Sam's palm.

"Did you hit your head, Lanie?" Sam asked, a cross between mortification and worry on her angelic face.

I shrugged and looked at Stephanie to see if she knew. She had the same shocked look on her face as Sam did. She shook her head.

"I...I don't know. I turned around and saw her on the ground," Stephanie said.

Samantha stood and put her fingers on Lanie's head, searching for a bump. Closing our eyes, I reveled in the sensation of her touch. Until Stephanie kicked us in the leg.

"I don't feel any bumps or see any scrapes," Sam said.

"No, I...uh... I don't... I mean. I don't think I hit my head. Just my knee and elbow," we said, our words tripping over the other while Lanie's soul pulsed in and out inside her head.

I could not understand why I felt such love and attraction for Samantha. She ruined my existence. I hated her? So I thought. But simply being physically close to her, inside my home, gave me such comfort. My feelings confounded me.

Sam stared at us. Her blue eyes searched our face. The intensity in her gaze made me wonder again if she could somehow see me.

"Lanie, are you high?" Sam asked.

Lanie's stomach flipped and knotted. She looked at Stephanie with wide-eyed paranoia.

I felt Lanie's consciousness pressing against mine, getting stronger. Her soul pushed me down out of her head once more and attempted to fill our legs. We needed to leave before Lanie said something to reveal her confusion. We tried to stand but our power struggle created a jerky motion with one leg pushing to stand and the other staying bent.

"I'm not feeling well. Maybe I'm coming down with something. We should go," Lanie said after I relented control. I would practice speaking when Lanie and I were alone. We stood together and I slid to a vacant corner in Lanie's mind, an ugly place she kept hidden.

The memories she kept locked away perplexed me. They were blissful. Roller skating in the kitchen with her parents laughing and encouraging; her dad teaching her to ride a bike. Walks around the neighborhood at dusk, her mother making up silly stories about how the snapdragons came to life when no one saw. It seemed her father's death had turned the happy memories painful.

We were outside now, stomping down the sidewalk. Stephanie followed.

"Lanie, I can help you," Sam yelled.

Footsteps on the porch had us walking faster. The two girls argued in hushed whispers until they stopped outside the fence.

"Why did you drag me in there?" Lanie whispered. "So I could get caught? I know you hate that I smoke, but don't be a fucking baby and get me busted."

"Whatever Lanie," Stephanie said. We hurried away from her. And from Sam.

"You might want to lay off the drugs, though, if it's going to turn you into a bitch!" Stephanie yelled at our backs as we stormed off toward home.

SAMANTHA

Lanie's vacant, glassy eyes reminded me of my own looking back at me in mirrors over the years. Her eyes reflected loss, pain, emptiness. Hate. And why in the hell did she touch me like she did? I could explain the loss because I'd heard her father died a few years before in some kind of accident, but the way she touched me creeped me the hell out. It felt slimy, like Jim Hasting's treatment of me when we met all those years ago.

Stephanie paused outside my fence, staring after her friend. I hesitated before joining her on the sidewalk, outside the safety of my yard. My hands flitted up to the amethyst and tourmaline necklace around my throat—a gift from Brian before his death, his attempt to protect me from Bartholomew.

Bartholomew took away my independence, replacing it with fear and uncertainty. I never returned to the wildlife reserve. I never put the top down on my convertible; I didn't even roll my car windows down to feel the wind through my hair. Crystals hung from my rearview mirror and were tucked in the seat and door pockets. I never went on walks through the neighborhood. I wanted my freedom, but I didn't know how to get it back. I wanted to live in peace without a demon haunting my life.

I opened the gate and stepped beyond the safeguards.

"What's going on, Stephanie?"

Stephanie's dark brown eyes were clear, focused. They still showed innocence, unlike Lanie's. Although, she looked like a caged bird, ready to take flight as soon as she had an opening. I didn't understand what happened. They'd both been helpers in my first-grade class when they were in sixth grade.

They had been straight-A students. Besides being a little chatty, they were really good girls.

"I don't know. She tripped over a crack. Maybe she hit her head. I didn't see."

"I heard you say she was high," I said.

Silence.

"Stephanie, how often is she like this?"

Avoidance.

"I might be able to help."

She shuffled her feet, still not responding.

"I'm no stranger to drugs. I know you're sober."

"It's just pot. It's no big deal."

Normally I would agree. Pot helped me cope. Still helped me relax occasionally. But Lanie was so young.

"Lanie couldn't stand. I think that's a big deal," I said, trying to keep any accusation out of my tone.

Her gaze dropped to the sidewalk.

"Look, if you ever need to talk, or if Lanie needs to talk, I'm here. Sometimes life is tough and it helps to have someone other than a parent to talk to."

No response. I looked down the sidewalk, not seeing any sign of Lanie.

"Hurry and go find your friend. Make sure she gets home okay."

My heart hurt to see so much pain and despair in Lanie's eyes, so much helplessness in Stephanie's. I watched her dash down the street. A feeling of disquiet and...fear settled over me as I watched her walk away. I needed to get back inside the fence.

Instead of going inside like I should have, knowing from my friend Max's reports Bartholomew watched me and the house, I sat on the porch waiting for my husband, Alex, to arrive home. I felt brazen, determined. There was no sign, no sense of Bartholomew, but this was nothing unusual. I hadn't sensed him in six years. My courage would fade, the fear would creep back in, but for now I basked in my daring. During times like these I wished I could see him like Max or Alex's uncle Brian could. Even with the amethyst and tourmaline jewelry, Max could see him. The crystals prevented Bartholomew from getting close to them and it blocked his thoughts from theirs. For me, without the jewelry I could only ever hear his thoughts or feel his emotions. There were rare occasions when he physically touched me. The thought made me nauseous; bile rose in my throat at the memory of him saying he lay with me in the last weeks before he tried to kill me for the third time. If I could see him, at least I would know whether he stayed far enough away not to hurt me again.

Over the years Max continued helping me garden, making sure the crystals remained in place and uncovered. Some days his white-blond hair would catch my eye as I walked by the living room window. Other days he knocked so we could sit in the rockers and talk. Max was autistic. Some days he felt overstimulated and wanted to be left alone, so I let him lead on whether he wanted my company. I always felt better with him around, because he could see Bartholomew. Max's reports had been the same over the years: Bartholomew could not get back in, but he said Bartholomew's image had begun to fade. I hoped it meant his soul weakened.

Stephanie would tell Lanie I asked about the drugs. Maybe Lanie would feel safe talking to me again. She'd talked to me before in sixth grade—I watched a boy knock Lanie to the ground a couple times. She got up and brushed herself off each time, but she never said anything. The third time I saw it happen, I pulled her aside and told her some boys didn't know how to show affection, so they thought behavior like pulling hair or shoving girls was acceptable. She told me he'd been shoving her since the first day of school, no matter if she tried avoiding him or not. I brought the boy out into the hall with Lanie and told him the same. He blushed and left her alone afterward. Maybe I earned her trust enough then for her to allow me to help her now.

Rosemary finished sweeping up, then sashayed across the street to my yard, the bulk of her hips causing her skirt to swish around her legs. The white in her gray hair glinted in the sun. I'd tried to give her crystals to wear without telling her why she needed them, but I never saw her wear them. She never mentioned any odd interactions, so I assumed Bartholomew steered clear of her. I had hoped the newness of me would have worn off over the years, but she still popped over on occasion. Of course these days she discussed her own woes instead of everyone else's.

"That poor girl fainted outside your fence? I didn't think it was hot enough for heat stroke."

Lanie fainted? I thought she tripped, I thought.

"Maybe she didn't drink enough water," Rosemary continued. "I get light-headed some days when I forget to drink."

She still carried the broom she had been using to sweep the sidewalk. As often as she swept these days, I wouldn't think there'd be a speck of dust to be found. She sat down next to me, uninvited, typical Rosemary style. She brushed her hands onto her apron, smearing a light coating of dirt. At least she never bothered us when we were inside.

"How's Jim?" I said, changing the subject.

Her doughy face dropped and she reached across the table with a sun-spotted white hand to clutch my arm. "He still calls her, you know," she said.

I gently slid my arm away from her and stood to put some space between us. I didn't want to comfort the woman. I knew who Rosemary referenced as she often complained to me about Jim's obsession with his ex-wife. For the life of me I never understood why Jim would cheat on his wife with Rosemary if he loved his wife so much.

"His ex-wife?" I asked.

She nodded, and tears pooled in her eyes. I felt little compassion for Rosemary after the shit she put me and Alex through, but it'd been six years. She took Jim Hastings, the bastard, in after his wife threw him out for cheating on her with Rosemary. Every once in a while I would do a check-in with myself. Did I feel guilty for exposing them?

Nope. Not one bit.

"I take care of him, make him three home-cooked meals a day, with freshly baked muffins and cookies. Still he won't say 'I love you' when I say it to him. But every time he hangs up with that...that...woman, he says it."

I tried to keep the smile off my face because I felt sure she didn't want to say "woman." But Rosemary pretended to be too polite to call her a bitch.

Alex arrived home, interrupting our conversation. I was grateful. I could handle Rosemary in small doses. I could not handle an in-depth heart-to-heart.

"Well, speaking of taking care of men, I suppose I'll get back so you can take care of yours," she said and hurried off the porch. I could see Alex in the cab of his truck waiting, watching. He tolerated less from her than I did these days, which made me laugh. He'd thought she was a harmless, sweet lady when he and I first met.

My stomach still flipped with excitement when his red Chevy truck pulled into the driveway each day. He drove the same truck he had the first day I met him; the day I interviewed him to remodel the house a little over six years ago. It now had a small scratch on the passenger side where he'd scraped it with a ladder. His black hair had a few small streaks of gray, and I blamed each one of them on his abusive father. Daniel passed away two years ago from cirrhosis of the liver. Even though he stopped drinking after Brian's death, the disease still caught up with him. After the diagnosis, he started drinking again and didn't stop. He died within three months.

"Hey," he said, walking up the front steps. I stood to greet him with a kiss. His Irish heritage gave him a unique beauty. Light olive-colored skin, bright green eyes, and black hair. Some days I couldn't stop staring.

"What are you doing sitting out here?" He looked around the yard, a bit of panic in his voice.

"Waiting for you. We can go inside."

After Alex took his tools to the back porch, he joined me on the over-stuffed couch inside. Two Tiffany lamps on either side of the couch lit the living room, gifts to myself after the completed remodel. They didn't provide a lot of light in the dim room. *Mood lighting*, Alex called it. We used applewood and sage in the fireplace, so those smells lingered, clinging to the fabrics in the room. The photograph of me swinging between my parents when I was little sat on the fireplace mantle next to one of Alex and Brian in front of Alex's house after they completed the build. Our angels watching over us. Alex didn't want a picture of his dad. I'd asked him about it, but he hadn't figured out how to forgive him yet. Several mismatched votive candles were interspersed with the pictures, and white twinkle lights twisted up the banister. Since I didn't want Bartholomew spying on our life, I never opened the curtains. I did what I could to make the living room cozy, now my favorite room in the house.

"Okay, so what's wrong?" Alex searched my face.

"How do you know something's wrong?"

"I've been able to see through your mask for years."

I propped my bare feet into his lap then started to tell him what happened. He automatically started rubbing the soles.

"Wait, I remember them from a few years ago because you were so fond of them, but I don't know which girl is which. Who was high—the one whose dad died or the one whose dad is Black?"

"The one whose dad died."

After I finished talking he said, "I'm sorry," and gently squeezed my toes.

"How do kids become so lost, so quickly?" I asked. "I don't understand."

"You forget, it's not just kids. You know how people become lost: trauma. For kids it's combined with not knowing how to deal with it. It's not so hard to get lost; the hard part is finding our way back."

I looked at Alex's face, searching, almost expecting to see Brian sitting there.

"How'd you get to be so wise?" I asked, with a smirk.

"Trauma."

Lying my head back on the arm of the couch I said, "Yeah."

We'd both seen our fair share of traumatic loss, which caused somberness to penetrate our lives. It seemed we rarely laughed anymore.

First my parents' death, then Alex's uncle Brian died in a horrible car accident, then Alex's father. I'd only known Brian a few months, but his genuine kindness left an imprint on my life. The loss of Alex's uncle hit him harder than his own dad's death. After Brian's funeral, Alex pulled inward for a few months. We'd sit for hours and not say anything.

He never drank alcohol to cope, for fear of turning into his father.

I dreamed of Brian regularly after he died. Not the Brian I had known, with a weathered tan, wrinkly face, and white beard. He looked young, a lot like Alex did now with shiny black hair. He always wore a red flannel, along with his toolbelt, the initials *BK* burned into the hammer pouch. In the dreams, sometimes he was simply there, sitting next to me or Alex while we went about our lives in the dream. Sometimes alone, sometimes with my parents. The more time passed since his death, the harder it was for me to remember what he said in the dreams and the more infrequent they became. Now it seemed he stopped by to let me know he still watched over us. I missed him less and less, but when a Louis Armstrong song randomly played while I shopped, or on the rare occasion on the radio, my breath would catch.

When I moved home after Bartholomew's attack, I moved from the third-floor loft to the room with the window seat on the second floor so I didn't have to climb two sets of stairs. The attic once again sat empty.

After a few weeks of Alex and I attempting to sleep in separate houses, he moved his clothes and tools into my house and I didn't object. We never really made the decision for him to move in with me, it sort of just happened.

Over the years, Alex mentioned having children once. I expressed my fear of being able to keep them safe from Bartholomew; we had a hard enough time making sure Alex, Max, and I were safe.

Alex bought my excuse. And I lived with the heavy guilt of lying to my husband about the back-alley abortion I had when I was eighteen that caused irreparable damage to my body. If I thought about it too much, the not telling Alex part, I felt physically sick.

I looked over at Alex. He'd fallen asleep. His hand had stopped moving and rested on the top of my foot. I let him snooze and watched his breathing slow. It put me at ease being next to him. He made me feel safe.

BARTHOLOMEW

As Lanie and I hurried away from Samantha, I picked up foreign terms from her brain—*freshman, pot, joint, dude, MTV, bunk*. None of them held any meaning for me. I needed to learn the current vernacular to remain hidden. If Samantha discovered me, she could end me. Somehow.

Lanie lived in a small, squat, brick house behind a two-story complementary Victorian; I presumed it had been servants' quarters in the past. We walked down an alley to access the house. Neither structure had been kept up, except for the neatly mowed grass, but unruly hedges separated the two houses. Tree limbs grew low and haphazardly, creating treacherous walking conditions. We ducked under a crabapple tree near the back of the house, and the small red globes popped and squished under our shoes.

We slowed when Lanie saw her mom's car parked in the short driveway next to the front door of the house. Hate, then guilt bubbled up from deep inside her stomach, making the acid churn. Both hate and guilt were familiar emotions to me; the physical pain they caused was not.

Pop doesn't upset my stomach, so why does interacting with my mom make me feel like I want to puke?

I pushed up into Lanie's brain, sliding through the streaks of void, searching her memories again, and found what I sought. She believed everything wrong with her life occurred because of her mother. Lanie blamed her mother for her father's death because her mother had fought with him before he left. Then, instead of using his life insurance to ensure they could keep their home, her mother spent it on an extravagant funeral. They had to move into the miniscule four-room house they now called home. Lanie often dawdled after school, even going so far as to get after-school detention some days, in the hopes of avoiding her mother between jobs. Some days it did not work.

Of all days she has to be home, why today? she thought.

What an odd, ungrateful girl, I thought.

What do I have to be grateful for? she replied.

So she *could* hear my thoughts, like I could hear hers. Useful.

We walked past a small, surprisingly neat garden with penny flowers and catmint without a single weed, a contrast to the hedges and trees. Maybe the mother only had time to tend one garden, not an entire yard.

Ugh! I don't know why she had to plant that shit. It smells like cat piss, Lanie thought.

So vulgar!

What's with the self-reprimands all of a sudden, Lanie? she wondered.

Idiot child.

I felt our face frown at my remark, but we continued on.

Inside, the living room had floral-patterned furniture, much too large for the space. The couch and a matching overstuffed chair spanned an entire wall. A blanket and pillow were neatly stacked on one corner of the couch. Lanie's mother sat on the other end reading a book. Her mostly gray hair was pulled into a ponytail; only traces of black could be seen. As we entered the house, she set down the book and stood to greet Lanie, an expectant smile on her face. She wore gray slacks and an off-white blouse, her bra clearly visible through the thin fabric.

Lanie ignored her. As we passed, I noticed we were a taller version of the mother, but with no gray hair. And the mother wore no heavy black eye makeup. We continued past her to a room behind the living room. A sweet smell greeted us when we walked into her room, not pleasant like the butterfly bushes, but a syrupy and invasive smell that shoved its way up our nose into our brain. Large pictures of masculine-looking women covered the walls of Lanie's room, their mouths hung open in silent screams. Their lips smeared

red. No wonder the girl was broken—she lived in a room wallpapered with anger and despair. How could she live like this?

We lit a small packed cone on a saucer—the culprit for the smell—then moved an end table in front of the door, lifted her mattress, and pulled back the cover of the box spring. Hidden below was a small bag with one half of a rolled cigarette, a round cardboard tube stuffed with a piece of clear sickly sweet-smelling fabric, and a lighter. Sitting at her bedroom window, we smoked, exhaling through the tube out the window. Did she really think blowing the smoke through the tube would cover the smell?

It smelled and tasted unlike any tobacco I had ever tried. *It tastes like...*

Sunflower seeds, she replied as she exhaled. Of course, she thought she spoke only to herself.

This is better, she thought once her head returned to the haze it had been in when she and I first collided. *Why does everything have to be so intense? I don't know why Stephanie got so mad—she's the one who dragged me into the stupid house. She blames me for everything, like I have to twist her arm to hang out with me.*

As she smoked and sunk into self-pity, her soul receded and I spread out, filling every empty space. Drugs and liquor were the devil's tools, so I never consumed them when I lived. This would be a new experience for me and I wondered how they would affect me.

I suppose I didn't have to call her a fucking baby. But she acted like one! And I could have gotten into so much trouble. Ugh!

I went deeper into her recessed mind to find the source of her pain and discovered more memories with her parents. They walked hand in hand behind her as she ran through the grass, spinning and laughing. I watched as Lanie bent to pick a dandelion flower gone to seed and made a wish for a new pair of roller skates. She turned to see her father embrace her mother and kiss her slow and sweet, stroking her mother's cheek as the kiss ended. Her mother smiled up at him, their eyes locked until Lanie squeezed between them. She thought maybe she could physically feel the adoration she watched them share. Her heart swelled with the belief the three of them would always exist like they did in that moment.

Fast forward. I observed as Lanie learned how to maneuver her feet with wheels on them. Her mom stood at one end of the room, her dad at the opposite end. They pushed her back and forth between them as she learned to balance on wheels.

Then, in another memory, the phone rang. The scene, vivid in Lanie's mind, was like watching a picture show. It was the evening of November 15. Her dad had been gone for several hours after her parents' fight. The fight where Lanie took her mother's side because she feared the snow. The fight where her father had stormed out of the house, where Lanie ran out the door after him and asked, "When will you be back?"

He responded with silence as he glared at her and slammed the car door.

The ring of the phone shattered the silence. Lanie and her mother had been curled up reading. Her mother almost didn't answer, but the answering machine never clicked on, so the trilling had gone on and on. The phone sat on a wooden spindle table with a crocheted lace doily behind her dad's recliner. Her mother finally answered with her normal, false cheer.

Then silence.

Lanie remembered the silence. It triggered her to look up, to see white shock on her mother's face, a stark contrast to her black hair. Her mother stood immobilized, the phone pressed to her ear so tightly it seemed she wanted to shove it into her brain. Then Lanie's mother collapsed. Her legs buckled, unable to hold the weight of the news. Lanie heard the voice on the phone saying, "Hello? Mrs. Schnell, Mrs. Schnell!"

Lanie rushed to her mother, picked up the phone, and told the man on the line her mother had fallen. He sent an ambulance.

Lanie's mother woke a few minutes later and dragged Lanie into her arms.

Her mother did not speak. She held her daughter and screamed into the top of Lanie's head. Muffled vibrations rattled Lanie's brain. Tears soaked into her hair. Her mother's hug hurt—it was too tight, too constricting. Lanie cried, unsure why. She'd never seen her mother so utterly devastated.

Later, after the doctors sedated her mother, Stephanie and her mother arrived. They told her the news of her father's death. Lanie felt numb from then on. Life became unreal, like it had happened to some other girl and Lanie simply went through the motions of living. The joy she felt at new experiences no longer invigorated her. A mundane flatness consumed her.

Six months after her father's death, her mother sold their house because she couldn't afford the payments. The new house didn't have a hardened blue paint smudge on the beige carpet where Lanie's father let her use fingerpaints while he watched the Bronco game. The new house didn't smell like the sweet tobacco he smoked. There was no room in the new house for the dining set where they laughed and joked over dinner. Instead, Lanie and her mother sat in the kitchen at a small metal folding table room enough for two. A white tablecloth, hand-painted with bright red roses, covered it. Lanie often refused to have dinner with her mom; punishing her mother for her father's death made Lanie feel better.

Tears dripped down her selfish cheeks as she fell into sleep. I had difficulty understanding the wallowing brat's despair. People made their beds, regardless of their age. And this moronic girl was plenty old enough to make good decisions.

My wife, Abby, had been fifteen when she made the decision to marry me. I had courted her for three years, taking her fishing, even though I abhorred the activity. It was not proper for a young lady to enjoy fishing, so to earn her trust, I helped her hide it from her parents. I even let her wear my breeches so as not to soil her dresses. Abby knew she would not find a more virtuous man, even if her parents influenced her decision. What a lovely young girl she had been. I often wondered what turned her into an adulterous whore.

Lanie snored softly. In death, I never slept. I did not yearn for sleep.

My soul slipped into her legs and I moved them to the side of the bed. Would Lanie wake from the movement?

I waited.

No response.

I rose slowly, shifting inside, expanding until I opened our eyes.

Still she slept.

SAMANTHA

The phone rang, interrupting our peace and quiet. Alex stirred. I groaned as I stood to answer it.

"You know, you could ignore it," Alex said, trying to wrangle me back down to the couch.

"Does it make it worse that I know I could?" I replied after escaping. My bare feet drummed lightly on the hardwood floors as I walked to the kitchen where the phone hung just inside the doorway.

"No," Alex said.

I smiled, even though he couldn't see me, then picked up the white cradle receiver and said, "Hello."

"Heya gorgeous, it's Kimber."

"Hi lovely! What's up?" I said as I sat on the bottom step of the stairs in our foyer.

"I wanted to call and make sure you guys are still on for Friday. I'll go to the store tomorrow."

Friday night, Alex and I had dinner plans with our group of friends. Eight of us met at a different house each month for dinner and games. This week we were meeting at Kimber and Colin Jones' house. Kimber was one of my closest friends. She married Colin a few years after we became friends. Colin was the cop who accused Alex of abusing me when it had been Bartholomew. Dinners were fun, but occasionally strained because of his suspicions.

"Of course! We wouldn't miss it," I said.

"I assumed, but you know me. I've got to be certain," she laughed. "How was work? Still avoiding the other teachers?"

"You know, it's not the same since you left to teach middle schoolers." Something occurred to me then, like a lightbulb. "Question for you. Did you have Lanie Schnell in any of your classes?"

"I did, actually. She was in my seventh grade social studies class the first year I transferred. Super bright. Why?"

"She fell outside my house today and came to me to get a band-aid. Is Colin nearby?"

"No, it's his night to make dinner. Why? Did you do something illegal?" she teased.

"Promise you won't say anything. I know how he can get a little obsessed. Not that being obsessed is a bad thing!" I recovered, not wanting Kimber to feel I disliked her husband. She laughed and I breathed a sigh of relief.

"He's intense for sure, but I promise, I won't say anything."

Alex brushed past me and mouthed "shower," then caressed the top of my head and went upstairs.

I continued my conversation.

"Lanie was high. It shocked me because I had her in sixth grade and she had been so outgoing, friendly. Smart, like you said. Today she seemed...lifeless."

Kimber got quiet for a moment, perhaps processing what she heard me say.

"You still there?"

"Yeah. Sorry. She had a rough go of it after her dad died, but I never saw her high."

"I don't know if I should be worried or not. Or even if it's any of my business. She just happened to fall outside *my* house."

"She's a good kid. It's rare to see empathy in thirteen-year-olds; they're mostly self-absorbed," she laughed then continued, "But she had it. Everyone genuinely liked her. After her dad died, she withdrew. She even tried to push Stephanie away. Stephanie never let her, though. They have one tight bond, those two." She huffed a little then said, "They made me envious."

31

"What should I do? Anything?"

"I don't know, Sam. I guess all any of us can do is be there when she needs us."

"What if she never asks?"

Kimber went silent again. "I'll call Olivia, her mom, to check in. She and I connected. I can say I've been thinking about them."

"Thanks, Kimber. I don't know why, but something feels unsettling about the whole situation."

"I'll let you know Friday what I find out. Okay?"

"Yeah, okay," I said, then we hung up.

Kimber and I taught first grade together for a few years. She met Colin about a year after she and I became friends. Colin hadn't realized I was the "Sam" Kimber had been telling him about and he had slipped my mind since Bartholomew's attacks stopped. I sensed he still knew Alex and I hid what actually happened, but not having a hospital visit in six years made him a little less suspicious.

I pushed Colin, Kimber and Lanie out of my mind and went to find Alex. I hoped I'd find him naked.

I knocked on the bathroom door and he immediately told me to come in. He stood in the middle of the room, pulling a comb through his black hair; a towel around his waist. Water droplets still clung to his chest.

"You missed some," I said. Squeezing between him and the sink, I ran my tongue up his neck.

"And you're overdressed," he said. "But, I think we can manage."

He slid my skirt up, raked his fingers up my thighs, and had his way with me on the bathroom counter.

BARTHOLOMEW

A clock on Lanie's bedside table said 5:47. I wondered how long the effects of the drug would last.

Lanie dreamed of her father carrying her to bed after falling asleep on the couch listening to her parents play cribbage. In reality, I ambled around her room. In her dream, she pretended to sleep.

Moving Lanie's body fascinated me. I manipulated her arms to pick up a brush and run it through her tangled hair. I sat at her dressing table and wiggled her toes, unsuccessfully attempting to move one at a time.

Lanie slept on.

Her room was small, maybe eight feet square and crammed with *things*: a vanity piled with lipsticks, perfume and eye makeup; a calendar hung on the wall with giant black X's. I assumed the X's meant the days had passed, which meant today was September 10, 1984—a few days after my 118th wedding anniversary.

I continued my exploration of the small room. Academic awards hung on the walls, interspersed with the over-sized pictures of women. The words on the pictures were all misspelled—Ratt, Mötley Crüe. As I scrutinized them, trying to decipher why the words were misspelled, I realized something more horrific: The pictures were not of women—they were of men. Shirtless young men with long teased hair and bright red seductive lips! Musicians with gaping mouths, black and silver cylinders gripped in their hands. Understanding dawned on me—this girl could not be helped if these were the role models she surrounded herself with. A drugged-out, demented girl like her was a waste of life.

I sat at the vanity looking through her belongings, searching for something redeeming. Brightly colored ribbons stuffed one drawer, hiding a small pocket knife with the initials *H.S.* engraved on the side. Another drawer contained photographs, many of her father and mother. Camping photos, zoo photos, park photos. They looked like a happy family.

The light outside faded to darkness, and still we sat. Lanie slept while I explored the girl's life. I found a pink journal with a fake lock buried beneath the ribbons. The confessions written inside disturbed me as much as the photographs of the half-naked men on the wall. They told of her first drug experience, a party one month after her father died. The night she had premarital sex simply said, *I had sex. It was weird.* I shook my head in disgust. How would the world ever evolve if these were the types of children who would one day lead, who would one day teach?

An odd pressure developed in the girl's belly. I ignored it and whispered aloud so the girl would not wake. I formed the words with slow deliberation, rolling the L's, bouncing the D's off the roof of my mouth. I taught myself once again how to speak.

"*Today was an amazing day. I met Mark. He has the best weed.*"

Strange, the date on the entry was one week after the party. How quickly she became an expert.

"*He's so sweet and kind and mature! Not like the brats I go to school with. He showed up after school with a single, long stem pink rose. I might be in love.*"

The pressure in her belly turned to pain. I pushed on our stomach, trying to make the pain stop. It persisted.

The next entry whined about her mom.

"*I can't believe she complained about me being ungrateful! Me? She's lucky I still even live in this house with her after what she did! I hate her! I hate this house! I hate my room! So what, she has to work a lot. She has no idea what I'm going through. Dad dies and all she does is work. She leaves me all alone and complains when I won't have dinner with her on her one fucking night off. She should have thought about what life would be like without Dad before sending him off alone. If she hadn't fought with him before he left, he'd still be here. I won't go to that stupid shrink. I don't care what she says. No one is going to tell me how to feel, especially some over-educated jerk who has no idea what it's like..."*

A black smudge on the page smeared the last few words of her absurd rationale. At the bottom of each of the most recent pages, written in shaky ink were the words *I want to die.*

Maybe I could oblige her. Once I learned how to master this new body and used it to get back into my house, of course. Did her death wish allow me to so easily possess her?

The discomfort in our belly became unbearable. I relaxed the body and immediately regretted the action. Something warm and wet spread out around our bottom. Urine.

And then Lanie woke up.

Confusion filled her mind, reflected in the mirror we sat in front of. She looked down to see her darkened pants. Then I felt Lanie's shame.

"Oh my God!" she said, trying to stand. She told our body to move, but our legs were heavy and refused to stand. We would have to get more coordinated or people would wonder.

Why am I sitting?! Did I sleepwalk? she thought.

We stood and looked down at the dark stain between our legs. She hadn't peed her pants since she had been a small child. Mortified, she stepped away from the mirror so she didn't have to look at her body, and stripped off the sodden clothes.

I had not inhabited a body in almost a hundred years. The physical sensations felt strange, unfamiliar. If she had not been high, maybe she would have been more conscious of her body's needs.

God! This has been such a weird day, she thought.

We walked to the door, pulled a robe off the hook, opened her bedroom door, and listened. No noise came from the house. We crept across the hallway to the bathroom while listening for any sound from her mother. Lanie hid her soiled laundry at the bottom of a wicker hamper.

We stepped into the shower and Lanie set the water as hot as she could stand it, to the point of pain. She tried to burn her shame. I receded away from her nerve endings in a struggle to escape the excruciating pain. Her skin felt hot and swollen. And it itched.

At last, she turned the temperature down. She relaxed. Then I relaxed, filling The Darkness, letting the streams flow over our head, onto our shoulders. An affusion of sorts. She washed with lavender shampoo and I thought of Sam when she bathed. This must have been how she smelled.

What the hell?! Why am I thinking about Ms. Blaine naked?! Oh my god, am I turning lesbo?! She shivered in disgust and smacked the side of her head saying, "Out, out, out!"

The repeated smacks rattled me. I did not understand the girl's use of self-punishment. A word bounced around our head.

Masochrist? Masochist? I can't remember exactly what those seniors said.

What on God's Green Earth are you talking about?

I think it means someone who likes pain, she thought.

Then you are most certainly one of those.

We were having an internal conversation and she had no awareness she spoke to anyone but herself. I needed to be cautious with my thoughts until I knew how I could use the girl.

Lanie's consciousness grew stronger, pushing me deeper into The Darkness. The more she relaxed, the more she crowded and squeezed until The Light grew stronger. Ignoring my panic, I shoved against her, using everything I had until I exhausted myself and succumbed to her pressure, feeling small and insignificant in the center of her belly.

Would I become nothing?

She finished showering then dressed in a hurry, once again avoiding mirrors. She despised her body, a reaction I had not anticipated. She felt disgust remembering how a group of boys in school had acted earlier in the afternoon, asking her to lift her arms up to the side. Then they all broke into hysterical laughter because as she lifted her arms, they could see her breasts through the loose holes of her sleeves. Her budding breasts only caused gawking from the boys and even in the privacy of her own room, she crossed her arms over her chest to cover them.

Were all teenage girls as ashamed of their bodies as she was? Such a strange, dark little creature.

The clock next to her bed now said 7:52 p.m. Two hours felt like such a small interval to learn and control the body. I would need to find another means to extend my time.

After Lanie dressed, she started laundry so her mother would not discover the urine-soaked pants. She surprised me when she added her mother's clothes to the wash basket. If she hated her so, why would she help her mother? Lanie's stomach growled as she pressed start on the machine, so we went in search of food.

A plate covered in tin foil rested on the counter with a note. *Made your favorite. Seemed like you had a rough day. I'll be home late. Love, Mom.*

Somewhere deep inside she felt sad—not that she had any awareness of the feeling. Before she could process the emotion, it turned into resentment, into anger. Her mother did something kind for her and it made her despondent, so of course her logical course of action turned the feeling negative.

She couldn't even come and ask me if I wanted to have dinner with her. She thinks leaving me a note is a way to communicate. Boy, her parenting skills need some work.

But she sat at the table in her pajamas, the only light coming from the oven hood, and ate her favorite meal. Alone.

I forced my soul to get as close to her mouth as possible to experience taste. Mashed potatoes, gravy, salt and pepper green beans, and a deep-fried pork chop, a little warm even. The pork chop would have been better without something called ketchup, but for my first meal in this new lifetime, I found it delicious.

While we ate, Lanie thought about the times she sat around the dinner table with her parents. Her brain spun out of control. She tried not to remember the good times—those memories hurt. The more she fought against them, the more the memories found their way to the forefront of her thoughts. She remembered the dinner right before her dad died when he told them about the strange letter he received from an aunt he had never met and the phone call preceding it. He'd been so excited because he never knew his dad or that he even had an aunt. His contagious excitement caused her mom's face to light up. The intense memory hurt—the ecstasy she saw in her father and her mother's delight, filled with happiness for him. When had she last seen her mom smile?

Well, if she was home more, maybe I'd have time to notice, she thought, turning the empathy she felt into blame.

No wonder I possessed the girl so easily. Anger and bitterness filled her soul, turning it into something viscous. Even I could be an optimist...at times.

She finished eating, then went back to her room where she layered on makeup, jeans so tight she had to lay on the bed to zip them up, and a T-shirt. Then she hurried out the door and walked down the road, under the glow of the streetlights.

As we walked, she wondered what her dad would think of her if he could see her now. Her soul receded at the thought, giving me more space. So, something besides marijuana expanded The Darkness.

She pushed the thoughts of her father out of her mind and focused on Mark. He helped with the pain. He helped her become numb.

I have to get home from Mark's before Mom gets off work, she thought. *Last time, she almost caught me.*

After six blocks, she paused in front of a small clapboard house with a dirt yard. A couch with stuffing protruding from both arms sat perpendicular to the driveway. A gigantic car with a peeling vinyl top was parked behind the couch. The torn screen on the front door of the house flapped in the cool September breeze.

I had assumed this Mark would be a school friend, but a grown man with an odd-shaped beard opened the door. He had a bald chin and dark brown hair longer than Lanie's. So strange! The man greeted Lanie by shoving his tongue down her throat. Repulsed, I filled every space of Darkness to disentangle us from the man, but Lanie pushed what she believed to be her conscience to the back of her mind.

Chill, Lanie, she thought. *This is no big deal, besides he makes me feel grown up.* She pushed against my soul. Oddly enough this time, The Darkness, not her golden light, forced me down into the pit of her stomach. *He has good pot. Pot to help me sleep*, she thought.

They stepped inside the door and he slid it closed behind her. The living room had one couch, a lamp without a lampshade, and a television. Piles of cans, crumpled papers, and paper sacks littered the floor. A large tube as tall as the couch smoldered near one of the arms. He clasped her hand and guided her to the filthy couch. We felt his dry, cracked hand in ours, the fingernails greasy black. She recoiled internally at his kiss, her soul contracting, pulling away from her lips. It continued sliding away from the places his slimy fingers touched. I pushed to fill the spaces her soul left so I could prevent this atrocity from going any further. But once again, The Darkness solidified.

Oh, please God, what Hell have you put me in? I will do anything if you make this stop, I prayed, for the first time in decades, and continued to force my way into the void her soul left.

We pulled away.

"What's the matter, Lanie? That time of the month?"

"No. I don't know what's wrong. I'm feeling like I shouldn't do this."

"Hey, you showed up at my door. It's no skin off my nose, but you won't get any more pot from me unless you pay for it. One way or another."

She "purchased" her drugs with sex?

I don't have the money to buy it, she thought. Once again she understood my thoughts, making me unsure of which ones she could "hear" and which ones she could not. I had to figure out this puzzle.

Get a job!

She sat for a minute and he leaned over to kiss her once more. The Darkness pulsed and grew while The Light shrank away from the man's touches, confounding me once again. Why had The Darkness become so powerful? I pushed against her, but she resisted me. He pulled her shirt over her head, then sat back.

"You are beautiful," he said.

Her soul lit up, reconnecting to tissue, to muscle, forcing me into the center of our body. She forced me to give in to her repulsive hormones.

Please God, make this stop!

Lanie did not respond to my plea; God did not stop the horrendous act.

They would stop at kissing, right?

Right?

Right?!

I am a man! This cannot be happening!

His strange beard scratched her cheek, and she reached up to itch her face. We could taste the man's rancid breath, reminding me of burned flesh, transporting me from one atrocious act to the childhood memory of another.

It was dinnertime, one of the few moments in the day when my father paid me any mind. I was seven. Three of my six siblings sat at the table with us; the other three were old enough to live elsewhere. They spent so little time with us I could scarcely remember them. Three brothers later perished in the war. Only one brother survived, as well as my two sisters. I resembled none of them—I had brown hair like my eyes; their eyes were all blue like my father's or green like my mother's. My pale skin burned in the sun, whereas my siblings' and parents' complexions turned a golden brown. My brothers teased me about this, calling me Mother's Little Abomination.

My mother treated me with kindness, kept my secrets. Kept me safe from Father's wrath. As a small child, I could do nothing to please him and received whippings for the slightest infractions—placing my elbows on the table, bringing in a cracked egg for breakfast, forgetting to call him sir. I confided in my mother and she soothed my tears and tended to the welts left by his belt.

She passed me the white gravy in a delicate gravy boat for my mashed potatoes, and her smile warmed my insides. I felt loved by her at least.

Then my father spoke: "Mother tells me you have a new friend."

My stomach dropped. She promised me she would not tell him. I looked at her, but she would not meet my gaze.

"After you finish your dinner, you and I will speak. Alone," he said.

No longer hungry, I wondered if he would use the belt, a switch, or his hand.

I pushed food around my plate until he roared, "Stop playing with your food! Eat!"

I did as he instructed. Forcing the food into my mouth, making me gag.

"We will have a good crop this year. Tom says everything is going smooth," my father said without any of the previous trace of malice. Dinner continued on in this way as I shoved each bite down my throat.

Father stood before the dishes were cleared. I turned to see Tom, my father's slave driver, standing behind me. His Black face looked grim.

"Come," Father said, laying his napkin across his plate. I followed suit, then did as he asked.

Instead of taking me to his study where he doled out my punishment, he continued past the room and out the doors into the cool spring air. Gravel crunched beneath my shoes. Cicadas sang in the distance. I could not see much farther than the light of the porch, but a large shape loomed beyond the edge of our circular drive. As we got closer, I could hear whimpering.

No. No. No!

"Father, please, I won't speak to him again, I won't even look his way."

"He refused an order from me this afternoon, Bartholomew," he replied.

I imagined the order he disobeyed was he that did not stand up straight, or did not jump as quickly as Father required. Still, I did this. I was responsible, because I knew Father, I knew his wrath.

As we got closer, the dark mass took shape: a pyre. Scattered among twigs, logs, and branches were my wooden blocks, the rocking horse I had shared with my only friend, my wooden rifles.

I tugged at my father's arm, trying to get him to stop walking. He backhanded me. I flew across the gravel, and sharp rocks cut into my forearm. Through the tears in my eyes, I saw him smile.

"You will learn one way or another. Slaves are not friends."

Tom would not look at me; he only stared at the boy strapped to a board protruding from the center. Did my father make him do this? Why would he have complied? I witnessed my father whip the slaves, gleefully, never asking the overseer or Tom to bestow punishment. But this? This order should have been disobeyed. In my small mind, I knew this. My father was wrong.

My father took my hand and for a moment, I thought maybe he had seen reason, changed his mind, refused to burn my friend alive. Until I felt the box of matches in my hand.

"You did this, so you will light the pyre," he said.

"No! No! No!" I cried. I begged. "Please! I promise, I won't do it again."

"You will light the fire, or you will join him."

I looked up at Father, confused.

"You are a product of your mother's whoring. I know this. She knows this. You are not mine. So toss the match, or I will solve two problems tonight." His calm voice seemed as if he spoke about the weather, not about ending the lives of two children.

"No," I said.

My father laughed, then dragged me to the pile. A scream broke the night and I heard footsteps running.

"You will not take my son!" my mother called out. She reached for me, pulled me away then took the matchbox from my father, lit the match, and flung it into the pyre. The gunpowder lit up the skies and for the first time I could see Andre's face. Tears stained his innocent cheeks.

His screams filled the night, then I smelled his burning flesh. Above his screams, I heard Father's laughter.

My screams joined Andre's and Father laughed even louder. I turned away, but my father yanked me from my mother's arms and forced me to face the flames. I closed my eyes, but that did nothing to block out the screams, nor the stench of my friend's life ending.

I became aware of my current surroundings, the rancid breath close by, bringing me back to the present. I tasted marijuana. The girl's soul had shrunk again. I shoved my way into The Darkness. Anger, revenge filled my mind—for the memory of my father or the heinous act I had just been forced to endure? I forced the memory out of my thoughts and looked around the room, wanting to escape. A prophylactic lay on the floor near Mark's feet, oozing semen onto the carpeted floor. The girl would pay for her indecent act. If I could figure out how to get out of this body, I swore to never possess another female.

Tuesday morning, Lanie's mother woke her saying she made breakfast. Lanie moaned and complained about the early time. She dragged herself out of bed and threw on the closest clothes she could find. I tried to stop her from putting on clothing with holes showing her bare skin. I could not.

Lanie sat in front of her vanity and said, "Tut, tut, looks like hell," combed out her hair, and went downstairs. Her mother sat, legs crossed with her back to the wall at the small kitchen table drinking coffee. She looked at ease. The kitchen smelled heavenly! Fresh brewed coffee, smoky bacon, buttered toast. Were the smells worth the torture the girl put me through the night before? No, but maybe the taste of bacon was...

A plate of eggs, bacon and toast waited for Lanie.

"What, no coffee for me?"

"You know where the coffee pot is, Lanie."

Her mother stayed seated. Lanie felt slighted. *I have to make my own coffee? Spoiled rotten child*, I thought.

Guilt filled her belly.

"Lanie, you could say thank you. I just thought we could have breakfast together before we both had to rush out the door."

"Thank you," she mumbled.

"I don't have to work at the diner tonight. Want to go see a movie or something?"

"Sure."

Lanie sat down and sipped her coffee. I felt it had too much sugar, not enough cream. Would her tastes always be so different from my own or could I manipulate her somehow to adjust them? The bacon and eggs, however, were divine! Just enough salt and pepper and the hickory seasoning on the bacon tasted delectable. I savored breakfast, even if the ungrateful child I possessed did not.

Before Lanie finished her breakfast, her mother left for work. She worked as a secretary for a real estate office during the day and apparently a waitress at the Stafford Diner in the evenings and on weekends. Lanie's mother kissed her on the forehead and wished her a good day.

"I love you," she said.

"I love you, too." Another mumbled response from Lanie.

After breakfast, Lanie rolled three joints and smoked one, burning our throat in the process. We coughed and sputtered, then smiled. *Oblivion is my favorite mindset*, she thought. We put the other two in our backpack, then hid the rest of the marijuana beneath the box spring cover.

Before we left the house, I tested my influence over the girl. Instead of turning to go down the alley as she wanted, we strolled into the yard and lay on the dew-kissed grass for a few moments. We did not mind the moistness, especially since I had power again.

Unsure how to find the school, I did not attempt to control her. We walked to Stephanie's house first. The girl wore bright purple sock-looking things up to her knees, black skin-tight pants, and a multi-colored top that hung below her coat. Her bushy red hair was tied up with a purple polka-dotted ribbon. And I thought *Lanie's* attire was awful...

We continued on past my empty house and paused. No cars in the driveway, tempting me to venture inside the gate and see if the doors were unlocked. To see if I could sit in my home undisturbed, but Stephanie grabbed our arm and moved us toward school.

Stafford High School was a prison-like two-story, red brick institution with small windows. *Letting in light must hinder the learning process.* I did not think there were enough intelligent females to warrant such a behemoth building, but as we stepped inside, realization dawned on me. Girls attended the school with the boys. Even more appalling, youth of all colors intermingled with the white students. They cajoled and laughed together, smacking one another's hands. Embracing! I attempted to avoid touching them, as they were certain to be disease-riddled, but the halls were too crowded.

We stopped at Lanie's locker and looked at the gadget for quite some time trying to figure out how it worked, fascinated with the numbers and dashes on the dial. Stephanie bumped us out of our stupor when she said we were going to be late to history.

History? This could be interesting. I let Lanie lead again. She spun the dial, then grabbed a couple of books and we were on our way.

We waited until the bell rang to enter the classroom. Stephanie gave the teacher a nervous smile; Lanie held our head defiantly.

"I asked you girls not to wait until the bell rang to take your seats. Another round of after-school detention then?"

Lanie ignored him. Stephanie said, "I'm sorry, Mr. Arnold."

Lanie slid into a desk at the back of the room. Stephanie sat next to her.

"Good morning," the teacher said.

I wondered if he knew Samantha. She probably had him in her bed, too.

"Good morning, my ass," Lanie whispered. "It would be good if I were still in bed." Lanie glanced over at Stephanie to see if her comment garnered a reaction.

Mr. Arnold glared in Lanie's direction, then nodded to a boy who entered the classroom. Stephanie smirked at Lanie and she puffed up with confidence.

45

Such an odd relationship. Lanie pretended to be indifferent to everyone around her, including her friend, yet she still wanted Stephanie's approval.

"I hope you did last night's reading on the events leading up to the Civil War."

I perked up. The Civil War? My era. Would the teacher talk about the atrocities the North committed in forcing their laws on the Confederate States? Would he tell stories about how the farmers were forced to pay their slaves or face prosecution, and how in paying the negroes, the farmers struggled to survive? Would he teach them about the war crimes committed by the North and how Lincoln broke federal law to go to war with the South?

"Can someone tell me what events led up to the Civil War?"

A boy in the front row blurted out that the war started because Lincoln freed the slaves.

The teacher shook his head no.

Then Stephanie countered also without raising her hand, "The war started because seven states seceded from the United States over the election of Abraham Lincoln."

"Raise your hand, but you are correct. South Carolina led the way for the other states to secede in 1861. It wasn't for several years after the war started when Abraham Lincoln issued the executive order..."

We looked around the classroom. Posters of historic people and events covered the walls. A globe sat on a small table next to the teacher's desk. A green chalkboard covered the wall behind him. Next to the chalkboard hung a poster showing the very man responsible for destroying my beloved Confederacy with Hero written across the bottom.

Hero? *Hero?* He was a criminal!

"...and he is one of the greatest American presidents in history."

We stood. Lanie struggled, lost somewhere in her haze, unsure why we were now standing. She wondered why she cared what the stupid teacher even said.

"What kind of dribble are you teaching here?" I said.

"Excuse me, Lanie. I'd prefer if you raised your hand before you spoke."

"Raise my hand? That is the injustice you notice? You are preaching about how the biggest criminal in history is a hero and you want me to raise my hand?" I threw my hands in the air in frustration.

"You're being disruptive to the class, Lanie. Please sit down and we can discuss why you think President Lincoln was a criminal."

The whole class stared at us now. Lanie tried to sit. *Why can't I just shut up and sit down? Why won't my body work?* she thought.

"Lincoln was nothing but a nigger-loving criminal who deserved to be shot!" I yelled, banging our hands on the desk. Gasps echoed from the students closest to us, and then a giggle from somewhere in the front of the room. How were such idiots allowed to teach impressionable children? "And you sir, are a moron if you think *hero* is a title he deserves." I pointed to the poster behind him.

Where'd all that come from? Lanie thought, struggling to get control of herself. She pushed to the front of her mind. It did not work. The Darkness permeated her soul. I controlled her now.

"Out! Get out of my classroom! I'm tired of your disruptions."

I did not move. The teacher stormed toward us, grabbed our arm, and escorted us to the principal's office. He didn't give us a chance to grab our backpack. We struggled against the man, clawed at his hand while he dragged us down the hall past the metal lockers. We tried to bite him, but he twisted our arm behind our back and pushed us in front of him. The girl did not have the strength to fight him.

We sat in the rigid plastic chair in the principal's office waiting for the principal to get ahold of Lanie's mom. He sat in a plush leather chair.

What was this world coming to? Teaching vulnerable minds Abraham Lincoln had been a hero? He decimated my country and plunged it into severe poverty! I fled as soon as I could to make a home far from his reconstruction. When I heard John Wilkes Booth shot him, I celebrated with a toast to his eternal damnation.

A few minutes after the teacher left, he came back holding Lanie's joints in his hands.

Thirty minutes later, Lanie and her mother both sat in the principal's office.

"Mrs. Schnell, we are very concerned about Lanie's behavior. She's consistently late to Mr. Arnold's class and she's disrespectful. Finding drugs in her backpack is even more disconcerting."

"Why hasn't anyone said anything to me about this before? She's a straight-A student, so I had no idea she was having issues. Lanie?"

Lanie stared at the ground.

"Lanie?" her mother said again.

"He doesn't like me. No matter what I do."

"Now Lanie, Mr. Arnold is a professional and he treats all of his students fairly," the principal said.

Bullshit, she thought. *Jack came in five minutes after Stephanie and me and didn't get so much as a reprimand.* I wondered why she kept this to herself. Instead, she shrugged.

"Mrs. Schnell—Olivia—I realize this has been a tough couple of years for you both, but schooling is important and Lanie needs to take it seriously. Her behavior is unacceptable. We don't tolerate racism."

"My racism?" Lanie said, glaring at the principal. "What about Mr. Arnold's? Ask Stephanie how he treats her."

How he treats Stephanie? I wondered. *The girl is white.*

The principal ignored Lanie's accusation and said, "For bringing drugs onto school property, she is suspended for a week."

"A week?" Lanie yelled. "You're afraid I'm not taking school serious and you're suspending me for a week? How does that help me?"

"There are consequences for your actions, Lanie."

We slumped in the chair. Her reaction confused me. A week without school? What fun she and I could have! My house would be empty during the day, we could go exploring...

48

The car ride home felt awkward and strained. The Darkness shifted and pulsed with Lanie's anger, but the effects of the marijuana had worn off, along with my control.

"I don't know what you were thinking today, Lanie. I know you and I have had a rough go of it, but your actions were inexcusable today. How do you think Stephanie felt hearing you say what you did? You can bet Stephanie was hurt by what you said." Olivia paused for a minute, her hands gripped the steering wheel.

Why did I say those things in class? Lanie thought. *I felt like it wasn't even me, like I was dreaming. I would never use the n-word. Maybe I do need to stop smoking. These past few days have been so weird!*

The n-word? I knew this modern society I lived in had changed for the worse. Slaves no longer knew their place. I'd seen it in the guests my previous tenants had allowed to eat at their table, in the language they used. And didn't use.

Olivia sighed, then said, "You never told me Mr. Arnold was a bigot. The principal wasn't much better. To be clear, just because I acknowledged they are bigots, doesn't excuse your behavior."

How could Lanie's mother accuse those men of being bigots when they allowed boys, girls and all variations of students to attend school together? All of it confounded me. Then to be censored for simply speaking the truth? The Yankees winning the Civil War destroyed more than my home, it seemed. They destroyed the entire country and a man's ability to speak openly and honestly.

When Lanie still didn't respond her mother said, "You're grounded for two weeks. No phone, no friends over, no going anywhere."

"But Stephanie's slumber party is next Friday! You promised I could go!" she yelled.

"Do not yell at me. One, you are going to have to do some groveling to get Stephanie to forgive you. Two, maybe if you miss out on something you like, you'll be more respectful."

Nothing we said warranted Stephanie's forgiveness.

Lanie stewed and turned her back to her mother then mumbled, "Doubtful."

When we arrived at the house, Lanie jumped out of the car, slamming the door behind her, and stormed to the front porch. Her hands shook as she unlocked the door. She stepped inside, and slammed it in her mother's face. Lanie did not wait for her mother to walk in the living room. She hurried to her bedroom, where she slammed the door. Again.

I expected Lanie's mother to go back to work, but she stayed home. Lanie hid in her room, but she could hear her mother's muffled voice making phone calls. The phone calls made Lanie nervous.

After forty-five minutes, Lanie's mom burst into the room without knocking, her face red and puffy.

"Get out!" Lanie yelled.

Ignoring Lanie, she started pulling out drawers, dumping their contents on the floor. Pictures, ribbons, clothes, like she was building a pyre...

My soul shivered.

Lanie sat up in bed and turned her back to her mother. Tears slid down her cheeks as her mother wreaked havoc on her room.

"Where are you hiding the rest?!"

"What?" She snapped her head around and glared at her mother. *She won't find the rest*, Lanie thought.

"Where are the rest of the drugs?"

"They didn't belong to me. I had them in my bag for a friend."

"Don't lie to me. I've ignored your glassy eyes thinking you were tired, believing you weren't sleeping well after...after the accident. But now I know."

"They weren't mine!"

Her mother stormed over to us and slapped us across the face. Stunned, unsure how to respond, Lanie's thoughts raced. *Did that really happen? How could she?!* Her mother had never hit her before. Lanie's cheek burned and when we touched it, we could feel the outline of her mom's fingers.

Lanie's mother looked as shocked as Lanie felt.

"Oh, God. I'm sorry. I'm so sorry," she said, reaching out to stroke Lanie's hair.

Lanie flinched, then knocked her hand away.

"Don't lie to me," her mom whispered. "You have an appointment this afternoon. I don't know how to help you deal with your grief. I should have forced you to go two years ago; maybe things would be better for you now."

"I'm not going to see some stupid shrink."

"You will. Or there will be consequences."

What could she do to me?

Oh, Lanie, people find ways, terrible ways to torture others, I thought. *Especially parents.*

After Olivia left, Lanie cried herself to sleep. Again. Forcing me to listen to her. The Darkness spread through the girl's body, extending almost as far as it did when she was high. I tried to move about the room, but every time I made the slightest attempt, she would wake. Yesterday, I could do whatever I wanted. The drugs gave me the ability to control her. So, for my situation to be bearable, Lanie could not be sober.

After several excruciating hours, Lanie's mother came into the room. I could not see her, only hear her. Even opening Lanie's eyes caused her consciousness to stir.

"Lanie, come on. It's time to get up," she said, sitting on the side of the bed. Her mother stroked the spot she'd slapped with tenderness. I felt Lanie stir, but she pretended to sleep. We both wondered if the welt remained.

"There's no mark." Lanie's mother must have been thinking the same thing.

"Do I really have to go?" Lanie said, opening her eyes.

"Yes. I found someone else. You don't have to go back to the jackass we tried before."

"Aren't they all the same? They only want to make me cry."

"No, honey," she said, still stroking Lanie's hair. "Most therapists want to help. He wanted to sell books."

"And we didn't need a book on heroin addicts."

"No," her mom laughed. "We certainly didn't."

Lanie sat up and leaned her head on her mother's shoulder. Her mom put her arm around Lanie.

"I've missed this. We haven't cuddled since your father died."

Love swelled up inside of Lanie and her soul expanded, crowding me. What would become of me if this broken girl healed? If The Light filled her body completely? Would it push me out—or in a manner of speaking, suffocate me? Could I escape? Her love didn't feel good. It felt as if a five-hundred-pound person were laying on me. Lanie did all the breathing and living, but I panicked, pushing back with everything I had.

She is manipulating you into talking to the shrink. They are all pretentious know-it-alls like the last guy. They'll brainwash you into believing they're smarter than you.

Maybe they are *smarter than me*, she thought.

The second car ride of the day felt even more miserable. Would I blink out of existence if Lanie's cracks healed closed? Would I become nothing? The thought terrified me. And it made me realize, possessing a fifteen-year-old girl might be better than the alternative. As long as I had control. I would have to convince her to continue smoking pot.

We arrived at a professional-looking building and I rode in an elevator for the first time in my life. The sensation of weightlessness gave me the sense of being free of the body I possessed, but it scared me to be inside a room that moved of its own accord.

I felt torn. I wanted to be free of this body, but I wanted to get past the barriers the whore put up. Lanie's body would help me obtain my goal of returning to my home. After, Lanie would be useless. So how did I get Lanie into the house and then get out of her body? Did she need to die for me to escape?

If I died, I'd be with my dad. I wouldn't hurt anymore.

My thoughts seeped into Lanie's brain. I should not be surprised, but I needed to remember the transmitter between us went both ways.

If I died, my mom would be alone, she thought.

She doesn't need you, Lanie. She would be free to live her own life without the burden of an ungrateful teenager.

Lanie looked over at her mother, who filled out paperwork. Dark circles lined Olivia's eyes. Wrinkles crossed her forehead and fanned out from her eyes and mouth. Her face scrunched in concentration, making the lines even more pronounced. Guilt filled Lanie and I had room to expand.

The memories I now saw were recent ones, right before Lanie's dad died. She and her mother had a spa day. Manicures, pedicures. They both had red highlights added to their black hair. Lanie remembered her mother's shiny and healthy hair. Now it hung down past her shoulders, dry and lifeless.

All she does is work to provide a home for you and food for your plate. It's a hard life raising a child, I thought.

Am I really as ungrateful as she says I am? she wondered.

Yes. An ungrateful burden.

By the time the shrink called us into her office, I had stretched from the small patch of Darkness in her center all the way down to her fingertips and her toes.

Much better.

A petite woman, with a much too welcoming demeanor greeted us. After seeing the kids in Lanie's school, I felt relieved to see a white woman, even though I distrusted her kind smile and truthful eyes. What would she convince Lanie to say? A spider plant hung in front of the only window. Pictures of the woman and her ugly family were on the desk behind her. The whole lot of them were unworthy of being publicly displayed.

"It's nice to meet you, Olivia and Lanie," she said, offering her hand for Lanie to shake. "I'm Sara Raddison. Call me Sara."

Lanie refused to shake her hand, crossing her arms instead.

Seemingly unfazed, the woman motioned for Lanie and Olivia to sit on the couch. Then she sat in an office chair with wheels and looked over papers on a clipboard, her expression unreadable.

"You've both had quite a rough go of it, it seems. Why don't we start today by telling me what prompted you to reach out?"

"Well," Olivia said, "Lanie got suspended this morning because she had an outburst in class and the teacher found pot in her backpack. I think she's been smoking for some time now. I just didn't want to believe it."

Lanie sat upright with her hands clasped between her knees, refusing to relax or let her guard down. She glared at them both.

"Her father died in a car accident almost two years ago and we tried to find a counselor then, but we didn't find the right fit. I think he did more damage because now Lanie doesn't want to talk to anyone. I don't know what to say or how to help her. I feel like I say the wrong things and make everything worse. I'm walking on eggshells."

Olivia paused, looking to Lanie to say something. Lanie crossed her arms and looked away.

"Lanie was always so sweet and caring before her father died. People would comment to me about it. She genuinely cared about others—she volunteered at the nursing home every week. Since his death, she hides in her room. She maybe goes to the nursing home once a month. Instead, she zones out in front of the television and she pushed everyone out of her life except for her best friend Stephanie. Well, until today—"

"I hate that you're telling our secrets to some shrink who you don't even know," Lanie interrupted.

"I'm sorry life has been hard for you, Lanie. I'm actually not a shrink. I'm a licensed clinical social worker."

"So you're not even educated enough to help us," Lanie snapped.

"That's not correct. I have a master's degree in social work. I chose to provide resources for people to find their own ways to cope with the problems life throws at them, instead of prescribing drugs or treatments. It's a different approach."

"The last shrink put my mom on lithium. She got weird."

"Drugs help some people, but for others, stress management and tools to deal with triggers are more effective. Do you journal, Lanie?"

Lanie didn't answer.

"I wish you would talk to someone, Lanie," Olivia said. Lanie looked up at her and glared. Olivia turned to the therapist and said, "Sometimes I see her, the normal Lanie. Believe me, I was no picnic as a teenager, my mother will be the first to tell you. So I know Lanie is pushing normal boundaries sometimes when she lashes out, but drugs? Her withdrawal from life and friends? Those things worry me."

Still Lanie remained quiet.

Olivia sighed, then said, "Lanie, do you want to talk to Mrs. Radisson alone?"

"Please, call me Sara. It is up to you both as to whether you want to talk to me separately or together."

Do not say anything, Lanie, I thought.

Lanie obliged. *I'm not going to talk. No matter what they say. They don't know anything about what I'm going through.*

Her defiance made me feel something... Pride? Maybe the girl had more strength than I gave her credit for.

"Maybe it will be better with just you and Lanie," Olivia said. "Honey, I'll be right out in the lobby."

Lanie glared at her mother. I felt a part of her wanted her mom to stay, another part said it did not matter. *Sara* would not get her talking.

Olivia left the room and Sara set the clipboard on the desk. "I want to make sure you know everything you tell me is confidential. By law, I can't tell your mother. I can't promise you'll feel better, but I'll try to help. I need you to talk to me, though. I'm good at reading people, but I am no mind reader."

Keep quiet, Lanie. She is not to be trusted.

Except her eyes say something different, especially when she smiles, Lanie thought.

Sara watched us for a moment, then said, "Nothing you tell me will shock me. I've been a LCSW for almost twenty years and I work with a lot of teens and families."

What if she can help?

Sara picked up the clipboard, read a few lines, then put it back down and waited. "Your mom listed music as something you enjoy. Do you have a favorite band?"

"Not really."

"I heard a really good song on the radio the other day, 'Purple Rain,'" the therapist said.

Lanie volunteered, "My mom took me to see the movie. She didn't know what it was. But she thought it would be a cool mom thing to take me to see an R-rated movie."

"The character in the movie had a pretty troubled life. Didn't he? Do you feel your life is as bad?" Sara said.

Lanie kept quiet.

"I've heard a couple other songs from the movie, but 'Purple Rain' is definitely the most powerful. Every time I hear it, it catches me right here." Sara pointed to her chest.

"Yeah, it's a good song."

"Want to tell me about the pot?"

"It wasn't mine." Lanie realized she answered too quickly, too defensively. *Shit.*

"I hear that a lot. Like I said, everything here is confidential. How long have you been smoking?"

Lanie looked at the floor. She didn't want to trust the woman. I did not want her to trust the woman. She had just gotten to the point where I could move with less constriction, and now this woman attempted to get her to open up again. I would not have it. I pushed up against The Light, trying to reach the muscles of her mouth.

"I tried it at a party about a year ago," she said looking up, then said, "but I'm not an addict. I don't smoke all the time or even every day," she lied. "Only when…"

It's partially true. Sara doesn't need to know everything. But maybe if I give her a little bit of honesty, she'll cut me some slack, Lanie thought.

Shut up! I thought, forcing myself up. Maybe I could burst through The Light as though it were a thin membrane.

"When things get a little difficult to deal with," Sara finished.

"Yeah."

"It's okay to miss him. It's okay to be angry, sad. There's a mourning process you need to let yourself go through so you can heal."

At the woman's words, Lanie's soul lit up and spread, engulfing The Darkness I inhabited, pushing me down into her belly again.

"I don't want to heal. I don't want to forget him."

"Healing doesn't mean forgetting him. It means remembering him and loving him, but in turn, living your life again and not letting the hurt become calcified into angry hate. What's your favorite memory of your dad?"

Do not answer her! She will twist everything you say, make you look crazy. She's lying about not telling anyone. See, she's writing everything down!

"I don't have a favorite really. But every Friday he'd pick me up after school and we'd go get dessert at a different restaurant. Just me and him. My mom worked part time at the real estate office she works for now and she had to work all day on Thursdays and Fridays and on Saturday mornings. So we made it kind of a tradition to do something special. He even let me have coffee, even though Mom said it would stunt my growth."

"What a great memory. Do you journal?"

She already asked that question, she is trying to trap you. If you answer her, your mom will know and she will find it. You will be grounded for life if she reads it.

"Yeah, but just stuff I do all day."

"That's okay. There's no right way to journal, but the more you can write down your emotions and your feelings, the better. Why don't you try to write down all your favorite memories of your dad? Then when you're sad or angry, you can look at them and remember the good. It might hurt a little at first, but I think you're stronger than you know." Sara stayed quiet for a moment then said, "Lanie, I need to ask you something. I see your eyes darting back and forth. Are you high right now?"

I felt our eyes widen—at my shock or hers, I was unsure. Were our eyes really moving quickly?

Lanie blinked and shook her head. "No. I'm not high. Just thinking about everything you're saying."

Sara nodded. "Okay." And scribbled another note.

"I swear. I'm not high," Lanie said. "I haven't smoked since this morning..."

"It's okay, Lanie. I believe you. I'm sure this is a stressful situation for you, especially with what you said about the last person you talked to. I promise you can trust me. I know it's hard for you to believe, but I hope you'll let me prove it to you."

Sara smiled and Lanie, to my dismay, believed her.

By the time we left Sara's office, Lanie felt better. The constriction returned, containing me in a small space within her stomach, making me glad for the foresight to insert doubt in the lobby, otherwise the session might have been the end of me.

"Can we schedule a time for next week?" Sara asked Olivia. Olivia looked at Lanie and Lanie shrugged. Inside she felt lighter after talking to Sara, but she would not admit it to her mother.

In the car, Lanie asked if they could go get dessert. Her mother smiled and tears pooled in her eyes.

"Of course. Where do you want to go?"

I had to figure out a way to prevent Lanie from going back to that woman.

SAMANTHA

Lanie dominated my mind all day on Tuesday. Something about her felt off, but I didn't know what exactly. She wasn't the first high school student I'd seen who smoked pot. But none of them distracted me enough to accidentally give my kids an extra ten minutes of recess. If it hadn't been for the art teacher coming to find me, they might have had the rest of the afternoon off.

Once school let out, I hurried home, hoping to catch Lanie and Stephanie walking home again. Stephanie didn't walk by until almost five o'clock. Alone.

"Stephanie, can I talk to you for a minute?" I walked down the porch steps toward the fence to meet her. She looked startled, then afraid.

"Um, I'm already late."

"I noticed. Is everything okay?"

"Yeah, I just... I had an after-school thing."

She was lying to me, which I understood. She had no reason to trust me.

"Where's Lanie?"

"She left school early. Her mom came and got her. I really have to go, Ms. Blaine. I'm sorry."

"Stephanie, if you girls won't talk to me, I'll have to call your parents. I'm concerned."

She glared at me, then hurried down the sidewalk without looking back, providing no resolution to my obsession with Lanie. I'd give them a day or two. Maybe Kimber would have some news for me Friday. If not, would I really call their parents? Was I one of those teachers? I wasn't sure...

I stood at the fence for a moment wondering how far away Bartholomew was from me. I reached up and slid the crystal pendant back and forth on its chain, tempted to take it off to see if I could hear him. Bad idea. I turned and went inside the protection of my home. Curtains closed, doors closed, blocked off from him completely.

The phone rang as I stepped inside.

"Hey, Sam."

"Maggie! Hi!"

My best friend Maggie, her husband Russ, and their three boys had moved to Colorado this past summer. Russ had been having a hard time finding work in California and Alex's business grew, so he needed another carpenter. Russ didn't have a lot of experience remodeling houses, but he had been a cabinet-maker for years. Alex and Russ complemented each other.

The five of them were getting settled in at Brian's two-bedroom house, a tight fit for now while they got on their feet.

We did the normal chit-chat about Russ, the boys, and Alex. Then I asked Maggie about how to help me with the girls.

"One of my former students stopped by the house yesterday. She was high. Do you think it's normal for kids so young to smoke pot now? It seemed awfully young to me."

"I don't think we were much older."

"Yes we were! I didn't start until after my senior year when all the shit happened."

"Yeah, we only snuck booze into your parents' basement. So much better."

"Really, Mags?" I laughed. "It was better. I don't know why exactly."

"Because liquor is legal for adults and pot isn't? Your ideologies are a little off. Neither one is good for kids. The damage they do to their brains is the same."

I knew this; she didn't need to preach about it.

"Anyway, I'm worried about this girl. Straight A's, outgoing, optimistic. She doesn't fit the type."

"Sam, I think you've lived in this small town too long. There isn't a type. You know that. We weren't the type either."

"Well, I wasn't."

"Whatever!"

"I miss you, Maggie. Let's have breakfast on Saturday. Alex has a project he's finishing up, so he'll be working."

"I'll check with Russ to make sure we don't have plans, but that should work. How about we go to the French bistro in downtown Denver?"

"Perfect." I heard Alex's truck pull into the driveway. "Alex is home."

"Okay, well Sam, don't worry too much about the girl. I'm sure she's fine."

We hung up and I moved to the kitchen where I waited for Alex. Could Maggie be right—Lanie would be fine and I didn't need to worry? I hoped so, because I didn't know what to do if Lanie wasn't fine. A few minutes later Alex walked in the back door. He didn't look happy.

"You okay?" I asked.

"Yeah. No. I don't know. John is going to be a grandpa."

John? Who was he and why did this matter? Alex stared at me while I tried to figure it out. "John. The guy I'm doing work for. Jeez, Sam. I can't believe you don't remember."

Whoa...I'm supposed to remember every one of his client's names? He had more than one at a time now. I got them all mixed up.

"Well, his son is a few years younger than me and he's already starting a family. Here we are trapped in this fucking house." He gestured at the kitchen where we were standing.

Alex didn't swear, unless he was really distraught. Of course, he felt angry. He'd been honest with me about wanting a family. And he had no idea I hid a dark secret from him.

"Alex, I'm sorry this is upsetting to you. But you know we can't bring a child into this house." *Or into this world at all—at least in my case*, I thought.

"You don't think we can protect the baby? We've done fine protecting ourselves and Max. Why would a baby be any different?"

"A baby wouldn't be different, but a child would. Are we not supposed to let our kid play outside? Have friends over?" Bartholomew, my convenient excuse.

"We can sell it."

"The kid, once it's grown?"

He scowled at me. I guess now was not the time for humor.

"You know as well as I do, it's not a good time to sell. Inflation is high, buyers are hesitant. Besides, I'm not ready to give up the house. It means too much to me," I said.

Besides, if we moved, what would I tell him then, the truth? Then what? He'd leave. That's what.

"Something has to give, Sam. I want a family and you won't have one while we're trapped."

"So, what do you want me to do? Rent the house to some unsuspecting family who will be terrorized by Bartholomew? In good conscience, I can't do it."

"Fine, fine. I'll stop wishing for a normal life with you and live in this twisted reality."

"Don't be mad, Alex. Please."

"I'm tired of putting our lives on hold because he's out there and we have no idea if he'll ever leave us alone."

My stomach twisted at realizing maybe I somehow held Bartholomew to me because he gave me a reason not to have a family with Alex. Maybe I wanted him near enough for an excuse, but far enough away he couldn't harm us. I felt disgusted, because somewhere deep inside, I knew this to be true.

I did believe Bartholomew would wear down and move on, find somewhere else to haunt. His persistence terrified me, immobilized me. But Max would come in and report back; Bartholomew still lingered outside the fence. Limbo gave me nightmares, where I found myself back in the reserve where Bartholomew attacked me. I'd wander around trying to find my way out, like a gauntlet. Bartholomew lurked out of sight, but I never could see him. I only felt the fear. I'd run, but never get very far. My legs moved slowly, like my feet were weighted down with mud. My arms didn't feel like my own. An invisible something would ensnare me, restrain my arms and legs, take control of my body. Right before I woke, I would think, *Just give in, let him have sex with you. It's just a body. Then Bartholomew will let you live.*

The fear and the sense of being lost, out of control, never resolved itself. I would fight to stay awake to prevent the dream from taking hold, without success. When the nightmares got really bad, I'd force myself to get out of bed and walk through the house, praying Bartholomew still resided outside the fence and not inside the house.

There were so many layers of protection, I couldn't imagine him actually getting inside, but I never stopped being vigilant. The windows and doors stayed closed, as well as the curtains. My car had the same kind of protections and I never went anywhere without the necklace and earrings Brian had given me. During the daylight hours, I refused to let him win. At night, I felt different.

"Call Max," Alex said, interrupting my thoughts.

"And do what? Invite him over for dinner? That'd be nice."

"Sure, invite him to dinner. But call him and see if he'll come over. Maybe we can figure out some way to get rid of Bartholomew permanently."

"Okay."

Shit...he wouldn't drop this. Maybe we could "try" to have kids. I could stop taking the unnecessary birth control pill and when we didn't get pregnant, I could pretend I didn't know I was infertile. Lots of couples couldn't have kids and most of them didn't have a procedure gone horribly wrong haunting their lives.

"When should we have him over?"

"Tonight. See if he'll come over tonight. I'll cook and go to the grocery store even."

I reached for him and pulled him close to me. "I love you so much right now for wanting to have a family with me, for loving me enough to want me to be the mother to your children."

He bent down and kissed me, then said, "Call him."

"Fine!"

Alex and Max were almost as close as Max and me. They went fishing a few times and Alex taught Max how to play chess. Alex would make a great dad. Which made the whole situation even worse.

Max came over for dinner at seven o'clock—a little late for him, he'd said, but he came anyway because I told him how important it was to Alex. It took him ten minutes to come inside the house. I watched him from inside as he walked back and forth inside the fence, pacing like a caged tiger. *Bartholomew must be antagonizing him.*

Outside on the porch I saw he wasn't anxious, but excited. "Max, are you okay?"

"I don't see him!"

"What?" I asked.

"He's not here anymore."

I met Max in the yard, then we ventured outside the gate. My heart jumped into my throat at the thought that we could be rid of him. Then the guilt hit my gut. I watched Max look up and down the sidewalk and still he said he saw no sign of Bartholomew. I took off my earrings and necklace and set them on a fence post. Nothing. I could never see him, but I felt him and heard him—if he chose to talk to me.

"Are you sure?"

"Yes. Sometimes I would see him a few houses down, but he's never been gone. I don't see him anywhere."

"Could he have gotten into the house?" I asked.

His face paled and we hurried into the house to look. I tentatively set my jewelry on the kitchen table. I couldn't hear or feel him with them on. Then we searched, looking in the shadows.

"I don't feel him. Can you see him?"

He shook his head and said, "I'll come back every day."

Has Bartholomew finally moved on? Intuition told me no. I quickly put the necklace and earrings back on.

"I wish Ella was alive," Max said.

Ella, Brian's dog, kept watch after we took her in when he died. Sitting on the porch, she'd move her gaze slowly down the sidewalk then back up. Max had seen her do this one day and realized she had been tracking Bartholomew's movements. If Bartholomew stood in one place, she sat perfectly still. She died this past spring. I missed her, too, but for more reasons than her ability to sense ghosts.

We sat at the kitchen table to eat our spaghetti and salad. Alex sat on the bench seat.

"You amaze me, Max," Alex said, rolling noodles around his fork. "Your bravery. I'm terrified of the unknown, but you aren't." He shook his head and smiled. "I am constantly amazed."

I watched Max's face while he thought, his white eyebrows dipped. His lips twitched. "I'm the unknown to most people—at least that's what my mom says. People are afraid of me because I'm not like them. I look different, talk different. Ghosts don't scare me. Evil scares me. Bartholomew is evil."

I hated that people were afraid of Max. He'd told me stories from when he was little and had been bullied in school. His mom homeschooled him because of how kids treated him. People could be such assholes, something I had a difficult time understanding.

"I think we're all a little different," I said. "And we're all the same. To me, that's why people are fascinating. Take Alex and me. We don't agree on everything..."

"That's an understatement," Alex said, laughing.

I smiled and continued, "But our differences make life rich. Especially when we talk about them without any intention behind our conversation. I'm not trying to change his mind, and he's not trying to change mine."

"Well, it depends on the topic..." He winked.

I shook my head, and Max laughed. I felt pretty sure Alex referenced sex, but I hoped Max thought he meant something else.

"Anyway... It's a matter of learning who we are and how we think."

"How did we get from fear to differences?" Alex asked.

"Fear is *caused* by differences," Max said.

"I think fear is caused by ignorance," I said.

Max nodded and Alex studied me for a minute, twirling noodles round and round his fork, never taking a bite.

"So, you are saying my fear of ghosts is caused by my ignorance? I have to disagree. I'm afraid of them because I can't see them, hear them, touch them. I have no control over the situation. That's what scares me."

"Your point is valid, but I never experienced a ghost who hurt me before Bartholomew. Before him, were you afraid?"

"No, because he 'educated' me to what ghosts were capable of," Alex replied.

"I guess I meant people who are afraid of Max. That's ignorance," I said.

Max looked at me, his turn to process what I said. I felt like I shouldn't be talking for him. I just felt so angry at people who didn't take the time to get to know him before judging him. I witnessed people being afraid of Max over the years, unsure how to talk to him, avoiding eye contact, pretending he didn't exist. It frustrated me and I felt helpless in those situations.

"So, if people got to know me, they wouldn't be afraid? They'd stop crossing the street when they saw me walking?"

His comment hurt my heart. I studied him for a moment. His pale eyes reflected kindness, gentleness.

"People cross the street when they see you? I'm sorry, Max. I can only imagine how that makes you feel."

"They used to not. It's only been the last few years. It's because I'm a man now."

"It has nothing to do with you. It's them. Remember that," I said, reaching for his hand.

"Wave and smile when you see them," Alex said.

"Or raise your arms like Frankenstein and really scare the fuck out of them," I said. He laughed.

"I read *Frankenstein*. He was a misunderstood monster, kind of like me."

"You are no monster," Alex said.

The rest of dinner we discussed the garden, Alex's newest job, and my students. We avoided the conversation of our ghost. Until dessert. I stood to get the store-bought cheesecake out of the refrigerator and Alex dropped the question.

"We can't keep living like prisoners. Max, if he returns, how do we banish him, permanently?"

"He's stubborn," Max said, then went quiet.

My back faced them as I plated their desserts. I dreaded going back to the table. The lying and hiding plagued me. Riddled with guilt, I turned and gave them their cheesecake, hoping the sweet wouldn't turn sour in my stomach.

"I don't know how to make him leave. The other ones always left when I helped with a cleanse, but they weren't evil. He's evil and it makes his aura dark and ugly, like brown sewage."

Alex slumped in his chair, defeated. My heart ached for him. *Just come clean, Sam. That's all you have to do. Come clean and let him decide whether to stay or go.*

But what if he chose to go?

Max finished off his cheesecake, but mine and Alex's were barely touched.

"Let me take you home, Max. We can look for Bartholomew on the way. Can I take your truck, Alex?"

He nodded. Max and I left him sitting at the table.

Alex's truck rumbled to life beneath me. It smelled like sawdust and I noticed some scattered on the floor. It shocked me to see the untidiness. He was always so meticulous.

"Do you see him?" I asked Max as we drove.

"No, but it's dark. I'll be able to look better tomorrow. He can hide in the shadows at night."

"If he isn't gone or if he comes back, is there someone we can ask about getting rid of him?"

"A priest can do an exorcism."

I didn't know any priests. But maybe Alex did. He was raised Catholic, even if he no longer practiced. Why hadn't he suggested it after all these years?

"Thank you for coming to dinner tonight. It's nice having your company."

"Thank you for making my favorite."

"I didn't realize spaghetti was your favorite." I smiled over at him. "I'll have to remember that."

I dropped him safely at his house, then drove around Stafford, in no hurry to get home to resume the *have-a-family* conversation. Avoidance wasn't the solution, but I didn't know what to do and driving often gave me time to think.

I knew how Alex felt about abortions, so I knew I couldn't tell him the truth. He'd used the words *immoral* and *murderer* when his sister had come to him for advice a few years ago. She had been pregnant with their sixth and she felt exhausted. Honesty conjured images where Alex pointed his finger at me and called me a murderer, shame and disgust visible on his face.

In all my life, I'd never been so afraid of losing someone. I knew my parents would die one day—not that their deaths weren't difficult, but this felt so very different. Alex would leave because of a choice he didn't agree with and my deceit. If I'd have told him in the beginning, would he have stayed anyway? Fear prevented me from being honest. I needed him then and I needed him now.

He was an extension of me and I hoped he felt the same way. If he didn't, I didn't know what I'd do. What if having a family meant more to him than me?

I drove down my street and slowed in front of my house. Something Lanie said, then Rosemary contradicted, stuck in my head. I parked, flipped the switch for the electric gate, and stepped onto the sidewalk before it closed. Then I took off my jewelry and set it on the fence post. I hesitated just a moment before letting go of it.

Do I really want to do this, alone? If he's here, he'll try something if I'm alone.

I walked up and down the sidewalk, looking for a crack high enough to catch a toe. Waiting to hear or feel Bartholomew. Alex stood watching me from the front door.

Nothing. No crack. No Bartholomew.

"The girl fainted," Rosemary had said.

"I tripped," Lanie had said.

Something didn't add up—I was missing something. Fear crept up my neck. Could Bartholomew have had something to do with Lanie falling?

No. Ridiculous. He'd passed through me several times when we lived together and I never fell. I turned to face Alex now.

I could do this. I grabbed the jewelry and put it back on as I walked up to the house. Still better to be safe than sorry.

"Well?" he said, pushing open the screen door for me.

"We didn't see him. And I didn't feel him or hear him just now."

"If Max keeps watch and there's no sign of him... The thought feels so damn good, Sam. You know?"

"I know."

But deep down, I didn't believe he left. He hid somewhere—in a neighbor's house, on the next street over—biding his time, waiting for us to let our guard down. I felt it. Or maybe hoped. God, I was fucking sick.

BARTHOLOMEW

Lanie's thoughts and feelings grew stronger. I heard her unconscious thoughts, the ones she did not know she felt. The ones where she admitted to herself how much she loved her mom. How she feared something would happen to her, so she pushed her away. Such an odd sensation. If I had not known, I would think there were voices in my "head." They blended with my own and I wondered if mine were doing the same to her. Could I influence the girl through her conscience? Would she take on my own personality, my beliefs?

After they left the appointment, Lanie and her mother talked for hours. As soon as the girl finished half her coffee, she rambled about everything. Coffee was her truth serum—and for me a huge problem. The more the girl talked, the more her soul filled our body. I felt confined.

"This is nice. I'm sorry we haven't had more chances to do this," Lanie's mom said. "I need to make more time for you. I get caught up in work and making sure we have food and a roof over our heads. I forget, even though you seem so grown up, you still need me."

Lanie looked at her dessert, not at her mother. Her soul pulsed with the shift of her emotions. Guilt allowed me a little more space.

"So, are you going to help with Halloween decorations at the nursing home again this year?" Olivia said, changing the subject.

"I think so. They want me to come in once a week to set up a nail painting station again. Ms. Morris called a few weeks ago and said the ladies are asking me to come back. I just...school is crazy this year."

I don't want to go back because so many people there smell like death, Lanie thought.

"It's your decision, but you seemed happier when you were volunteering." Olivia paused briefly then said, "Lanie, I need to know. Have you tried anything other than pot?"

"No!" she said, looking up. Then seeing the questioning look on her mother's face she said, "Except I've had a couple of wine coolers."

The lies expanded The Darkness.

"They're pretty tasty. I could see why you'd like them."

Why is Mom being so cool? No freak out? Lanie thought.

"I'd be lying to you if I didn't say I tried things when I was a teenager. Granted, not when I was fifteen."

"No way."

"I know. I'm your mom, I'm not supposed to admit it. But how can I expect you to be honest with me, if I'm not being honest with you?"

Lanie looked back at her dessert. Her mom wouldn't be okay with everything she'd done. The vodka she drank when she partied with Mark and his friends. Sex. Lanie knew her mom would definitely freak over that secret.

"So just pot and a few wine coolers?"

"Yeah. I've tried beer. It's gross."

Lanie's mom studied her face. She seemed to be looking for a lie somewhere. *Don't ask me about sex*, Lanie thought.

"You're so smart, Lanie. And a really good girl."

Lanie smirked at her mother's comment.

"Even on the bitchy days," Olivia added with her own crooked smile. "Promise me you won't do anything worse, like cocaine or amphetamines. I know pot doesn't seem like a big deal, but it's not good for you. Your brain is so young. Who knows what kind of damage it could do? You're smart and you have so much life ahead of you."

Lanie ate her chocolate cream pie and her mother took bites of her lemon meringue. She did not promise Olivia anything.

"Does Stephanie smoke with you?"

"Nah. She's too chicken."

Her mom laughed. "I'm not sure I'd call her chicken. She's just not been through what you have. It's not a bad thing she doesn't smoke with you. Lanie, I do hope you'll quit. I know it's hard. I miss him so much, but the hurt lessens. If you hide your pain and your feelings, you won't be able to get through this."

"I'm not an addict, Mom. I know what I'm doing."

Her mom sighed.

Lanie knew she didn't believe her, otherwise she wouldn't be making her go to the stupid shrink. She didn't trust Lanie to know how to deal with her own issues. Did her mom think she was too immature? Too dumb to know the difference between doing hard drugs and smoking a little pot once in a while? *Well, maybe I do smoke every day. But not that much!* She didn't need to make such a big deal out of it. She did wonder, could her mother be right? Would the hurt she felt in her heart and stomach lessen if she faced the death of her father? How could it ever get better? She felt like the sun would never rise on a cloudy day, like she'd be sick forever.

Her wavering between love and guilt and pride and hurt and happiness and anger left me weak. I tried resisting her emotions, but they were part of my being, manipulating me. I had to do something! I pushed against her, but the more I pushed, the more she resisted until her soul forced me into a tiny corner of her brain.

Misery. Pure misery.

Lanie's suspension was worse than hell, I was sure. I had difficulties understanding my spatial space, even before I possessed her, but now I felt like I lived in a one-inch-by-one-inch square. Confined and trapped. I could not get out. When I forced my way up into her skull, I thought she would push me right out the back of her head. Then she would see something on television or hear a song and anger would bubble up and she would start bawling. The girl's emotions were all over the place! She still lashed out, yelling and screaming when her mother asked her to do something, but she never relapsed to smoking pot. During her temper tantrums, I got a little reprieve from my corner, but not much.

On Wednesday when her mother left, she put on the television. She flipped between *The Wizard of Oz* and MTV. I felt disoriented between the children's show and the obnoxious music. She popped popcorn and poured a glass of dark-colored liquid, then lay on the floor. The drink fizzed and bubbled down our throat. *The rock stars are so glamorous, with their big, blond hair. I could be a groupie for Mötley Crüe or Ratt. I bet they wouldn't care if I smoked pot. They might even have better stuff than Mark*, she thought.

Cross-dressers on television, in public?! What has this world come to? I thought. They had been visitors of Thaddeus all those years ago, but they had been discreet.

Mmm...but fine cross-dressers.

Lanie grew stronger. She refused to smoke, afraid her mother would catch her. I could not get a grasp on her, could not control her. It proved to me the drugs allowed me access to our body.

She lay around watching television all day, stuffing our body full of chips, candy, and soda. Occasionally she would stand up quickly and rush to her vanity where she scribbled into the journal, all rubbish about how she felt this way or that. Such a waste.

Her mother arrived home after five, even though she said she had been scheduled at the diner.

"I called in. You need me more. We're going to have dinner together," Olivia said.

Lanie beamed inwardly, answering her questions and letting her mother engage her in conversation. On the outside, she rolled her eyes and crossed her arms. Had it always been this difficult to be a teenager? No wonder I could possess her so easily. She did not know who she was or what she wanted. I became another nagging voice inside her head.

When we went to bed, I thought I would be able to move free and unchecked. Wrong. She struggled, even in sleep, and kept me at bay. Each time she fell asleep and I tried to move, she would jerk awake as though she had fallen. No matter how long I waited for her to sleep, as soon as I stirred, she would wake.

I had to regain control.

SAMANTHA

Rumors trickled down to the elementary school about Lanie's outburst in the history class on Wednesday morning. Lanie's history teacher and the sixth grade teacher at Stafford Elementary were married. Since Kimber moved to middle school, I often avoided the teacher's lounge. I had fond memories of meeting Kimber on the day we both came in to decorate our classrooms. There had been a cute, sea-green Victorianesque couch we would sit on and pretend to be prim and proper ladies, where we would whisper "fuck" every so often to remind us who we really were. A year after we met, a not-so-generous someone donated their autumn-patterned faux velvet couch, and the cute sea-green couch disappeared. Tired of rug burns from the scratchy fabric on the backs of our legs, we opted to sit in each other's classrooms thereafter. Since her leave, we only saw each other at our monthly gathering of friends. I missed working with her.

The teacher's lounge had become a gossip-fest and bitch session about students and parents. At this point in my career, I hadn't become cynical. I wasn't naïve enough to think it would never happen, but I still had hope. Surrounding myself with negative energy would only ensure cynicism's speedy progression. Today, though, I had gotten out of bed late and needed a cup of coffee before facing the boundless energy of twenty first-graders.

As I walked into the room, I glanced at the group of five teachers sitting around a retired cafeteria table. Kimber and I dubbed them the IBs—Icky Bitches. In their late fifties, they were the usual suspects, burnt out and past their expiration date. I didn't understand why they continued to teach if they hated their job so much, especially a job where their actions influenced so many impressionable minds.

Get your coffee and get out, I thought.

"My poor husband has the worst students this year," I heard Joyce Arnold say. "These two girls refuse to respect him. They weren't much better when I had them. Thankfully, you, Samantha, gave me a reprieve by allowing them to read to your first graders."

I kept my back turned to the group. Usually I could sidestep being triggered and dragged into Joyce's drama. She rarely had anything nice to say about her students, so I avoided her. Maybe she wanted my attention, so she chose to use my name this time, to try to draw me in. I kept stirring my coffee, attempting to ignore her.

"Yesterday, Lanie used the n-word in class—even worse, she interrupted my husband during his lecture. Then he found pot in her backpack. Thankfully, the principal agreed with my husband and suspended her for a week. At least he'll have a week free of her interruptions. Her friend though he still has to deal with. The things we have to put up with as teachers. Parents should really instill better manners in their children."

I turned around, coffee in hand, to look at the group.

"Joyce, someone should have taught *you* it's unprofessional to gossip about students. We don't know what they're going through," I said and walked out of the room.

I hated to learn of Lanie's actions through the gossip gaggle, but the language she used disturbed me. Lanie didn't strike me as the racist type. *So what would push her to use that word?* I felt sad knowing she struggled.

I tried talking to Stephanie on Wednesday after school, but she brushed me off again. She must have taken a different route home the rest of the week, as I didn't see her.

I sat on the front porch waiting for Alex, sipping a cup of tea, daring Bartholomew to show himself, to see if he really had moved on.

Jim Hastings pulled up across the street, still wearing his creepy toupee.

Occasionally I would see it slip forward so the bald spot at the back of his head left a gap. *The man should really just accept his baldness.*

Jim got out of his car and waved. I did not wave back. I refused to be neighborly with him. Rosemary was bad enough, but she never hit on me. I suppose if we moved, we'd be rid of Bartholomew *and* him.

Thankfully, Jim didn't push the issue. He grabbed his briefcase out of the back seat and went inside. Our other neighbors kept to themselves. Sometimes they would wave. After we finished the house, they stopped to tell us how great it looked. I was happy to be cordial, but not become friends. I needed my space, damn it.

BARTHOLOMEW

Thursday afternoon, Lanie had a visit from Stephanie. We had not seen or talked to her since Lanie had been suspended. She walked in the door agitated and nervous.

Why would she still want to be friends with me after what I said? Lanie thought.

I didn't understand Lanie's dramatics about the incident. The drugs in her backpack caused the suspension, not what we said. Words were just words, after all.

Olivia was at work, so the girls sat on the flower-patterned couch. Stephanie wore her usual atrocious attire; today she wore orange and green. She looked like a pumpkin too long on the vine. Her hair, the rotting leaves.

"Ms. Blaine is driving me crazy!" she said. Then, looking around the house, she asked in a hushed voice, "Is your mom home?"

At "Ms. Blaine" she had my attention. What was Samantha up to? Did she know I possessed Lanie?

"No, she's at work."

"Good. Anyway, Tuesday and Wednesday she stopped me in front of her house and asked me about you. Today I went a different way."

"You better not snitch, Stephanie. My mom already had me see a shrink after I got suspended."

"I didn't. I swear, but she's a pain in the ass. You should never have gone into her house."

Lanie's memory of walking into the house felt foggy, confusing her as to why Stephanie still blamed her for the problem. "You shouldn't have taken me *into* the house. I didn't need a stupid band-aid."

Stephanie sat quietly for a minute, looking anywhere but at Lanie. "That was an awful thing you said in class," she finally said, glaring at Lanie. Anger flared in her eyes. "It's bad enough how Mr. Arnold treats me. We're friends, how could you?! I really didn't want to come here, you know. But Ms. Blaine said she was going to call my parents. My mom and dad don't know you party or they wouldn't let me hang out with you." She paused for a minute then said, "After what you said in class, I don't know if I want to hang out with you anyway."

Everyone was so worried about what I said in class! I could not understand the outrage, why they felt affronted. No one seemed concerned about the drugs the girl had in her backpack, they were only concerned about a single word, a moment in time. The fixation dumbfounded me.

"I know. I'm really sorry. I don't know why I said that. You know I didn't mean it, right?" Lanie's soul shrank. Anger, sadness, guilt filled our body. The Darkness felt gloriously expansive.

"It didn't seem like you. Maybe going to talk to someone isn't such a bad thing," Stephanie said.

Lanie's temper flared and she wondered, *Why does Stephanie always have to side with my mom?* "What do you know about anything? You're so naïve, Stephanie. Little Miss Goody Two Shoes won't even drink a fucking beer, afraid to have a teacher say 'boo' to you."

Ah...much better. I stretched out a little bit. *Keep going, Lanie. Tell her how you really feel.*

"You have a perfect life, with a perfect house and a perfect fucking family. You don't get looked at like a troublemaker—"

"Only when I'm with you!" Stephanie yelled.

"Well, don't hang out with me. I'm fine on my own. And just walk a different way home if you can't deal with the bitch."

"Fine, Lanie, you got it! I'm done." Stephanie left, slamming the door on her way out. Lanie stewed and I spread out even more, the first time I could in days. What if the rift with Stephanie got really bad? Would Lanie sneak upstairs, risk her mother finding out? *A stupid fight with Stephanie and all I want is to go smoke a joint. What the hell am I thinking?* Lanie thought.

Tires crunched in the driveway. Lanie's mother was home.

Maybe I should talk to Mom about Stephanie. She'd know what to do.

So she can chastise you for hurting Stephanie's feelings? What happens if she starts asking questions about why you had a fight? About why you went into Samantha's house?

Who is Samantha and why do I know the name?

Ms. Blaine, I thought.

That's right.

The door opened and Lanie's mother walked in with two bags of groceries. Lanie watched her struggle with holding the door open while carrying the groceries, her briefcase, and her purse.

"A little help, here?" her mother said.

Lanie stood and helped her carry the groceries.

"Thank you, Lanie. There's a present for you in there."

"From the grocery store?"

"No, there's a small bag inside. Put the groceries away though, or you can't have it."

Lanie pulled groceries out of the bags and put them away. At the bottom of one of the bags she found a small teal-green plastic bag.

"No way! Really?!"

Lanie pulled the rectangular plastic box out of the bag. It had a blue cover with some strange name on the front. Lightning streaked down from the letters. I wondered if it was foreign.

Lanie's joy squeezed me back into a corner. She rushed through putting the groceries away and gave her mom a hug, then hurried to her room, giddy with excitement. I couldn't understand the excitement she felt about the box that said Metallica.

She ripped off the outer plastic, opened the box, and put the tape in her music player, a boombox. A blast of something horrendous erupted from the machine. I had no idea what the electrical instruments were. Then the angry growls and screaming began. Lanie jumped up and down, shaking her head back and forth. Her soul grew brighter than I'd ever seen it. I shrank away, afraid and dizzy from her movement. What in God's name was she listening to and why on earth would she dance this way? She spun, making herself dizzy, her hair flying every which way, and fell onto her bed laughing.

Her mom poked her head in during one of the mellower songs to let her know dinner would be ready soon. Olivia smiled at her daughter's reaction. "I guess I did good."

"This is the best!" Lanie shouted over the noise.

The best? I had to get out of this body. Or get control of her again. One way or another, I could not survive much longer like this. The music should have made her angry. It should have agitated her, but it did not. I felt confused. It agitated *me*, but what could I do with her feeling so good? Nothing. I could do nothing. I resigned myself to being trapped in the body of a fifteen-year-old.

After her mom left the room again, Lanie lifted her mattress, stuffed the rolled cigarettes into her pockets, then walked to the bathroom where she flushed them.

No! No! No! No! No! I screamed. The drugs were my only hope.

She ignored my pleas.

I'm going to try, really try, she thought. Then we joined her mother for dinner.

Lanie's soul still glowed, except for one small space near her stomach. I could not expand. What had her mother done to me by giving her the awful music?!

I could almost forgive her as we stepped into the kitchen. The smell of garlic and cream greeted us first, then we saw the table.

Olivia had set it with two Blue Willow patterned plates, silverware with rose embellishments on the handles, orange linen napkins, and glass tumblers.

A toasted caramel-colored tablecloth embroidered with bright fall leaves covered the battered table. A small votive candle enclosed in a metal pumpkin cage flickered. Didn't Olivia know her ungrateful daughter would never admit to being impressed by her mother?

"Wow!" Lanie said, sitting on the shabby wooden chair, a tattered contrast to the adornments on the table. "I haven't seen this stuff in a while." She smoothed her hand over the stitching.

I stand corrected...

"I thought it would be nice," Olivia said, bringing a large bowl of pasta with cream sauce and a salad to the table, then she sat down. "I'm really proud of you, Lanie. It took courage to talk to Sara. I'm glad you want to go back; she can really help us, I think."

The food tasted as delectable as it smelled. Pine nuts crunched in our mouth and mingled with the saltiness of capers, the tang of lemon, and the cream. Oh, the cream! Tasting food again would be my undoing. The torture the girl put me through was almost worth it to taste.

The phone rang, interrupting dinner. Lanie didn't move from her seat. *It's not for me*, she thought. Her stomach dropped knowing she wouldn't hear from Stephanie. *Why did I say that in class?* I felt our face frown.

Her mother lay her napkin next to the plate of pasta and went to answer the phone.

Because I spoke the truth, I responded.

No, I didn't.

"Well, hello Mrs. Jones! It's been a while," we heard Lanie's mom say.

Mrs. Jones, why would she be calling? Lanie thought. I had no idea who the woman was, so I paid no attention. Instead I focused on getting Lanie to take another bite of the creamy deliciousness. Her soul still glowed, impeding my progress.

"It's very kind of you to worry. But I think she's finally willing to talk about everything..." Her voice became muffled, as though she didn't want Lanie to hear what she said. Lanie scowled.

She's talking about me again. Embarrassment filled her, and betrayal. She didn't understand why her mother felt the need to share everything with the whole world. By the time Olivia returned to the table, anger allowed me to spread out a bit. But she had stopped eating.

"Mrs. Jones called to check on you."

"Why? She's not my teacher anymore. Why does it matter to her?"

"Well, honey. She cares about you."

"What did you tell her? That I'm a freak. That you can't control me. That you finally forced me to see a shrink—"

"She's not a shrink."

"Whatever! I hate when you talk about me. It's no one's business."

"She said you fell the other day and might have hit your head?"

Ms. Blaine! Lanie thought. *She really is a bitch.* "Yeah, I tripped and banged up my knee and elbow. That's all. I went to Ms. Blaine's house for a fucking band-aid—"

"Language!"

Lanie rolled her eyes then said, "I'm fine. It wasn't a big deal." She picked up her fork, pushed her food around. I hoped she would put just one more bite into her mouth. Just one!

"Okay, well I let her know you were doing much better. I didn't tell her anything else," Olivia said. *She* put a bite of food in her mouth. Why couldn't I body jump?!

Lanie shoved her plate away and stood.

"Ah, ah. Please scrape your plate and rinse it." Olivia motioned to the dishes left on the table with her fork. We glanced at her briefly and saw sadness. Then she said, "I'm sorry I answered the phone. We were having a nice dinner."

"Yeah, you ruined it. Like you ruin everything," Lanie said and stormed out of the room. To my great disappointment, she put the music back on and turned it up as loud as it would go. Except this time, her soul did not glow. It did not expand. But I did...

My life sucks, I thought, pushing the girl so The Darkness could expand.

I hate living in this house with her. I wish she would die, she thought. I could tell she didn't mean it, not truly. Her soul darkened at the thought of losing her mom and fear clawed at her belly. Something black as night grew inside of her then, an acidic pain ate at her stomach. I relished the space; she would not push me out. I knew I would remain in this different emptiness no matter what the girl felt.

SAMANTHA

During lunch on Friday, I went to the office to print new ABC coloring sheets for my kids. Our two secretaries stood just inside the door of the copy room, where they could see their desk, but not be overheard. They nodded in greeting to me, but continued their hushed conversation. As I pulled a ream of white paper to refill the printer, I understood why they whispered. They were talking about the rash of abortion clinic bombings. My stomach twisted in disgust. Such senseless violence over a personal choice, something strangers should have no say in.

"Thankfully no one has been killed yet. But there have been dozens of bombings across the country. My sister-in-law works for one here in Colorado, and she gave her notice because she's so afraid," one said.

"It's only a matter of time before someone is hurt, or worse," the other replied.

They returned to their posts at the front of the office and I went about my task, a heaviness in my body now. Maybe I could talk to Alex about the bombings; it could be a conversation starter.

Once I made up my mind to feel him out, I felt a little better. The guilt still filled my belly, but I had to make peace with my decision. Why were life decisions so difficult to make? Being an adult weighed so heavy on me some days. It seemed all my decisions affected someone else. Maybe that was the beauty of being young, the oblivion of self-absorption.

I won't talk to him tonight though, I thought. *I don't want to fight before we go to dinner at Kimber's.*

And I feared it could turn into a fight.

Kimber and Colin lived on the east side of Stafford in a stone bungalow, only about a mile away. They were the only couple who had children—three-year-old Sally and nine-month-old C.J.—and their house held signs of them everywhere. Crates of blocks sat in the living room, finger-painted pictures hung on the refrigerator, and a swing set took up a large portion of the backyard. In the summer, Kimber and Colin would host BBQs with their neighbors and family, complete with a ton of kids. Alex especially enjoyed us being around the babies. I think he believed it would make me get the itch.

On the drive, Alex brought up children. The topic I definitely wanted to avoid...

"If Max says Bartholomew is gone, we can start trying right away."

"What if it's already too late for me to have a baby, Alex?" Maybe if I planted the seed of doubt now, it wouldn't be such a shock when he found out the truth.

"Don't say that. It's not." He looked too long at me and drifted over the centerline.

"Please keep your eyes on the road, Alex," I said.

He turned his focus back to the road but continued, "You can't think that way. Look at your parents. They had kids late. How old was your mom again?"

"Thirty-eight."

"We have a few years, then!" He sounded so hopeful.

I know. I was a terrible person. We'd been married four years, together for six and I still couldn't tell him. I felt terrified. Living without Alex would be like living without a lung—I wouldn't be able to breathe. *Fear is a bitch.* It seemed no matter what I did, it followed me around. Just like the fucking ghost outside my house.

Alex sensed my change from apprehensive to sullen.

"You okay?"

Sometimes I liked when Alex picked up on my feelings because he knew when I needed him and when I needed space.

"I'm excited, you know," he said. "I've wanted to be a dad for a long time. Every time I bring up kids though, you act this way. I know you're scared, but I'm tired of putting our life on hold."

Right now...he annoyed me.

"I'm fine, but I don't want to talk about kids right now."

He sighed. "Sure, Sam. Whatever."

Damn it, I knew I shouldn't blame him. None of this was his fault. But, it felt easier to take my frustrations out on him than on myself. Even if I felt guilty. I could handle the guilt. I couldn't handle him leaving.

We pulled up outside Colin and Kimber's. A tricycle lay on its side near the front door, lit up like a stage prop from the porch light. God, I hoped the kids weren't home.

I started to open the truck door when Alex reached for my hand and said, "Thank you for coming out tonight. The house is really getting to me. I hate feeling like a prisoner in my own home, worrying about whether he can see inside or if he'll somehow get in. I hope Max is right and he's gone. If not, we should talk seriously about moving, Sam. Let him have the damn house."

"And what if a family with small children moves in, Alex? What happens if he gets annoyed with a cute little pigtailed three-year-old and impales her with a screwdriver? What happens then? Let's get this over with," I said and climbed out of the car. I heard his door close as I opened the chain-link gate. I didn't want to walk inside angry.

"Look," I said, turning to face him. "I know how bad you want a family. Let's talk about it, just not tonight. Okay? I love you and I don't want to fight."

I reached for him and he stepped into my hug.

"Okay, but soon, please."

"Soon," I said.

We turned and walked up the sidewalk hand in hand. As we approached the door, male voices drifted out the open window.

"You guys don't think it's weird they never invite us over? They're hiding something and I'm positive the something is he's an abusive drunk like his father."

Alex and I froze, almost in sync. The memory of Colin coming to the house after Bartholomew attacked me in the shower came back to me. He'd warned me away from Alex, saying his family had a history of abuse. He told me not to trust him, even reported the conversation to the ER doctor. I had hoped after getting to know Alex, and me for that matter, he would see Alex would never hurt me.

But, in the five years since the dinners started, we avoided having our friends over. It wasn't safe. Bartholomew could have followed any one of them home and latched on to their lives. They wouldn't even know. We successfully dodged the questions saying the house was still a construction zone, or we had a problem with the electricity in the kitchen and the breakers kept blowing. At least we thought we had been successful.

Then we heard our other friend Anthony say, "Colin, until she shows up with a black eye or bruises we can see, there's nothing we can do."

"They're hiding something. Kimber swears she's never seen a bruise on Sam's body, but I still think Alex could be violent. He's just gotten smarter about it. There are bigger hospitals in Denver. Sam could be going to one of them and we'd never be the wiser."

Alex looked at me, hurt evident on his face.

I whispered, "After all this time, Colin still sees you as my abuser. I can't believe it."

"I can handle this, Sam. But we should offer to host next month."

"If you don't handle it, I'll have to go to the next dinner with nothing on but an overcoat."

He laughed, but I was serious. Did I really have to walk around naked to stop the gossip about Alex? I squeezed Alex's hand and we walked side by side up to the door and knocked.

Colin opened the door and greeted us as if he hadn't been talking shit. His squared shoulders said confidence, but falsity showed in his pale blue eyes and the slight blush in his cheeks. Six years ago, I'd have stormed in and told him exactly what I thought. Things were different now. I was different, whether I liked it or not.

After Colin took our coats, Alex took him aside. Anthony and Tim greeted me with hugs. Did they know we heard them talking? They didn't let on if they did.

I left the guys and walked through the low café doors separating the dining room and kitchen. Thea and Kimber leaned against the butcher block counters sipping glasses of wine. Jillian sat across from them at the small kitchen table. Kimber had on an apron over her slacks and silk blouse. Her blonde hair was curled and pulled up in a banana clip with a few loose strands framing her pale-freckled cheeks. Thea did everything big, including her hot-pink makeup, shoulder pads, and teased light-brown hair. Thea never missed a trip to the tanning bed either; she always looked like she'd just come from the beach.

"I guess we both felt sassy tonight," I said to Jilli, motioning to our tops. I chose to wear a short-sleeved red silk blouse with faux buttons; she wore jeans and a chunky red sweater. The red made her natural copper skin glow.

"Twinsies!" she said, laughing.

"I need a glass of wine. It's been a week," I said. I could see the guys from where I stood and the look on Colin's face belied he didn't buy whatever Alex said. "I have to ask you guys something," I began as Kimber moved to get a glass. "Alex and I heard Colin talking when we walked up to the door. He still insists Alex is abusive. Do you feel the same way?"

Thea ducked her head. Jillian and Kimber gave each other an awkward look.

"So, that's a yes."

"Not necessarily," Kimber said, pouring me a glass of wine. "Jilli and I were talking about this the other day. Colin won't stop. He's a good man and he thinks he's looking out for you. I've tried to talk him out of it, but he's convinced. In the six years I've known you, I've never seen Alex treat you with anything but respect. But the whole thing with him investigating your injuries all those years ago and you not inviting us over? I'm sorry, Sam, but it's a little odd."

"Doesn't say much about me, does it?" I said, taking the glass she handed me. A peace offering?

"That's not it, Sam. Women often get into situations they don't know how to get out of."

"Look, when I first moved here I lived in a death trap. With helping do the remodel, I had a couple of accidents. And I'm pretty sure the neighbor broke in and attacked me in the shower, but we couldn't prove it," I said. Even though I knew now, it wasn't Jim. It had been Bartholomew all along. I continued, "Alex doesn't hit me. He never has." I paused and looked at each of them. Jilli and Kimber met my gaze. Thea looked at the floor. "Alex saw what abuse does to people. Shit, he rarely raises his voice to me. I promise. The house has been such a disaster zone, but I think we've finally got it where we want it. Maybe we can host dinner next month."

"Oh, Sam, that would be awesome!" Jilli said.

Thea avoided my eye contact through the whole exchange. She and I weren't super close. We'd gone out dancing several times, but we'd never really gotten into any deep conversations. Still, I had a hard time believing she'd think I would stay in an abusive relationship. I did not give off that kind of impression.

Colin came into the kitchen, interrupting our conversation. Kimber slid a roast chicken out of the oven, transferred it to a ceramic platter where Colin started carving it. I could smell the rosemary and brussels sprouts. Thea, Jilli, and I knew better than to help. We learned early on that Kimber refused to have us help, insisting we were guests. So we moved to the living room so she and Colin could finish up. Alex, Anthony, and Tim were deeply engaged in a conversation about the current economic climate. I heard *inflation* and *housing crash*. Both topics brought up my feelings of dishonesty, so I stayed away. Alex and I had talked about moving to get away from Bartholomew. I even had a realtor give me a property analysis a few times, but I never pushed and then the market dropped which gave me a convenient excuse.

Thea joined the guys, leaving Jilli and me alone. She drank a bubbly ginger ale, while I drank my second glass of wine.

"You okay? Stomach bothering you?" I said, noticing the tiny sips she took.

"Yeah, um...just nerves. We're trying to buy a new house. Listening to those guys talk makes it worse—maybe it's a bad time to buy. But we're tired of our apartment."

"Ah...well, ignore them. There's always a fluctuation. Comes and goes. I shouldn't have bought my house either, should have found something that needed less work and upkeep. But I wanted a Victorian. Now...I'm not sure we could sell it if we wanted to in this market. Not for what I put into it for sure."

Jillian nodded and Kimber announced dinner was almost ready. I started to walk to the dining room, but Kimber pulled me aside. She held a bottle of wine in one hand and salad tongs in the other.

"Hey, I talked to Lanie's mom last night. She said Lanie's doing okay; she finally opened up this week and they found a good therapist."

"That's a relief. The Icky Bitches said she blew up in class on Tuesday and said some awful stuff."

"I heard. This town is full of gossips," Kimber said, shaking her head. "But her mom said she's hopeful because Lanie has been doing really well since then. Maybe it was her rock bottom."

"I hope so. Thanks, Kimber," I said, squeezing her arm.

"No problem." She smiled, then motioned with the wine bottle. "Refill?"

I nodded. She poured.

By the time we started eating, I was halfway through my third glass of wine and felt pretty darn good. My head buzzed, my limbs felt light. Life was good. And I couldn't stop smiling. Kimber's beautiful décor always set the tone. Stemmed crystal goblets, china plates, and antique silverware—all passed down from her grandmother—adorned the table. Three taper candles in low floral centerpieces flickered along its length. Kimber raised her glass and said, "To good friends!"

"And incredible cooks!" Colin added. Kimber blushed a little and we all laughed.

"So modest," Thea said.

Voices of my friends hummed in conversation around me and I basked in the ease I felt. I had a bite of chicken on my fork when Alex stood up. I froze.

"Hey, um, I need to say something."

He put his hand on my shoulder and looked down at me. I steeled my gaze and urged him on.

"Sam and I heard Colin and Anthony talking when we walked up to the house. I know this isn't great dinner conversation, but I need to clear the air. It's been pretty obvious actually, these past few years, you still suspect me of hurting Sam. It might not mean much to you, but I have never laid a hand on her in anger or in frustration. You all know about my dad. I watched him beat my mother my entire life and I swore I would never be like him. I'm tired of the whispers. I'm tired of the accusations. They end tonight."

I swallowed my wine, proud of him. I wanted to take him home and do whatever he wanted. It took a lot for him to stand up to people after being belittled and beat down by his father.

Our friends were still, forks frozen over their plates.

And then I saw Colin give Tim a look. A look that said, *Yeah, right*. So, I did what any self-respecting woman would do: I stood up and took off my blouse.

Well, I tried to take it off, but Alex stopped me before I could get it all the way over my head. If it had real buttons, I could have just popped the sucker open. Instead, I got it up over my bra when he grabbed my arms. Maybe later I'd be glad I chose to wear a bra, a new red satin one even, but at the moment, I wished I hadn't worn anything beneath my shirt. The faces around the table were mortified.

"Look! Take a good look!" I twisted away from Alex and turned my back to them. The intake of breath told me maybe showing them my back wasn't the most convincing way to prove I didn't have any bruises. The scars from the back door glass still crisscrossed my back in white streaks.

"Alex didn't do that, okay? The scars were from a creaky goddamned house with weak window panes and a good blast of wind."

I turned and caught Kimber's eye. She beamed at me. Was she beaming? Holy shit, she was. Everyone else looked mortified, but she looked as proud of me as I felt of Alex. Huh…I guess I had her on my side.

"Anyway, do you see any bruises? Here, look at my stomach. My neck." By this time, I'd gotten the shirt completely off. I stood at my friends' beautifully decorated table in my bra, surrounded by crystal and china and silverware.

Classy. Real classy, Sam.

Now what? Should I put the shirt back on? Or own it and finish my dinner without it? I decided to own it and sat down.

Alex shook his head. Kimber burst out laughing, followed by Jillian. The guys did everything they could to avoid looking at me. And Thea was beet red, from anger or embarrassment?

Who cares? I thought.

"Dinner is scrumptious, as always, Kimber," I said, stuffing a bite into my mouth. "Colin, can you pass me the wine?"

He picked it up and handed it to me, but he avoided eye contact. He didn't even once glance at my breasts. *Impressive.* Maybe he was a good guy.

Alex leaned over, kissed my cheek, and nonchalantly whispered in my ear, "Damn, I love you, but can I suggest half a glass instead of a full glass?" He winked at me and I saw the wisdom in his words.

I poured myself half a glass.

"So, is this proof enough, Colin? Or do you need me to take off my pants?" I said, reaching down for the buttons on my 501s.

"No! No, I'm good," he said, holding up his hands, a knife in one hand, fork in the other. Still, he did not look at me.

He didn't apologize to Alex and if I'd have had more wine, I might have threatened him with more clothing removal unless he apologized. But, we had a civil discussion about domestic violence. Thea didn't participate. I didn't think my actions warranted her silence, but so be it.

Jillian had been quiet through dinner, too. She interjected a few times, but she wasn't as talkative as usual. I noticed a few goo-goo eyes between her and Anthony.

"Jilli, what's new with you?" I asked, giving her a pointed look. A slow smile slid across her face and she looked at Anthony. He nodded and she burst out.

"We're pregnant!"

"That's why you rejected my offer of wine earlier!" Kimber said, smiling.

There were cheers and another toast. Kimber brought out an amazing crème brûlée and the dinner ended on a very good note.

The drive home flew by in a drunken haze. I slid into the truck as close to Alex as I could get and he wrapped his arm around me. I clutched his hand. With only the glow of the dashboard lighting up Alex's face, I could see his happiness.

"Did I tell you I'm proud of you?" I asked.

"Like a hundred times," he laughed.

I kissed the back of his hand and said, "A hundred and one, now."

He slid his fingers beneath the edge of my shirt and made slow circles on my bare shoulder.

"Mmm...you're giving me goosebumps," I said.

"I know," he laughed. "I can feel them. Should I stop?"

"No. Should I?" I said, sliding my hand up and down his thigh.

"No."

We pulled into our driveway, and after he turned off the truck, he shifted so he faced me.

"I love you, everything about you. Even when you take off your clothes in front of our closest friends and embarrass the hell out of me." He kissed me and my toes curled. I felt the tip of his tongue on my lip, sending zings down between my thighs.

He pulled away to open the door. "Wait there."

He hurried around to the other side of the truck and opened my door. I laughed.

"Mr. Chivalry," I said, stepping down into the driveway. Panic interrupted the moment I saw the gate behind us open. He followed my gaze, then quickly hit the switch to close it.

"He's not here anymore, remember?" Alex said.

"He could be, though. I'm sorry. Let's begin again," I said, pulling him close so I could kiss him once more. Before I could, he scooped me up and carried a laughing, very drunk me onto the porch. He paused, looking at the door.

"Keys are in my pocket," he said and I laughed again. A light across the street turned on. Rosemary? Or Jim? I flipped them the bird, unsure whether they could see me. Alex set me down, pulled the keys out, unlocked the door, gathered me up again, and carried me over the threshold.

"I don't think I've done this before," he said, kicking the door closed behind us.

"You definitely have not. Lock it, please."

We paused in the foyer. The stairs loomed in front of us.

"Couch," we said simultaneously. He carried me to the sofa. I skimmed my fingertips over his jawline, onto his lips. He took one in his mouth and sucked.

He lay me down, more gently than I thought possible, then turned on the Tiffany lamps.

"I want to see you," he said. I stood then and began slowly peeling off my clothes, first the delicate blouse, then my button-up blue jeans, slipping each metal disc slowly out of each hole. He'd seen the satin red bra, but not the matching thong.

"Mesmerizing," he said.

"I love you, Alexander Zane Kearney."

A shudder went through me and he hadn't touched me yet; he just stood there gazing at me, the words I said to him repeated back to me in his eyes. I felt it from the tips of my toes, to the tips of my brown hair. The invisible connection between Alex and me felt like I could almost touch it. I held out my hand to him and he took it and we stood, holding hands, kissing, before we made love on the couch.

I lay in his arms after, delirious with our lovemaking, almost asleep when he whispered, "I love you, Samantha Aileen Kearney. Forever and always."

The next morning I woke, still on the couch with Alex's arm and leg wrapped around me. I wished I hadn't made plans so early, but it had been a few weeks since I'd seen Maggie, so I disentangled myself from Alex and dragged my ass upstairs to get ready. I even showered, then waited for Maggie to pick me up at nine. I was on time, she was ten minutes late.

"Sorry I'm late," Maggie said when I slid into the car next to her.

"What's your excuse? I'm hungover and *I'm* on time," I said.

"Oh, Morgan was mad because I wouldn't bring him with me. He threw a fit, so Russ wouldn't let me leave until we got him calmed down. I keep thinking he'll outgrow the tantrums." She shoved her hair back away from her face and pulled away from the curb. She wore the amethyst and tourmaline earrings and necklace I gave her and I breathed a sigh of relief. We'd given them all jewelry, even necklaces for the boys, before they were allowed to come over. It didn't mean Bartholomew couldn't follow them, but we hoped it would deter him if he knew they were as vigilant as we were.

"Alex needs to witness one of Morgan's tantrums. Maybe he'll drop the baby issue then," I said.

Maggie laughed and nodded. "He very well might!"

We went to Chez Louis, a French bistro near downtown Denver. White lights hung draped across the top of the butter-colored stucco outside. The sidewalk was lined with yellow zinnias, white petunias, and violet wisteria. Inside, it had mismatched padded cane chairs and spindly wooden tables. One taper candle rested in the center of each table; some of the candles were burned down to nubs. Chalk-printed menus hung above the small wine bar.

We were seated with a view of the garden, where the ruby red tomatoes nearly burst on the vines. Basil, rosemary, and sage scents drifted in from the partially open windows. Whoever tended their garden was equally as talented as Max.

I sipped my café au lait and listened to the noise while Maggie used the bathroom. The smell of cream and pancake batter filled the air, making my stomach grumble and turn at the same time. Hangovers were nonexistent in my twenties, but they slowly made their appearance now and I did not like them. I didn't think I was an alcoholic, but did waking up with a hangover make me one? Well, if it became a regular weekend habit, I'd have to consider the possibility... For now, I would have my wine. It was healthy, right?

We ordered beignets and eggs benedict, mine with salmon, hers with ham. Then I recounted the night before. She had a good laugh when I told her I sat through most of dinner in my bra.

"Your friends have a point, though, Sam. It is weird you don't ever invite them over. Do you think Bartholomew is still a threat?"

"We aren't sure. Max came over a few days ago and didn't see him, but he could be hiding somewhere. We would never know. I hate being prisoners in our own house. Alex is getting restless. He keeps asking me about kids."

"Sam, you know how I feel about this. You need to tell him. The longer you don't tell him, the more damage you're doing to your relationship."

"If I told him, we wouldn't *have* a relationship. Did I tell you about when his sister got pregnant after we moved in together?"

"Refresh my memory, please. My memory hasn't come back after having kids," she laughed.

"It was Kate's sixth. She went to Alex for advice. Since he and I were 'living in sin,' she thought he'd be more supportive. She didn't want to have another, but her husband didn't believe in birth control. Alex told her she didn't have a choice—he said it was immoral to have an abortion. I couldn't tell him after that. I'd hoped maybe he would change his mind about women who had abortions, but I've been afraid to even broach the subject. Some of his views have shifted a bit, like about pot and drinking. And every once in a while he even says 'fuck.'" Maggie laughed and I continued, "But this, this is different. I don't think he'd be able to forgive me."

"You still should have been honest and let him decide whether to forgive you or not."

"Thanks for the support," I said, turning my gaze away from her toward the garden. Someone hidden from view snipped fresh herbs. The scent of dill drifted in from the open window.

"Oh, don't even give me that attitude. You know if you come to me with something, I'm going to be honest." She paused and stared pointedly at me. I could see her out of the corner of my eye.

Our food arrived and I felt grateful, for a moment, to have our mouths busy with something other than talking. I blew on a bite of salmon benedict and slid it into my mouth. Delicious creaminess.

"What happened to Alex's sister?"

"She had the baby, but the doctor said she put her life at risk with each pregnancy, so her husband agreed to a tubal. I wondered if Kate asked her doctor for help. But I never asked."

"It is so crazy to me that we still live in a man's world. It's 1984, for fuck's sake," Maggie said.

After I finished my breakfast and brushed the beignet powdered sugar off the front of my shirt, I said, "So, are you guys thinking of staying in the house? It's quite an adjustment."

"Honestly, I think it's a little small. We're really grateful, but the boys are *not* enjoying squeezing into one room. Three's a bit too crowded. We do love Stafford, though. I wasn't sure we would. Dillon is struggling to make friends a little, but he joined the football team and is doing better. Shane and Morgan jumped right in; they had sleepover invites the first week. Cool new kids from California," she laughed.

"So, you think you'll stay?"

"In Colorado? Yeah, I think we'll stay. You got us for life, my friend."

BARTHOLOMEW

Stephanie did not call or stop by after their fight. Lanie alternated between feeling guilty and getting angry with Stephanie all over again for siding with her mom.

Why does everyone think they know what's best for me? I can make my own fucking decisions, she thought.

Yes, I replied. Because I knew the girl's decisions might not be beneficial for her, but they could benefit me. If only I could convince her.

Lanie spent Friday and Saturday rearranging her room, cleaning out her dresser, closet. She'd tossed everything into the middle of the room, similar to what her mom had done earlier in the week, but Lanie didn't feel angry. She just wanted to organize. The pile grew. She threw out babyish birthday cards her aunts and uncles had given her over the years. *Why do I keep all this stuff?*

She found a card her dad had given her for Halloween, a few weeks before he died. It had three pumpkins on the front with an awful pun inside. Her dad didn't buy greeting cards, except for on rare occasions. When he did, he always chose the cheesiest one he could find. Lanie pulled out her journal and started writing down the memory.

The last year I went trick-or-treating, my dad gave me a stupid card. It had three pumpkins jumping up and down. Inside it said, "Happy Halloween, from the Jumping Jacks." His note said, "Remember, you're never too old for Halloween, Love, Dracudad." He gave me ten dollars to buy hot apple ciders and candy apples from the candy shop.

I dressed up like a gypsy, Stephanie dressed up as a baby doll. I felt so grown up, staying out past dark by myself. My dad had to convince my mom it would be okay. He was always doing that. My mom was the worry wart; Dad could reason with her.

Maybe journaling isn't so bad. This doesn't hurt. It feels good. I'll have to see what Stephanie's doing for Halloween. Maybe she'll forgive me by then and we could go get hot apple ciders again and dress up.

She set down her pen. Her soul glowed brightly; happiness filled her body. I felt misery. Pure misery.

Early Sunday morning we dreamed. Mark grew claws, wicked and sharp, made of bone. He sliced open our belly with one swift stroke, buried his face in the gore, gnawing at our guts with his dull human teeth. Pain sliced through us, both sharp and blunt. I screamed, waking Lanie. Pain coursed through our middle, the bed soaked with sweat. Lanie reached down between her legs and felt something wet. She leaned over and pulled the cord to the bedside lamp.

Blood covered the sheets, her fingers. Soaked through her nightgown. I looked around for an intruder, sure someone had snuck in and stabbed us while we slept. A sharpness in our belly caused me to writhe.

It was a dream. Just a dream. No one's here, Lanie thought.

Then where is all this blood coming from?! I replied.

"Shit, I got my stupid period."

What in God's name did period mean? Was I experiencing her woman's curse?!

Abomination! I thought.

Abomination? What the fuck? Did I just call myself an abomination? It happens a few days every month. It's no big deal, Lanie, she thought.

Every month? A few days? No. Absolutely not. I had to get out! A cramp rolled through us and I crumpled. I felt blood gush from her...body. I tried to twist away from the pain, pushing against my confinements, attempting to escape with no success.

Ahhh! I screamed.

Lanie rolled out of bed, moving carefully to limit the blood leaking to prevent further damage to the bed linens.

Linens? She worried about linens when blood poured from her orifice! Why did she not scream and cry and claw at her belly?!

Lanie peeled off the nightgown and shoved it between her legs.

Better a cheap nightgown than dripping blood all over the floor, she thought.

She wobbled to the bathroom where she sat on the toilet and opened a plastic cylinder. She shoved a piece of rolled cotton up inside her...lady part, then shifted it around. Using her bare fingers! Blood dripped from the tips of her nails as she reached for toilet paper.

She showered then, rinsing the vileness from her legs.

Is this why I never witnessed Abigail with her curse, or Samantha? I suppose they did one thing right—they protected me from this heinous experience.

Lanie felt unfazed.

She returned to the bedroom with the godforsaken cotton scraping against her insides with every step. There had to be something better than cotton to stop the bleeding. Remove the entire organ, maybe?! I didn't know which sensation felt worse—trying to force the thing up higher or move so it would slide lower. Every time we stepped, it jabbed. Jabbed! Jabbed!

She glanced at the bed then she said, "Oh, this isn't so bad."

Wasn't so bad?! The girl would certainly hemorrhage to death! How could there be so much blood?!

She pulled the sheets off and returned to the bathroom where she dabbed soap onto the blood spots. From my point of view, she would need more soap... The girl surprised me with her conscientiousness as she then took the soiled nightgown and linens and started a load of laundry. Without her mother prompting her.

"Everything okay, Lanie?" Her mother stood in the hallway, hair mussed.

"Yeah, I just got my period."

"Okay, need anything? Midol?"

"Nah, it's not too bad."

Not too bad?! I shouted.

She ignored me, remade the bed, and promptly fell back to sleep. All the while we were pummeled in the stomach every few minutes. How could she sleep? I tossed and turned inside our body, wishing for some sort of relief. I felt certain she would be dead from blood loss within the hour. I hoped her death would release me…

I waited, anticipating the last beat of her heart as it pushed more blood from her body.

Another punch, another stab. My soul screamed.

The girl did not stir. Even when her mother slipped in to give her a kiss goodbye, just before the sun began lighting up our room.

SAMANTHA

Max stopped by mid-Sunday morning. Alex and I were preparing a picnic lunch to take up to Lair O' the Bear park. I'd stopped going to the reserve after Bartholomew's last attack so we ventured farther away where it would be impossible for him to follow.

"I still don't see him. I've walked up and down three blocks on either side of you. He's gone," Max said.

I stared at him, stunned. Had Bartholomew finally moved on? I shook my head in disbelief. I knew deep down he was too stubborn. Despite my doubts, I breathed out and felt myself relax. For the moment, he didn't occupy the space outside my fence glaring at us and I would take the little victories when I could.

I had Max walk through the house again to be sure. We saw no sign of Bartholomew.

"Well, he's fooled us before. It's going to take a little more time for me to let my guard down. Still, it feels good to know he's not out there right now," I said.

"I'll keep watch," Max said, then left.

What would life be like without the fear of Bartholomew watching everything we did? I'd shut him out of my life so completely, but still lived in fear of his continuous presence. My house never saw the sun rays and felt dreary all the time because I refused to open any curtains. It could be depressing, especially in the freezing winter.

Alex looked ecstatic at Max's news. I felt anxious.

We were back in the kitchen finishing up preparations for our lunch.

"Sam, now can we have a family? He's gone. We're free of him."

My stomach flipped. Instead of answering for a minute, I pulled lettuce leaves apart and placed them on our sandwiches.

"I don't know, Alex. I have this feeling he's not—"

A knock at the front door interrupted me.

Alex and I looked at each other for a moment, then he went to answer the door.

I heard him say, "Can I help you?"

"Is Ms. Blaine home?" a girl's voice asked. I wiped my hands on a dish towel and walked to the front door where I saw Lanie standing on the porch.

"Hey Lanie, what's up?" I stepped outside and motioned for her to sit in one of the rocking chairs. She waved me off, so I stood as well.

"Stephanie said you freaked out. And you called Mrs. Jones?" She looked at her feet while she talked to me. I could sense her nervousness and then I picked up on another emotion, resentment maybe? "I just wanted to tell you I was sorry for whatever happened last week. I'm okay. So, um, could you chill?"

She looked up at me then, her face contorted from serious to partial smile to...hate? Her eyes shifted. I felt an odd conflict coming from her, something like scorn. She looked sober. No glassy eyes today.

"I know I don't have a good reason to worry about you. It shouldn't be my business. But when you walked through my door last week, I felt like you needed someone."

"I don't need you," she growled. "I have a mother."

It definitely felt like scorn radiating off of her now. She dropped her arms and squeezed her fist closed, then open, then closed again. I took a step away from her, feeling afraid. This girl, who couldn't have been more than five feet tall, maybe eighty pounds, suddenly terrified me. I felt irrational, crazy.

"Okay, I'm sorry. I'll leave you and Stephanie alone."

Lanie turned and left without another word. I stood, leaning against the porch railing for a moment watching her walk away, feeling like I had grossly overstepped my boundaries. Could that have been why I felt afraid?

No. Something felt wrong.

Alex came out the door. "Everything okay?"

"Yeah...I think so. Lanie put in my place, but I'm fine."

He came up behind me and wrapped his arms around my waist. I leaned back into the embrace.

"It feels nice to stand out here without worrying about being watched by Bartholomew," I said.

"It does," he replied, kissing my hair. "I'm serious about starting a family."

I rolled my eyes, sure he couldn't see me. I had to talk to him. Today.

We finished packing up our lunch, then headed up the hill. We took my 1963 black convertible Nova. Once we were on the outskirts of the foothills, we stopped and took the top down.

I'd been thinking about how to talk to Alex, to see if maybe he somehow changed his mind about abortions. I almost brought it up a couple of times after I heard the ladies in the office talking, but I chickened out. With the top down, I felt less claustrophobic. Before I could talk myself out of it again, I jumped.

"Have you heard about the bombings happening at the abortion clinics around the country? My co-workers have been talking about them. There've been dozens this year alone," I said.

He turned to look at me, a scowl on his face. I pointed to the windy road.

"Why are you bringing that up?"

"I just heard a couple of people talking about it on Friday and I haven't stopped thinking about it."

"I've heard about them," he said with a slight shrug. "No one got hurt. Maybe they'll stop murdering innocent babies now," he said, almost nonchalantly.

I felt my face get red and I had to look away. He had the right to believe whatever he wanted, but how would he feel if he knew the woman he loved "murdered a baby"?

"So, it's okay to bomb these buildings as long as no one gets hurt?" I asked, still staring at the passing road cutouts, trying not to get dizzy as the uneven streaks sped past. I could not look at him.

"It's just money the clinics are out and it's not like they have to pay for it. Insurance covers that kind of stuff."

"What happens when someone does get hurt, because they inevitably will? What if someone dies?"

He shrugged. "I don't know what you want me to say, Sam. They're committing murder. You believe in karma, so...they're getting their karma."

I don't know what I thought his reaction would be. Did I need to hear him say it? That he believed women who aborted babies were murderers? I suppose I did. I wanted to jump out of the car as we did fifty up the mountain road. The claustrophobia I'd felt with the top up returned, so maybe I didn't feel claustrophobic after all. Anxiety? My stomach felt sick, my throat constricted, my vision pulsed. Breathing felt difficult. I wanted to scream and shout at him, ask him if he believed I was a murderer. But somehow the words would not come out. My mouth stayed closed.

"Can you pull off at the next town?"

"We're almost there. What's going on with you?"

I continued staring at the window, trying to calm myself, attempting to understand why he felt the way he did. Why did he think he had any say about a woman's body? Our beliefs didn't always align and I understood he was raised differently than me. I accepted our differences, loved them even. This felt different and I hadn't expected such a visceral reaction at his words.

"What?" he asked when I didn't respond.

I stared out the window instead of answering him. I couldn't look at him then—he disgusted me and I felt afraid of my disgust. My hands shook.

He pulled into the empty parking lot, the reason we liked this spot—very few other people came here. I jumped out of the car before he turned it off and hurried to the closest trail. It led through a copse of dark pine trees. Fear slowed me down momentarily, but I pressed on.

"Hey!" he yelled.

"I just...I need to be alone," I said without looking back. I hurried down the trail, getting lost in the woods. It'd been so long since I walked alone, surrounded by trees and rustling pine needles. Trees that could be manipulated by an evil spirit making them crash down at any minute. Limbs that could break my bones, knock me unconscious. But right then, I would rather face Bartholomew than the feelings I had for my husband.

I couldn't tell him the truth. I would never be able to tell him the truth.

"Sam!" I heard him calling.

I ran. The trail ended at the creek, so I turned right. I knew he could see me once the trees cleared; still I ran, my breath coming in painful gulps. I never did take up running, even though I swore I would after Bartholomew attacked me in the reserve. The exhilaration cleared the energy block I felt, releasing it so I no longer felt clogged, heavy. I still couldn't breathe, but for a very different reason. I crossed the bridge over Bear Creek and looked back. Alex stood on the trail, hands loose against his sides. Empty. He raised them in a *what the fuck* motion, then turned and walked back the way he came.

I kept running.

Before I realized it, I'd reached an incline, and I felt completely out of breath. I stopped. The tears came then; sobs shook my body. I bent over, resting my hands on my knees and instantly felt nauseous, then stood.

I screamed until my vocal chords burned, hearing my voice echo back to me. Could Alex hear me?

I screamed again, not caring if he could. Forcing myself to stop crying. I climbed, pushed my body to its limits. My leg muscles burned with exertion. I wished I had grabbed one of the bottles of water we brought, but they were in the picnic basket, in the trunk of the Nova.

Murderer. I murdered my baby. The only baby I would give life to. After a few paces, I collapsed on the rocky ground. Jagged pieces dug into my knees. If I could undo it so Alex and I could have a family, I would. God, I would. *But I can't, so now what the fuck do I do?*

Murderer. My husband believed I committed the ultimate sin. I dropped back onto my butt, relieving the pain from my knees, but not from my heart. Snot ran down my face; I wiped at it with my sweaty T-shirt.

I realized something, then. I'd talked about it to Brian and Maggie and even Bartholomew, but still I hadn't forgiven myself. I believed I had, so many times. But now? Right now I could feel the guilt, the pain, the devastation of losing my only child, buried deep in my gut, like a giant serrated stone. I still punished myself. Why?

Did I ever grieve the child? Or just the loss of my ability to have more children? I couldn't remember. There had been so much agony at the time, I don't know what I processed and what I didn't.

I deserve to be punished, I thought. Yes, that felt right. And wrong all at the same time. I'd been punishing myself for sixteen years. Why the fuck couldn't I forgive myself? I sat on the side of the mountain, overlooking the park. Watching the miniscule cars drift by on the serpentine road.

I breathed. And listened. All I could hear was the wind.

A quiet solitude overcame me then, and a voice said, *Let go, it's okay. We got you.*

I closed my eyes and rested my head on my knees. The sun beat down on the top of my head. I imagined it filling my body, healing the hurt as it slid down my neck, through my lungs, into my belly and my womb.

My empty womb.

I don't know how long I sat there with my eyes closed letting the sun's rays heal me.

"I thought you might be thirsty after your hike."

I looked up to see Alex standing on the trail, holding the picnic basket and blanket. Why did I have to fall in love with someone who would hate me if he knew what I'd done? Tears welled in my eyes again. He took a tentative step toward me. "There's some shade, just over there." He motioned with the wicker picnic basket. "Let's have our picnic."

He walked past me and I stood to follow. He lay the blanket out beneath the shade of a blue spruce, the only Colorado pine tree I could identify.

I drank my entire bottle of water, not caring that I didn't have any for the walk back to the car. It was all downhill from here.

"Sam?" he said softly. "Will you tell me why you were so upset?"

I shook my head. Resolved to never tell him, to never think of it again. I would just pretend. I could not have the man I gave my heart to look at me and call me a murderer.

BARTHOLOMEW

To my chagrin, Lanie did not die. I could not fathom why she did not with the amount of blood loss. "Periods," as she called them, were more proof women were devils and their monthly bleeding and pain proved God hated them. The girl should have spent Sunday relaxing, lying about and massaging our belly. Instead, she insisted on walking to Sam's house to "tell her off" and then she frantically finished cleaning her room.

I wanted to strangle Sam. Lanie felt angry at Sam's interference and threats. I fed on her anger, pushing The Darkness, expanding it. I clenched our fists in frustration.

Since Lanie's suspension, I had been unsuccessful at controlling her. She'd been sober and I realized, without drugs, I had no power over her. I didn't know what I would do. I had no idea how to get out. Panic took over when I thought about being trapped inside this girl for the rest of eternity. Would our souls merge into one?

We walked to school the first day after Lanie's suspension. Stephanie was not waiting on her front porch for us, so we continued on alone.

The closer we got to school, the more Lanie panicked. She stopped several times to give herself a pep talk.

You can do this, Lanie, no reason to panic, she thought. *Just keep your head down.*

If Lanie thought wearing a Mötley Crüe T-shirt with a pentagram showed she "kept her head down," she was crazier than I originally thought.

We got through the morning without any outbursts, even in the history class. Stephanie refused to speak to us. Lanie would catch her eye and give her a quick smile. Stephanie ignored her. I paid close attention to what Lanie did. She wrote *September 20, 1984* on the top of one of her papers.

The year 1884, one hundred years before, had been a good year for me. I had been thirty-seven. My wife had finally moved to Colorado and adored the house I built for her. She slipped into her duties and reveled in the attention she received for her fine clothes and Southern manners. The seven years between Abigail joining me in the home I built for her and finding the love letters she wrote to her lover had been almost perfect.

Then I discovered the letters hidden beneath her lace-fringed combinations and satin chemises in a drawer of her bureau. As I read her letters, the ache within me grew. What an actress she had been! While she awaited my return from the war, she acquired another lover. In the letters she told him of my inability to show emotion, my lack of affection toward her, and how she wished for my death. She called me self-absorbed! A Yankee sympathizer! The one who gave her all she could possibly hope for and whisked her away from the poverty she detested living in. My Abby, my beautiful, angelic Abby.

Lanie skipped her fourth-hour PE class every day by hiding in the stairwell near the shop classes. She hated the gym clothes, changing in front of everyone, and everything about physical education. She learned very quickly how easy she could cut class. The school never called her mother and the teachers only confronted students if they returned to class without a signed excuse letter. I desperately wanted to look in the windows of the wood-working class, but Lanie would not move from the stairwell.

School lunch was an interesting ritual. Lanie didn't eat anything from the lunch line; instead she spent her money at the large glass machines, choosing chocolate-covered peanut butter cups and a fizzy soda. The bubbles tickled our tongue, but tasted horrible after the too-sweet candy.

She joined Stephanie on a concrete patio outside the lunchroom with a group of hooligans who smoked cigarettes.

"Hi," Lanie said.

"Hey," Stephanie replied.

"Look. I really am sorry. I don't know why I said what I did, but you know me. It's not a word I would use."

This again, I thought.

Stephanie remained quiet.

"I, uh, I stopped smoking pot. That was the last day. I think it made me feel too out of control. It's not an excuse, but I just wanted you to know."

Stephanie looked up at us then and smiled. "Really? I'm glad," she said.

The teens nearby discussed rowdy weekend parties while we choked on their secondhand smoke. Only one of the young smokers turned away from us when she blew out her smoke. Hearing this group of teens made me glad I was dead, as it would have terrified me otherwise to know these ruffians would be responsible adults one day.

A group of girls with dark hair at least three feet high, letter jackets, and flashy purses walked past us.

"That's her," one of them said and pointed at us.

"Racist bitch," another girl said, then threw her full paper cup of soda at us. It hit us smack in the chest and exploded into our face. Sticky brown liquid dripped from our chin, down our shirt. The straw snagged in the waistband of our jeans before flitting to the ground.

Lanie glared at them as they passed, fighting to keep the tears from falling. She refused to let them see her cry.

"What, bitch? Wanna fight?" a third girl said, throwing up her arms. She stopped a few feet from us.

Lanie dropped her gaze and the girls laughed.

While the soda felt unpleasant, I thought it nothing compared to Lanie's period, or the sex she had, so I could not understand why she became so upset.

As the girls walked around the corner out of sight, Lanie burst into tears and we ran for the bathroom.

The cold and echoey bathroom had large white tiles smudged with blacks, reds, and blues. I assumed they were caused by the lip and eye coloring these teens overused. Mirrors were scratched with sayings such as *Kelly + Adam* and *Sissy is a bitch*. Only idiot juveniles would go through the torture of scratching words into glass.

Lanie soaked a couple of paper towels and tried to wash the soda from her hair. The shirt was soaked in sticky fluid. Streaks dripped down the points of the pentagram design. I hoped they ruined the devil shirt. The door squeaked so we hurried to one of the stalls.

"Lanie," Stephanie called.

Opening the door a crack, we saw her standing there with a towel and a T-shirt.

"This is from my gym locker. There's no one in there if you want to hurry. I thought a towel would help, but I think it's going to make it worse. If you don't wash, the pop will dry sticky and hard."

"This is fucking mortifying," Lanie said, a sob escaping.

"Come on, I'll be a lookout and tell you when it's clear to cross the hall. Everyone is either eating lunch inside or hanging outside. No one will see you."

"Then what am I supposed to do? I have sixth period with Misty."

"Fuck them, Lanie," Stephanie said, shocking Lanie. She never used the F-word. "You shouldn't have said what you did, but I know you. You aren't racist. I've met plenty of them. We wouldn't be friends if you were. Don't let them get to you," she said, patting us on the arm.

"Okay, let's go before I chicken out, but I'm not going to class."

Stephanie rolled her eyes then walked to the bathroom door. We waited for a few minutes until Stephanie motioned us forward, then we hurried across the hall, not lifting up our head to see if anyone noticed.

It didn't take long to shower and dress, as we worried someone would walk in. The shirt Stephanie gave us was yellow with pink and orange flowers.

"There is no way I am going to class looking like this. I'm sorry, Stephanie, I'm not into your style. But, I love you! And I really am grateful for the shirt."

"I know it's too bright for you. It's okay. But you can't miss class again."

"It's fine. I'll grab a bus and go to the mall."

Stephanie sighed and shrugged. "I worry about you, but I'm not going with you. If I get in trouble, my parents will make me cancel my slumber party."

"I'll be fine. Go," Lanie said.

Stephanie turned to leave the locker room. Lanie ran to catch up to her, put her arms around her back, and said, "I don't know what I'd do without you, Anie."

Stephanie reached up and gave Lanie's arms a squeeze. "I wish you'd go to class, Anie. I don't want you to get in more trouble."

Isn't that cute...they have the same pet name for each other.

Lanie considered what her friend said, but we didn't leave. We hid in one of the locker room bathroom stalls until we heard tennis shoes shuffle up the stairs to the gym above. As soon as the bell rang and the hallways cleared, we snuck out the side door and hurried to the school stadium where we sat cross-legged under the shade of the bleachers. Lanie cried and cried and cried. And cried! Her shoulders shook, her whole body shook. She curled her legs up, wrapping her arms tightly around herself. Her thoughts raced between getting suspended, hurting her friend, the mean girls, her dad, her mother, back to the mean girls, and then to how she felt she let her best friend down. That brought on a fresh wave of self-pitying tears. I was trapped, listening to the whiny child. Oh the misery!

I couldn't do this. I had to get control or get out.

The school bell rang in the distance, distracting Lanie enough to stop her blubbering. Kids started pouring out of the gym doors walking toward the stadium. Lanie finally stood and walked the opposite direction of the school. We wandered the streets for a bit, unsure what to do or where to go.

We can always go to Mark's, I thought.

Mark. He didn't even call to see if I was okay. Did he know I got suspended? Why do I even bother with him? He only wants me around because I sleep with him. What a jerk.

Pity. A wonderful emotion. Her misery allowed me to spread out, fill The Darkness. I kept going with my thoughts. *People are cruel. They are selfish and mean. They only pretend to care about you when it's convenient, when they need something from you. Otherwise, they cast you aside and don't give you a second thought.*

My attempt at manipulating her still didn't allow me the control I needed. Instead, she meandered aimlessly, until she decided to walk to the nursing home where she volunteered. Perfect rectangular bushes lined the circular driveway, not a stick or a leaf out of place. Large pots of various-colored geraniums adorned the entrance and two concrete benches opposite each other. No one in their right mind would want to sit there for long stretches of time.

Do NOT go in there, Lanie. They'll rat on you.

No they won't, I cut school last year and came here. They didn't tell anyone.

She pulled the double doors open and the stench of disinfectant, sickness, and beef hit us. Lanie smiled; I retched. Lanie walked to the receptionist's desk, which sat empty, so she waited. The sterile white walls, floors, and counters reminded me of my previous tenants. A maddening absence of color. How did the inhabitants stay sane?

Some of them don't, Lanie thought.

"Lanie! We didn't expect you today."

We turned to see a Black women dressed in an all-white frock, with soft-soled white shoes that allowed her to sneak up on us.

Maybe there was too much color, I thought.

Our face frowned. Lanie's tolerance dumbfounded me.

My father would be proud.

Why did the painful memory of watching my father kill Andre keep resurfacing?! I buried it more than a hundred years ago. And now, in this, this time of assorted people, it returned. To remind me of what happened if I fraternized with non-whites. But, I had no choice now! The girl controlled me! I slipped down, deep inside our belly. Away from Lanie's Light, into the disappearing Darkness. Hiding from my own demons.

No, no. I have no demons.

"I had a...half-day. Teacher conference."

"Well, we aren't quite prepared for you, but I'm sure Ms. Valencia is up for a polish. She always loves to see you."

Lanie went quiet again. The image of a healthy woman with cropped dark brown hair, brown skin—*Like a permanent golden sun tan*, Lanie thought—filled her mind. The image shifted, replaced by one where the woman's hair had been exchanged with a scarf. Only her bright, welcoming smile remained the same.

"How...how is she?"

The woman's face grew sad and she shook her head. "She's in quite a bit of pain these days—the cancer is moving quick. I'm sorry. I know you two have grown fond of each other."

I felt an immense sadness within Lanie, but The Darkness didn't grow.

"She's heavily medicated, but she's still very aware." The woman motioned to a room next to the receptionist station. "Want to get your cart?"

Lanie hesitated for a moment, then nodded.

The woman unlocked the door and Lanie went inside to push out a two-columned blue plastic bureau on wheels. It smelled like chemicals.

Acetone and nail polish, Lanie thought and smiled.

"You know the way. I'm going to finish up my paperwork," the woman said. Before she walked away, she put a hand on Lanie's shoulder. "I'm really glad to see you. You brighten her day, you really do. She's missed you."

Lanie smiled, then pushed the cart down the corridor. We passed an old white man with cotton-colored tufts sticking out of the top of his head sitting in a wheelchair, crying. He smelled of urine. He paid us no attention. I wasn't sure he knew we passed. With killing myself, is that the fate I avoided?

The sadness in Lanie deepened.

I hate seeing them sit alone and cry, she thought.

After a short walk, we stopped in front of a closed door. Lanie knocked and a scratchy voice we barely heard said, "Come in."

We pushed the door open with one hand and guided the cart inside. The room was covered in pink and blue floral wallpaper. A beige plastic couch sat across from the occupied hospital bed. Surprise filled me. The woman who lay in in the bed was young—I expected an old decrepit lady like the man in the wheelchair. This woman had no hair, sunken bright brown eyes, but her skin held no wrinkles. No scarf covered her bald head now.

She's the same age as my mom, Lanie thought. *Forty. But she never had kids and her husband left her when she got sick. I shouldn't have stayed away so long.*

"Hermanita!" She whispered, but the woman's face lit up. "I haven't seen you in weeks. I'm so happy you're here. How's school? Your mom? Stephanie?"

Love welled up inside Lanie, pushing The Darkness away. Lanie pushed the cart around the bed next to a hard plastic chair.

"Hi, Ms. Valencia," Lanie said, ignoring her questions. *My problems are nothing right now*, she thought. "Want me to paint your nails?"

"Sure, sure. Help me up?"

Lanie moved to the side of the bed, raised it so the woman could sit, then wrapped her arms gently around the woman and helped her adjust.

She weighed nothing.

"Comfortable?"

"For now," the woman replied.

"What color?" Lanie asked.

"You pick your favorite."

I expected the girl to choose black, because it was the color she had on her own nails. Instead, she chose a soft pink. Lanie turned a bed tray so the woman could rest her hand on it. First Lanie washed the woman's hand with a tenderness I didn't think she possessed. She massaged the cuticles, gently rubbed her fingers. Her behavior surprised me. She treated her mother with such disdain, but this stranger she showed kindness.

Why do you hate your mom so much? I thought.

Because I can't hate my dad, Lanie replied. *She's the reason he's dead.*

"You didn't answer my questions," the woman said.

"Everyone's good. I got suspended from school, so my mom grounded me."

"You're smarter than that," the woman said with a smirk.

"I know. It was dumb."

"Don't be too hard on yourself—everyone makes mistakes. Did you learn from it?"

Lanie huffed, "Yeah. I quit smoking pot."

"There you go! God, I wish I had some good pot." The woman closed her eyes and smiled. Lanie laughed.

"Do your fingers hurt today?"

The woman laughed. "Everything hurts, but it's okay. Keep going. Your touch is soothing."

Lanie opened up the bottle of polish and held it to her nose. I slithered away from the revolting smell, but I could not get away from it.

"I love the smell of polish," Lanie said.

"Don't breathe too much of it or it'll replace your marijuana!" the woman laughed.

Lanie smiled and applied the polish to the woman's paper-thin nails. They sat quietly for a few moments.

"Lanie, I need to tell you. I don't have much time. The doctor said maybe a week. My body is shutting down."

Lanie fought back tears, and I felt our face grow hot.

"It's okay, you can cry."

Lanie dropped her head, trying to hide the tears sliding down her cheeks.

"I'm not scared. I'm ready to not be in pain anymore. Don't be afraid for me, okay? I know that's why you haven't been to see me. Because you were here when they told me chemo wouldn't help. La Muerte isn't scary for me. Not anymore."

Lanie nodded, wiped her face on her sleeve, then picked up the polish again. She finished one hand, then started on the next.

"I'll miss you," Lanie whispered.

"I'll miss you, too."

The woman touched Lanie's head with her diseased hand. I recoiled. Would the cancer transfer to us?!

"Be good to you, hermanita. Be good to your mamá, okay?" she said as Lanie closed the polish.

"I'll try."

"Don't try. Do," she said.

Lanie moved the tray and the cart out of the way, hugged the woman, then lowered the bed.

"Goodbye, Lanie," she said.

"I love you, Ms. Valencia," Lanie whispered as she walked out the door.

As we left, she pushed the encounter deep into her subconscious, burying the memory. Was this why I didn't know about the woman until today? Why did she bury her good memories? I suppose the same reason I buried mine.

They hurt too much, she replied.

We walked to the greenbelt to hide in a tunnel until school got out, then we climbed the hill to wait for Stephanie. All the while, Lanie repressed the emotions of the day, hiding them so she didn't have to feel.

SAMANTHA

I didn't know how to talk to Alex. He kept asking me what was wrong, but I didn't know what to say. A distance grew between us after our fight, something we hadn't experienced since the very beginning of our relationship. The more days passed, the more I worried I wouldn't be able to close the divide.

So Wednesday night, I made Maggie go to The Toadstool with me. I didn't feel I could talk to anyone else about Alex. None of my other friends knew about the secret I kept. I felt safer with them not knowing.

I hadn't been to the bar in years, but it hadn't changed, except for getting a little dingier. The bar stools seriously needed to be recovered; they were hardly recognizable as toadstools. Duct tape covered tears in a few of them. Maggie and I opted to sit in one of the booths at the back of the bar, instead of risking walking around with a piece of tape stuck to our ass. We slid into a booth opposite each other. I sat facing the darkened stage. No live band tonight, just the jukebox playing glam bands.

We each ordered a glass of wine and potato skins.

"So, we're talking about *the secret*?" Maggie said after our drinks arrived.

"Oh, Mags. I tried to talk to him about it on Sunday, in a roundabout way. I brought up all the bombings. He called the people who work there 'murderers' and said it was their karma. I swore on Sunday I wouldn't give it another thought, but it's consumed me. I can't seem to let go."

She sighed and put her hand on mine.

"Do you think if he knew about you, he might shift his thinking a little? If you told him how much it haunts you, how you live with your decision every day? Maybe he'd be able to find some empathy. You aren't going to change his mind. But maybe he could understand your situation."

"And what if you're wrong? What if I tell him and he can't forgive me, if he calls me a murderer and walks out of my life? I just..." My words caught in my throat. His rejection would break me.

"So, what would you rather happen?"

"Live with the guilt, even though it makes my stomach ache," I said. "At least he won't hate me or leave."

She shook her head and said, "It's your life, but you sound miserable."

"Sam?"

I looked up to see a clean-cut man in a blazer and slacks standing at our table holding a plate of potato skins. My mouth dropped open. "Holy shit, Joel? Um, hi. You work here?" Joel and I had slept together a few times when I first moved to Stafford. He was the last person I needed to see, or be seen with right now, especially since Alex and I were struggling.

Was he a cook? I wondered. *No, wrong clothing.*

He set the plate on the table, Maggie stared wide eyed, with a slight smirk on her face.

"Well sort of. I actually own it. Along with a couple other places in town. I bought it last year."

Right, business school.

"Cool, well congratulations!" I said, reaching for my glass with my left hand, hoping my wedding rings glinted in the dim light.

He looked at my hand, then lifted his. "I heard you were married. Me, too. I met her at school in Kansas."

Relief washed over me. *Whew. This wouldn't be awkward.* I risked a glance at Maggie, she stuffed a potato in her mouth, her eyes were still laughing at me.

"We're actually expecting our first kid in a few months."

Or maybe it would be awkward. *Fucking great*, I thought.

"Well, it's good seeing you. Enjoy your night," he said.

I nodded and took another sip of my wine. My glass was almost empty.

"Hey Joel?" I called, and he turned and walked back to the table. "Can I get another glass of wine?"

"Sure."

He walked away and Maggie said, "Ooof...harsh."

I rolled my eyes at her.

"I hope he's got some money to dump into this place," Maggie said. "It needs a facelift."

I felt grateful she didn't mention Joel starting a family.

"Okay, so Alex?" I said.

She raised her eyes at me and sipped her still-full glass of wine.

"Well, if you drink that glass as fast as the last one, he'll have to come and get us..."

I threw my napkin at her judgmental ass. It missed.

"Just fuck his brains out. He'll forget all about your moodiness."

I laughed. There was wisdom in her words.

I didn't finish my wine so I could drive us back to my house an hour later. I walked Maggie to her car.

"Thanks, Mags. Really. I'd go crazy without you."

"I know," she said and climbed into her car. I shook my head and turned to walk through the gate.

"Psst! Samantha!"

Oh dear God! I waited for Rosemary to wobble across the street.

"Look! He did it!" She held out her hand. A rock as big as a grape sat on her pudgy finger. I was sure he gave her a cubic zirconia. And I really didn't care, but maybe she had no one else to tell.

"Congratulations, Rosemary."

"He must have been saving up for years!"

"Oh yes, he must have." *Or his ex-wife paid for it,* I thought. "Look, Alex is waiting for me. Congratulations again." I walked through the gate, closing it behind me.

Alex lay in bed, reading a carpentry magazine, shirtless. Damn, he looked magnificent.

"I'm sorry I got upset," I said, walking to the dresser to change into a nightgown. Maybe a sexy nightgown and I'd take Maggie's advice...

"I forgive you," he said.

Forgive me?! I stopped. *Cool it, Sam. Trying to make up, remember?* I thought. I took a deep breath then said, "It's okay if we don't believe the same way. We will have to adjust. Can you do me a favor, though? Don't use the term *murder* around me."

"I'm sorry I upset you."

I breathed a sigh of relief. I wanted to avoid the whole topic for the rest of our lives. Hopefully he agreed.

He climbed out of bed, butt-ass naked, and took the nightgown out of my hand. I stood in my bra and panties. "You don't need this," he said.

"You know, if we have kids, *this*," I said, gesturing between us, "won't happen as often."

"Eh, worth it to find out," he said, shutting me up with a kiss.

Yep, Maggie was right. Make-up sex was the cure-all for a fight.

BARTHOLOMEW

We had an uneventful rest of the week, just day after day of living with the mundane, interrupted by a teenage girl's unpredictable hormones. Her period ended on Thursday, thank God! Lanie's mom caved and ended Lanie's punishment early because *we* had helped clean the house all week. It had been my idea after all. Which meant Friday night, Lanie packed an overnight bag, stuffing pajamas, a pillow, the new cassette tape her mother had given her, and all of her makeup inside.

I yearned to be released from the hell I now lived in.

Lanie walked to Stephanie's house in the fading light and from the friend's front yard, I could see the top peak of my house. Maybe the girls would spend their time outside and we could take a walk to spy on Samantha.

Stephanie lived in a brick ranch house in the middle of a neatly trimmed grassy lot. A pear tree hung heavy with fruit and a couple of aspens with their green leaves turning to gold framed a bay window. Light from inside spilled out onto the lawn.

The interior door stood open, so we could see inside the living room. Stephanie sat perched on the edge of a wingback chair. She looked up, saw Lanie in the doorway, then hurried to let us in. Behind Stephanie an ominous darkie stood. I shouldn't have felt fear because he was inferior. But still, terror coursed through me.

The man moved next to Stephanie and rested his hand on her shoulder, then smiled warmly at Lanie. She stepped toward Stephanie, hugged her, then hugged the man.

"Dad, you promised you'd be invisible tonight."

The man laughed. "Fine, fine. I'll just be in the kitchen helping your momma with snacks." He turned and walked out of view.

'Dad?' But Stephanie had light skin! *When did Stafford allow negroes to move in?! I* thought.

Why am I thinking like this? Lanie thought, feelings of disgust filling her belly.

Memories of spending time with Stephanie's family filled Lanie's mind. She loved Stephanie's dad. For the first few weeks after her own dad died, she'd spent several days and nights with Stephanie's parents while her mom took care of funeral arrangements, financial details, and numerous other things that kept her from Lanie. Stephanie's parents held her while she cried, made her hot cocoa, and cooked some of her favorite food. Lanie wasn't ever able to talk to them about her dad, but she hadn't been able to talk to anyone about him until Sara. They were always there for her, no matter what. The thoughts she had now disturbed her—something felt wrong, but she had no idea what. *My next appointment with Sara is Tuesday, maybe she can help me.*

"Come on, we get the whole downstairs. Lisa's at my cousin's house for the night. I even baked cookies on my own!"

"I hope you used the right kind of sugar this time," Lanie teased.

"I won't make that mistake again. Powdered sugar is *not* the same as sugar," Stephanie laughed.

We passed through the kitchen where I saw the cause of Stephanie's light skin and red hair—her mother. Traitor. The husband stood behind her with his arms around her waist.

"Mmm, baby, dinner smells divine!" he said.

She laughed and kissed him on the arm.

The memory of my father's face, laughing while my friend burned, rose to the surface once again. Hatred for my father, for Andre, for Lanie who forced me to interact with this family filled my soul, pushing against what little Darkness remained in Lanie's body. I had to get out!

Lanie's joy at being in the house, with her friend, her second family, forced me back down into the space, growing smaller by the minute.

The girls continued downstairs. Piles of pillows lay on the floor in front of a giant television console. Next to it stood a large stereo system with speakers almost as tall as Lanie. Records and small cassettes like the one Lanie's mom purchased were lined up along the wall. Bowles of chips, soda and candy piled on top of a wooden coffee table. We would surely be sick after devouring the junk.

Two other girls joined the party. They giggled about boys, gossiped about girls, and consumed so much grease and sugar, I felt sure their bodies would explode from clogged arteries.

Stephanie turned out the lights, and turned on the television.

"*Poltergeist*! Seriously?!" Lanie said, overcome with excitement. "I thought you were too scared to watch this."

The *squee* erupting every five seconds from a different girl had me jumping sporadically within The Darkness. I pushed again, trying to free myself, to escape from the torment Lanie put me through. My efforts did little but exhaust me. I could not escape. I resigned myself to hiding in the shrinking Darkness.

After drinking three soda pops, Lanie had to pee. Mr. Hatch sat in the living room reading a book. When she came out of the bathroom, he looked up and smiled at her.

"Hey Lanie, are you doing okay?"

Lanie paused, then went to sit on the couch next to him. She held his gaze as they talked. "I've been feeling really weird lately. Angry. Well, angrier than usual."

He nodded. "Anie told me what you said in class last week. Do you really believe what you said?"

"No. Not one bit. I don't know why I said what I did. It felt like it wasn't me, but it was me." She looked down now, away from the man and his intense eyes. "I try to be colorblind and just see people as people."

A short burst of a laugh escaped him, kind of a "ha," but not cruel, disbelieving. She felt silly for a minute until he said, "And how's that working out for you?"

"I don't know," she said, looking back up at him.

"Let me ask you this, what color is my skin?"

Lanie stared, unsure what to say, afraid of saying the wrong thing, of somehow making this man who she respected and loved ashamed of her.

Tell him, Lanie! Tell him, he's Black as the devil.

I felt her eyes widen.

Show this man he has no power!

Her mouth stayed firmly closed. What a fool!

"It's okay, Lanie. My skin is black. I'm proud to be Black. There's nothing wrong with seeing differences; it's how you treat people who look or act different than you. Being colorblind doesn't help anyone. Can I ask you a question?"

She nodded.

"Would you call me a nigger?"

Lanie went perfectly still, and blood drained from her face. Shame coursed through her small body. I couldn't understand her reaction.

"No. Never."

He nodded. "Would you call Stephanie that?"

Tears filled Lanie's eyes. She hurt them with her outburst in school. She'd hurt her best friend and her family.

What a disgusting beast! He should be ashamed, not you, Lanie.

He slid sit next to her on the couch, put his arms around her, and she sobbed into his chest. The wife walked into the room and sat on the other side of Lanie, rubbing her back.

"I'm so sorry, Mr. Hatch." Lanie looked up at the wife. "Mrs. Hatch, I'm so, so sorry," she choked out. "I remember feeling angry, but I didn't understand why I felt that way. Mr. Arnold is an – well, he's a jerk all the time. But I never got that mad at him. My body moved, talked almost like it wasn't me. Then I screamed and I couldn't stop. It was like, like I felt so angry, I blacked out and watched myself say those things."

Stupid blathering, idiot girl. Shut up!

The longer Stephanie's parents held Lanie, the more her heart swelled and squeezed me back into the tight place I'd been after her therapy sessions, but worse. The room slid in and out of focus and I felt as though I watched the scene from the end of a tunnel.

Stephanie came upstairs then, saw her friend embraced by her parents, and wiggled in to join the crew.

"We love you, Lanie," Stephanie said. "I forgive you, but if you say that word again, I'll punch you in the nose." They held her until her tears subsided and her soul swelled and filled, pushing against me. Her body surrounded by love, even while I raged inside of her.

Say it! Say it! N-

SAMANTHA

The more distant Bartholomew's domination of me became, the more my mind quieted. There were times over the years when I missed his sarcastic humor, as twisted as it had been. But the longer I went without him, the happier I became with myself. His negativity had inhibited my ability to heal.

A day had never gone by over the past six years when Max couldn't see Bartholomew. For Max to not have seen him for almost two weeks gave Alex and me hope again. We snuggled on the couch to read or watch television—with lamps on, curtains and front door open. Every night. The screen door let in the cool September breeze. The crystals and wind chimes on the front porch tinkled and sang for us. I felt free for the first time in years. I had a difficult time remembering what life without fear felt like; it infiltrated every aspect of our lives. As long as Alex and I had been together, we had never *not* lived in fear.

Friday night we opened up the doors and windows, lit the candles on the fireplace mantle, and brought out Brian's records. We stored them beneath the end tables in metal milk crates. The record player sat in the corner on a cherrywood table Alex built with hand-carved details around the edge and on the feet. It took him six months, but we wanted something special to hold the gift Brian willed to me when he died. I didn't add to the record collection; I bought cassettes these days. It felt sacred somehow, having only Brian's records in our home.

Alex and I grilled steaks, baked potatoes, and tossed a salad. The first meal the three of us had together; it almost felt like Brian sat there with us, celebrating our new freedom. We used Brian's kitchen table on our back porch. Alex had a hard time parting with so many of his uncle's things when we cleaned out his house, so we found new ways to use them. I poured three glasses of red wine, one for each of us. Alex rarely had alcohol, but we had something to celebrate tonight.

"To freedom," I said.

"To outlasting the fucking devil," he said. I laughed. Alex's sense of humor had improved over the years making me grateful. Bartholomew and I agreed couples should laugh together. After Brian's death, Alex and I didn't laugh much. But I suppose a melancholy mood was to be expected, as we hadn't had much to laugh about. I knew Bartholomew killed Brian, but what could I do about it? Have him arrested? Colin would love it if I showed up with some invisible being and tried to have the police put him in custody. I'd be locked up in an insane asylum. And who knows for how long.

I drank Brian's offering. I felt tempted to pour it in the grass, but I knew he wouldn't have wanted me to waste a drop.

Bartholomew was gone. Maybe not forever, but for tonight, we were safe, unobserved.

After dinner, we slid the furniture out of the way and put on *Ella and Louis*, our favorite Ella Fitzgerald and Louis Armstrong album. Alex and I started taking dance lessons shortly after we moved in together. Alex knew a few steps, so he became a much better dancer than me, but it didn't take long for me to catch up. We foxtrotted to "Cheek to Cheek," jitterbugged and two-stepped barefoot across the polished pinewood floor.

"I love dancing with you," Alex said.

"I love life with you," I replied.

He tipped his head low, gently kissing me. Our dancing slowed, then stopped altogether. He scooped me up and carried me out the front door, where we continued dancing in the cool grass, the music faint in the background. It was late, the neighborhood quiet with just the music and the buzz of the corner streetlamp. We danced our way to the side of the house, hidden from the eyes of the neighbors. We made love under the stars.

BARTHOLOMEW

I became conscious of a light filtering in from somewhere distant, seeking me out, reaching for me. Abigail's face came into view—lovely, angelic. Spiteful. Sneering.

"Lanie! Lanie, I told you to wake up!"

I couldn't open our eyes, but I felt her wake, pretending to sleep. She always pretended to sleep. Glorious irritation allowed me to expand in The Darkness. Where was she? Was Stephanie's repulsive mother shaking us?

Lanie tunneled farther under the blankets. Until someone took them away.

"It's not cold in here. You can take my blankets, but I'm not getting out of bed," Lanie said, finally opening her eyes. Her bedroom came into focus. Her mother stood over Lanie, blankets crumpled in a heap on the floor next to her feet, then everything went fuzzy again.

What in God's name happened? How did we return to Lanie's room?

"Lanie, if you don't get out of bed, you'll be grounded from the phone for two weeks."

That got Lanie's attention.

"I don't understand why we have to spend all day cleaning. It's just going to get dirty again," Lanie said, sitting up.

"I'm not arguing with you. Get up, get dressed, and help me."

Grudgingly, Lanie did as her mother asked. Her contrary mood allowed me to gain some sense of reality again. I'd lost time somehow, something that never happened before. Lanie glanced at the calendar and I saw an additional X. Two days since the sleepover and I had no recollection of what occurred during the time. Panicked, I knew I would never allow myself to blink out of existence again. I had to regain control.

It was a tedious day, but the fighting Lanie did with her mother gave me a little more room to stretch out. If only she knew her anger aided me. Granted, I did give her little nudges to push her in the direction of arguing with her mom. Instead of doing chores in a different room, Lanie followed her mother around.

"Cleaning is dumb," she shouted at her mother while she vacuumed.

"No one even comes over," Lanie said, swiping a rag over a dusty surface in the living room, while her mother straightened the couch pillows.

"You're wasting my Sunday. You could be making me lunch." They were in the kitchen now. Olivia washed dishes, while Lanie wiped down the counters... with the same filthy rag she used in the living room.

"Maybe if you were nicer, you'd have friends," Lanie said, standing in the doorway of the bathroom, watching her mom scrub the toilet.

Olivia had enough. She threw the toilet brush at Lanie, and it smacked her in the forehead.

"I can't believe you did that! Ugh! Now I need a shower!" She made gagging noises, but they were just noises. She felt grossed out, but not to the level of her outburst.

Olivia shoved a scrub brush and some cleanser at Lanie, then said, "Good. Take a shower and while you're in there, scrub it."

Lanie's mother left the bathroom and we heard the front door slam. Bitter satisfaction spread through Lanie. I filled and expanded The Darkness.

Lanie felt guilty the rest of the afternoon for picking a fight with her mom. Guilt had a positive effect on my predicament, like her anger and frustration, so I couldn't have been happier. Olivia spent the day outside until she went to work in the late afternoon. She attempted to give Lanie a hug before she left, but Lanie shrugged her away.

She watched her mom's car pull out of the driveway and as it disappeared down the street, panic set in. What if something happened to her mom, just like her dad, and Lanie didn't give her a hug?

What if my mother's last memory of me was of being a bitch over cleaning the house? I'll make it up to her, she thought.

Lanie finished cleaning the house, making her feel better. In doing so, she diminished the space I filled. She dusted the spots she'd barely passed over, she swept, she even cleaned out the refrigerator. It took her about three hours to do a thorough clean, then she pulled a twenty out of the babysitting money she'd been saving for a car and walked to the store where she bought her mom a single rose. The diner gave her mom a discount, but it wasn't free, so she would use the rest for dinner.

The diner was about eight blocks from Lanie's house. We passed my house on the walk, but Lanie wouldn't slow down for me to look in the windows. I did notice the curtains and front door were open. That was new.

I felt like a miniature person trying to walk a colossal dog. Absolutely no control over the situation. So, I did what I could do and paid close attention to the street names, houses, and other landmarks to ensure my familiarity with the neighborhood. I remembered the drive with Sam all those years ago when she pointed out the diner and the box-looking house at the end of my street so I could find my way home. The house, painted a different color now with a large porch, was the same.

It took about fifteen minutes for us to get to Lanie's mom's work. She opened the door and looked around. She saw no sign of her mother.

She must be on break because her car's in the parking lot. Lanie waved to the owner and he directed her to the back where a picnic table sat for employees. A large cottonwood shaded the picnic table, creating long shadows across the area.

Lanie stood at the back door of the kitchen and stared, the white rose held limply in her hand. She watched her mother's giggly demeanor with shock. She wasn't alone.

Olivia sat on the table in her waitress uniform, her apron spread beneath her like a blanket. A dark-haired man sat on the bench in front of her. He wore a light brown business suit and had gray streaks at his temples. Lanie's mother had her hand on the strange man's shoulder, and he had his hands on her thighs. She ducked her head, then laughed at something he said. Then Lanie's mother leaned forward and kissed him.

Whore.

What the fuck?!

Lanie slammed open the door.

"What are you doing?" she screamed. "I can't believe you're cheating on him! I knew you'd forget him! I hate you!"

Lanie threw the rose on the ground and took off running. Tears streamed down her cheeks. Her mother called after her, but Lanie kept going. She needed Mark. As much as I dreaded what would happen, he'd give her drugs—and this time, I'd ensure she stayed high. I would not let this girl have control again.

Get it together, Lanie. Before you get to Mark's, or he'll think you're an immature crybaby.

She didn't go straight to Mark's—instead she walked and walked, trying to calm down. She hiccoughed and stumbled over a crack in the sidewalk. The sun set, casting shadows across the neighborhood.

Ugh! My face is probably all blotchy, but I can't go home for makeup. That's the first place Mom will look. And I can't go to Stephanie's because she'll look there next. I'll have to stop crying. I can tell him its allergies. Yeah, my eyes are all puffy because of allergies...

She stopped and looked around to get her bearings. The middle school was a block east of our current location. She turned and walked toward Mark's house. *Hopefully he's not having one of his parties.* Any time a car came close, she stepped into the shadows, afraid it would be her mother.

SAMANTHA

Sunday morning we worked in the yard. The chilly nights meant we needed to put the garden to bed. The weatherman said it could snow this week, but I wasn't so sure. They were wrong so often. I thought Mother Nature had quite the sense of humor. I believed she thought, *Oh you think you can predict me, silly human? Think again!* And then she laughed and laughed. Unpredictable, temperamental, dramatic, fierce, and determined? Yep, definitely a Mother, not a Father. I smiled at the idea as I clipped another head of a sunflower.

"How many seeds do we really need to save, Sam? Shouldn't you save some for the birds?" Alex teased.

I looked up at him and smiled, then he snapped a picture of me in my floppy garden hat, dusty apron, cutoff sweats, and Keds.

"Got it," he said. "You have this look when we work in the yard—peaceful, serene. I wanted to capture it."

"Should I pose so you can be sure it turns out? You probably chopped my head off."

"Sure, but I don't think we can re-create your happiness."

Of course I felt happy. We worked in the front yard and I didn't feel afraid because an evil ghost lurked outside the fence. We loved our house, the home we built, the bounty it produced for us each year, the protection it provided. It hurt my heart to ever think of moving and I hoped Bartholomew had moved on, so we could stay.

I rolled my eyes at Alex and continued collecting seeds. The basket draped over my arm held about fifteen flower heads. I wanted to restart them along the six-foot fence on the south side of our yard. Sunflowers weren't the only ones I collected. I also gathered lemon balm, cleomes, and larkspur. I had jars of them in the cellar of the house—some I gifted to friends and family throughout the year, others I saved for us in case we had a late or early freeze that wiped out our gardens.

Alex took the camera inside then finished harvesting the tomatoes, cucumbers, carrots, and peppers. He and Max built a couple of cold frames off the back porch for herbs, lettuce, and cabbage.

We finished planting, harvesting, and collecting and sat on the back porch couch. My feet, sans shoes, lay across Alex's lap.

"I really do love this house," he said. "I don't want you to think I don't. We've built something pretty amazing. I hate feeling trapped. If he's still here, we need to move as far away as we can. Because as much as I love the house, I want a family more." He slid his hands up and down my bare legs, almost tickling.

"If he's still here or he comes back, I promise, we will move. Even though it might kill me to walk away from this house," I said.

We were quiet for a few minutes, listening to the crickets, to a dog bark in the distance, to a child laugh.

"I suppose he felt the same way, but even more so because he built it. We only remodeled it," I said.

"I don't understand how you feel empathy for him. Your ability to love and forgive is so vast."

"I haven't forgiven him, but I do still feel sad for him because he can't move on, because he has so much anger and bitterness it wrecked his soul. I wish he could find peace."

Alex leaned to the side and kissed my toes. I giggled and pulled them away.

"Gross! They're covered in dirt and sweat," I said.

"Haven't you learned anything these past six years? Seeing you dirty and sweaty turns me on." He slid out from under my legs and spread out above me, kissing my belly, my neck. Then he tugged my cut-offs down and slipped my shirt up and over. I lay naked on the couch with him staring over me. His face radiated love.

"I am still in awe of you. I always will be," he said before leaning down to kiss my lips.

Oh, Alex, I hope so, I thought before he took me with him to sensuous oblivion.

BARTHOLOMEW

All the lights were on at Mark's. *Damn it*, she thought. Lanie usually avoided his parties because they were all older and she felt immature and out of place. They only ever had beer, and beer was gross. People stood outside around a keg laughing and talking, oblivious of little Lanie.

The packed house cleared up why he owned so little furniture. The fewer obstacles, the more people he packed into his house. She found Mark in the kitchen drinking out of a tiny glass.

Shots, Lanie thought. *Don't be stupid.*

A grown version of Lanie with long black hair, a pale face and bright red lipstick stood close to Mark, her arm around his waist. It struck me as odd.

Lanie didn't care. She wanted to escape from the pain of seeing her mom betray her dad. She walked right up to him and whispered in his ear, "Can we go somewhere private?"

"Sure," he said, a look of surprise on his face. "I'll be right back." He untangled himself from the woman next to him and led Lanie through the crowd of people down a hallway. Perfume, cigarette smoke, and marijuana assaulted our nose. I couldn't stop staring at the people we passed. Men with brightly colored spikes where their hair should have been. Women wearing such little plastic clothing, they might as well be wearing nothing. Whores. All intermingling with people they shouldn't. China- men, greasers, Injuns, whites—all mixed together, celebrating, laughing. Sharing cigarettes even! The world as I knew it had been desecrated. Would I find any humans worthy of living?

Mark may have been too old for Lanie, but at least he was white. The shabby bedroom was occupied by a half-dressed, brown-skinned couple, but Mark had no problem kicking them out. His bed consisted of a box spring and mattress, the blankets and sheets mussed from the couple who just left. Last time I was here with Lanie, she and Mark hadn't made it past the living room. The room happened to be clean at least. Tapestries covered the windows instead of curtains.

"I got suspended because Mr. Arnold found my pot. He confiscated it all."

Mark locked the door. "He probably smoked it."

Lanie rolled her eyes. *Everyone's a pothead to Mark*, she thought.

He stepped closer and leaned in to kiss her, but she stopped him. His breath moldy and rancid.

"Can we—can you smoke me up first? I had a really shitty day," Lanie said.

"Sure. But don't ditch out on me."

"I have money. Not a lot, but some." She reached into her pocket for the rest of the twenty and looked at it. She had seventeen dollars left after she bought the rose.

"I don't want your money," he said, rubbing her arms. I couldn't understand the fascination he had with Lanie. The woman in the kitchen was much closer to his own age. What could he possibly see in Lanie? The lure of her innocence? It didn't matter. He would get me to my end goal. His scraggly beard itched our face.

I've been so good! she thought. A pit formed in her belly at the thought of her mom's betrayal. At seeing her laugh and flirt, then kiss the strange man. Her dad cold and buried alone in the ground, and her mother behaved like a...

Whore—she's a whore. I finished the thought for her.

It's her fault my dad's dead. I fucking hate her.

Lanie sat on one side of a padded, armless couch. Mark sat on the opposite side next to an end table where he loaded a bud of marijuana into a water pipe. His head faced away from Lanie, so he didn't see the tears slide down her face, or see her quickly wipe them away. He lit the bowl, took a hit, then scooted closer and passed it to Lanie. He rested his hand on her leg. I hoped the cloud would deaden whatever act he had in mind.

Lanie sat up and took another hit. Water bubbled and smoke filled the tube. She coughed and sputtered when the smoke hit her lungs, and then she took a second smaller hit. Mellowness settled over us instantly. We passed the pipe to Mark. They did this several times making our mind nice and fuzzy.

I would not lose control again.

We needed something her mom couldn't smell, wouldn't suspect. There had to be a different, more accessible option. Odorless and easy to conceal. The Darkness increased with each hit she took. I spread through her body, thrilled with the freedom and control I now had.

After ten minutes, Lanie leaned back against the couch and closed her eyes. *Yes, I missed this*, she thought. *Sweet oblivion.*

I lifted our arm, twirling it in the air. Making our fingers dance. I missed it, too.

"Do you have anything stronger?" we asked.

"You sure?"

Something stronger? she wondered. *Why do I want something stronger? Pot is fine.*

We leaned back, our head low enough to rest on the back of the couch.

"This feels nice," we said, closing our eyes.

Yes, but the pain is still there. I'm sure he has something to make it go away completely, I replied.

"What do you want?" Mark asked.

"Something to make me not feel."

I controlled her now.

"Ludes?" Mark asked.

We didn't know what "ludes" were, but we nodded anyway. He pulled back a tapestry, one I assumed covered a window. Instead it hid a large safe. He ducked under the tapestry so we couldn't see and he reappeared shortly with a small rattling bottle.

"Here, start with half of one and see how you do." He took a pocket knife off his belt, placed the pill on the end table, and cut it in half. "Don't want you ODing here tonight. They're $2 per pill, how many do you want?"

He handed us the pill and we swallowed it. She pulled out the money. "This is all I have."

He counted out five pills, in addition to the half, and gave her three rolled joints, placing them all in a baggie. "You don't have enough money..." he said, and leaned in to kiss us.

Someone knocked on the door, interrupting him. A woman's voice said, "Mark, we need more ice for the keg. It's foaming."

We shoved the money into his hand.

"It's too bad there are so many people here. I'm very interested to see how you react to quaaludes. You owe me," he said pointing at us, then opened the door.

The woman he'd been standing with earlier stepped inside the dimly lit room. I felt grateful for her intrusion, but Lanie felt slighted. In some sick part of her brain, she'd wanted Mark's attention.

"Time for you to go," Mark said and shuffled us out of his room. The woman stared after us, horrified as we staggered away from her. A clock in the living room of Mark's house said it was a little past eight o'clock. We smiled at the woman and Mark, flashed them two fingers, then strode through the crowd. I hadn't planned on staying for the party anyway.

"Are you dealing to kids?" I heard the women yell behind us.

"Only the ones who ask," Mark replied and then we were too far away to hear the rest of their argument.

I can't go home. I won't go home, Lanie thought.

No...I have other plans.

I wanted to see Sam, to see how she fared without me.

We walked through the dark night, Lanie drifted in and out of my thoughts. As the pill took hold, The Light dimmed, changing place with The Darkness. It spread to the edge of her muscles. It filled each appendage,

141

wrapped around each tendon. She wondered where we were going, why we'd left Mark's. She wanted to lay down, to stare up at the stars. They looked so pretty. She felt tired, wanted her bed. We staggered a bit, until I focused on the task of walking. The ludes seemed to have a small effect on my consciousness, whereas the marijuana had no effect, so it took more effort for me to control our body to not give us away.

Shhh, shhh... You're dreaming, it's okay.

This is a weird dream, she replied.

We made it to my house where we stood in the yard, swaying slightly, until I concentrated on holding still. We watched Sam and Alex inside my home. Their faces flickered blue and green from the light of the television, making gruesome reflections under their eyes and noses. Alex slid his hand up and down Sam's arm. I tiptoed closer to the house, grateful for no porch light. Spying had been easier when I didn't have a body, although I couldn't get this close to my house in recent years.

The room went black. A few minutes later, a lamp turned on behind the gauzy curtains covering my bedroom window, giving off enough light for me to see Sam's silhouette. Alex joined Sam soon after and the room went dark once again.

I looked for a way to climb to the balcony, but could see none. Instead, we sat in the grass and watched my darkened home. Alex and Sam's lives once again closed off to me.

Would they let Lanie into their lives? This poor lost soul in need of adult affection. How could I use her to my advantage?

The door kept my attention. Was it locked? We stood and crept up the porch, stepping close to the railing in case of creaking boards. The stairs didn't creak, but the porch did and we stopped to wait, listening for sounds coming from inside the house. Nothing. We reached for the screen door, grasped the knob, and turned. Locked.

We tried the back door, to no avail.

Walking down the steps, I noticed the garage. The doors were slightly ajar.

Sam's Nova was parked in the driveway with Alex's truck behind hers. The door creaked open, and there, covered in a gray cloth, was the 1950 Roadmaster— Sam's father's obsession. We stepped inside, closing the door behind us.

Dust flittered around as I lifted the car cover. It tickled our nose. Afraid a sneeze would disturb Lanie, I put a finger to my nose until the urge dissipated. They left the car door unlocked, so we opened the door and the smell of leather escaped. We slid inside. I'd never driven a car before and I'd only ridden in one with Sam. I gripped the steering wheel in my hands, wondering what it would feel like to have the car rumble beneath me, gliding over the asphalt roads.

Our knee bumped something near the steering wheel, creating a slight jingle. The keys...

The car couldn't go far because of Sam and Alex's cars blocking the way, as well as the electric gate. Still, I didn't understand how she could be so trusting to leave the keys in the ignition.

Lanie's consciousness began to stir. *Where am I?*

You're dreaming. Wishing for a car of your own. I lay down on the seat.

Her disorientation turned into dreams again. What if next time I wouldn't be able to lull her back to sleep?

Worried she'd wake again, we climbed out of the car, making sure to leave everything as we found it, and walked back to Lanie's house.

Olivia gushed over us when we entered the house with apologies, kisses, and hugs. She still wore her work attire, except grease stains were smeared down the front of the white apron. We tried to shrug her off, but she wouldn't let us go. Lanie stirred inside our mind, still angry with her mother. Did she really think Lanie would forgive her so quickly with such superficial attempts? The anger helped me stay in control and now that I had replenished her marijuana cigarettes and the little bottle of pills, I would not relent.

"Fine, fine. You're forgiven. I don't care who you whore around with as long as I don't have to see it."

"Lanie, it's not like that. He's a nice man."

Her mother moved us arm's length away, searching our eyes. Her face fell, disappointment evident on her weary features.

"I don't want to hear the details. Just don't bring him here."

"You're high. Lanie, you've been doing so good!"

How did she know? We weren't stumbling, our words were clear and concise. What gave us away? She squeezed our arms in frustration as we shook our head in defiance.

"Your eyes are bloodshot and I can smell it on you. I've been worried sick. You didn't have my permission to go out tonight. It's a school night."

"You didn't ask *me* if you could kiss a stranger!"

"I'm your mother, Lanie. I don't have to ask your permission. Where did you go?"

She pulled away from us, dropped her hands, and twisted her apron in her fists. Did she want to do that to Lanie? Twist our arms until we broke?

"Wherever I want."

Lanie's mother threw her hands in the air and yelled something incomprehensible.

"We're going to bed," I said.

Our voice silenced her and she cocked her head to the side.

"Who's 'we'? Is there someone outside? Did you bring a boy back here?" She stepped around us to look out the door.

"It was a slip up. Me. I'm going to bed."

We strode down the hall as she said to our back, "I should have told you about Scott."

I really didn't care about the man. Lanie felt concern, but at the moment, her feelings didn't matter to me either. I just wanted to be alone so I could figure out my next move. We had to be careful—I didn't want Lanie's mother grounding us or becoming suspicious. We climbed into bed a little after midnight.

OCTOBER

BARTHOLOMEW

The next morning before school, we woke to Lanie's mother dumping all Lanie's belongings onto the floor. Again. She was almost dressed for her office job—low pumps, skirt, and her hair was tied up neatly. She wore a beige bra, the straps digging into her shoulder. It seemed she interrupted her morning routine to go on a tirade. Dark circles pooled beneath her black feathered lashes.

Lanie shot out of bed and screamed, "What are you doing?!"

"I know you were high last night. Where's the pot?"

Well, we'd hid it, along with the pills, in Lanie's secret hiding place. Lanie plopped on the corner of the bed, above the stash, and promptly broke into tears. She could be an actress, this one, with all her dramatics.

"I hate you! I hate that you don't trust me," she yelled.

Lanie's mother stood with one of the desk drawers in her hand, the contents slipping onto the floor, and stared at Lanie. Shock, uncertainty, anger all mixed into Olivia's features.

"Lanie, I know you were high."

"I wasn't! My eyes were red from crying and I was at a friend's house. They smoke, not me," Lanie looked up at her mother, our gaze did not waver, false tears streaked down our face. Resolute. We would not break again.

We would, however, have to be more careful. Maybe we should stay away from the odorous drugs.

Lanie's mother dropped to the floor, surrounded by the detritus. Blue ribbons and baby pictures stuck to her calves. Lipsticks smeared into the carpet, their caps crushed and broken beneath Olivia's knees.

"I don't know how to help you," she whispered. Tears streamed down her face.

We didn't move from the bed, just stared at the woman unraveling in front of us. I hadn't anticipated the joy I'd feel at knowing I caused yet another woman's suffering. Lanie wasn't high, so I couldn't make our face smile, but I so wanted to.

Lanie felt confused by her emotions. Seeing her mother fall apart, unable to hold it together frightened her. She didn't understand why she felt joy, satisfaction. We stared at Olivia. Lanie didn't move, unsure of what to say, what to do. She only knew, she did not want her mother finding her hiding spot. Olivia looked up at us broken and defeated, her hands limp at her sides. She stood finally and walked out of our room.

Still we said nothing. Another hour passed before we heard her leave for work. Only then did Lanie move. She hurriedly dressed, ate a piece of toast, and was almost out the door when I thought, *It would be easier to get through the day with a little help. Especially if we run into Misty and her friends.*

Lanie slowly walked back to her room, but she hesitated outside her bedroom. *I don't want to get caught again,* she thought.

We won't, we'll be more careful this time, I thought.

We? Why am I all of a sudden thinking of me as we? Maybe I'm schizo.

Laughter filled her head and she smiled, but it wasn't my laughter. I didn't find my blunder amusing. I didn't want her to know, not now. Maybe not ever.

Take half of the little white pill—no one will suspect. They don't pay attention to you as long as you don't make a scene.

No scenes. Right, she thought.

We cut the five pills in half, swallowed one like the night before, and took one small hit from the joint. I was unsure how long the pill would last, so we found a small aspirin bottle and put half of the pills inside. Then we floated down the street to school.

We closed our locker and were walking down the hallway when Stephanie hollered, "Hey, Lanie, wait up."

We kept walking. The girl was unnecessary in our life, especially since I now knew what she was. A hand grabbed our arm.

"Hey, did you hear me? I looked for you this morning on the way to school. Where were you?"

Turning, I glared at the girl.

"You are a bothersome half-breed. You disgust me and I no longer have a use for you," I said and continued down the hall, leaving Stephanie stunned. Lanie stirred, causing a faint rustling within my body. She felt confused and frustrated as to why she couldn't control what she said or where she went. She didn't understand why she would push her friend away.

"Something is seriously wrong with you, Lanie!" Stephanie yelled. "You need mental help!"

I don't like this feeling.

She wanted to scream, to draw attention to the panic she felt inside at her inability to command her own body.

Maybe I do need help.

No scenes, remember?

She screamed inside her own head, with no power for the external expression. I smiled. Then walked to the nearest bathroom where I swallowed another pill. I did not want to listen to her. Then I hitched our backpack higher on our shoulder, and walked to the history class. I didn't want to risk another suspension as I had no idea what the repercussions would be, so I kept quiet through the classes, never volunteering to answer questions.

I had no difficulties keeping up. I received high marks on a quiz in geometry and on a grammar sheet in English. Stephanie avoided us for the rest of the day. I occasionally saw her glare at us from down the hall or across a room.

Today when we cut PE and hid near the shop classes, Lanie couldn't stop me from looking in the windows.

The students were crafting table legs and my fingers itched to show them how to carve scrolls or craft fluted legs by hand instead of using the mechanical lathes. It seemed only a moment had passed when the bell rang. We waited for the male group of students to scramble out of the class and then we went inside. The smell of sawdust surrounded us; piles of it hid in the corners where a broom hadn't reached. Aspen, cherry, balsa wood, and pine boards lay seemingly haphazard on metal shelving. Cubicles with safety glasses, aprons, chisels, and handsaws lined one wall. The shop teacher's back faced us as he swept up sawdust and small scraps of wood.

What am I doing here? Lanie thought, her consciousness returning after the long lapse.

"Can I help you?" the shop teacher said, turning to see us standing near one of the planers.

"I love the smell. It reminds me of my father," I said. "He died a few years ago. My apologies for the interruption." We turned to leave and Lanie wondered why she lied.

"I'm sorry for your loss," the teacher said as we left.

I needed another pill, so we hurried to the girls' restroom where we wouldn't be seen. The rest of the afternoon was rather uneventful, but we did have a nice stroll by my house where we waved cordially to Samantha. She smiled and waved back.

Perfect.

SAMANTHA

Alex was relentless—not that I minded attempting to make a baby every day. I buried the guilt and enjoyed the pretending. It had been almost two weeks since Max had seen Bartholomew. I'd stopped taking the pill the day after Alex and I made up. I told him I could not possibly get pregnant so fast, but it didn't seem to stop his desire to try.

We decided to celebrate my birthday with a masquerade dinner. And I went into full party planning mode. We slowly converted my house using purple string lights, cobwebs, and dyed cheesecloth. My kids laughed at me on Monday when I went to school with black hands. I needed to remember gloves the next time I decided to get crafty. Alex put together branches in a spray-painted black pot adding to the spooky feeling of our porch. Maybe we'd get extra trick-or-treaters this year with our decorations. I briefly considered cooking for the dinner, but I decided it would be much less stressful to have it catered.

I sat gluing creepy spiders and insects to the front porch with a hot glue gun when I heard a "Hi, Sam." I turned to see Lanie walking past. She was alone.

Sam? When did she start calling me by my first name?

The familiar fear I felt upon seeing her crept over me. My mind immediately went to Bartholomew. I shook the crazy thought out of my head and waved back. She continued on her way.

I watched her for a moment, until a bead of hot glue dripped onto my hand.

"Shit," I said, sucking on the burn spot and reminding myself not to give her much more thought, because even if she was struggling, she told me I wasn't someone who could help.

I dragged two fake skeletons out of the house and propped them up in our rocking chairs, giving them each a feather boa—one purple, one black. Then I went inside to look over the handwriting sheets my students completed that afternoon in class.

I stood with the refrigerator door open, debating whether to cook something or order takeout when Alex walked in.

"Nothing looks good," I said, closing the refrigerator. "Chinese takeout?"

"Sure," he said as I turned to wrap my arms around him. His overalls were covered in white dust and clumps of drywall mud were stuck in his hair. He had wiped his face clean—a strange contrast to his attire.

"Remember, I'm taking Shane out after school tomorrow in the Roadmaster, so I'll be home after you," I said to Alex.

"Shower?" he asked, waggling his eyebrows at me. I laughed and shook my head. Yep, relentless.

"You go. I'll order dinner. I want to get some more cobwebs hung in the living room," I said.

"The porch looks great," he said, leaning back to look at me. "We have the perfect house for Halloween."

"We certainly do," I said, reaching up to kiss his cheek.

"Be naked when I get out," he said.

I rolled my eyes and he smiled as he left the kitchen. I watched him walk out, loving the way he looked in his work attire. It reminded me of when he worked on the house and the sexual tension between us because he refused my advances for so long. Now, he was mine and I was his. My heart swelled, then dropped briefly. I pushed the secret out of my head, then called to order dinner. They said forty-five minutes. Enough time for me to join Alex in the shower, as long as we hurried.

BARTHOLOMEW

Lanie's mother was not home when we returned after school. The pills Mark had given us proved to be very effective, but I would not subject myself to sexual relations with the man. So we searched Olivia's room for money. I rummaged through Lanie's memories for any hint where her mother might hide her valuables. We found her cash easy enough, hidden in the false bottom of her jewelry box, a place Lanie was very aware of, since Olivia didn't hide much from her daughter. We found almost $2,000 in twenties, fifties, and hundreds. She would not miss a few bills.

I have my own money, Lanie thought. *From babysitting. I don't need any from our vacation savings.*

You don't have nearly enough, my dear.

We heard Olivia's car pull into the driveway a little after five o'clock. We had tidied the house, including picking up the mess Olivia had made in our room, and were making dinner, much to her surprise. I'd taken another half of the little white pills soon after finding the money, worried Lanie would regain consciousness. I cleaned and cooked out of pure boredom, refusing to turn on the television to see more corruption of this modern age.

I made a very simple meal, something called a chef's salad. Her mother had it on the list of meals she would prepare for the week. It brought back the fond memories of the hemlock salad I had made for my dear wife and the pleasure I felt at watching her choke. If I didn't need Lanie's mother, I might have gone in search of the plant along the drainage ditches. I was sure I could find it again.

We sat down for dinner and Lanie's mother said, "What a lovely thing to do for me, Lanie. You had me so worried last night…"

I didn't do it for her. I sliced the hard-boiled egg, ham, and avocado into small bites.

"Mom, I wasn't high. I apologize for reacting so emotionally. You have to understand, it was quite a shock as I'd only seen you embrace Dad. I'm more composed today."

She tilted her head and squinted her eyes, obviously not buying what I said. I realized my mistake too late—it did not sound like something Lanie would say.

"Well, I called Sara today to ask her what other options there were for you. If you had a relapse. She suggested an in-patient drug rehab facility. I don't want to go that route, but I can't lose you, honey. I'll do whatever it takes to keep you safe." Reaching over, she put her hand on our arm and gently squeezed.

Internally, Lanie's consciousness stirred. I stopped cutting and stared at Olivia. Lanie felt a little foggy, and she wondered if maybe a facility wouldn't be a bad idea. She'd completely lost it today and felt her life spiraled down into a pit she couldn't climb out of. She still couldn't believe the things she'd said to Stephanie and she felt she'd ruined their friendship. She'd been surprised when Stephanie had forgiven her for the outburst two weeks ago, but today…today her words were directed *at* Stephanie. She would never forgive Lanie now.

You're fine, quit being dramatic, I thought.

I struggled to find Lanie's voice, to use words she would to ensure her mother would believe us. It was imperative.

"Okay fine, I smoked pot with some friends last night after I left the diner. I was so mad at you, I wanted to hurt you. But I only ended up hurting myself." I ducked our head in mock shame and looked up at her, pleading with her to believe me. "Honestly, I've been proud of myself these past two weeks, too. And I felt so much better. Today I felt so out of it, like, like… I was a zombie or something. I said awful things to Stephanie, even. I don't want to feel that way ever again."

"I'm glad you are being honest with me," Olivia said. "So what do we do now? What happens when you get mad at me again? Because you will."

"I'll ask Sara tomorrow. She said she can give me tools."

Lanie's mother nodded, then we ate in silence for a few moments.

I have to be more careful, walk the line. Olivia will not lock me up and prevent me from getting back into my home. I'll kill her daughter first, regardless of what happens to me. I will not be incarcerated.

Who said that? Lanie thought, then her soul went perfectly still, perfectly quiet in the center of our body. Waiting. Listening for me to continue thinking. I paused. Did I want her to know about me? Did I want her to know I'd accomplished this amazing feat of possessing her because of her broken soul? I could pretend the drugs made her hear things; it would be simpler. But it wouldn't be quite as entertaining.

A tremor of fear passed through our body and I smiled. Olivia was too busy staring at the salad to notice. Would she have said the old phrase "someone just walked over your grave" if she had seen us quiver? Now that I had experienced this phenomenon while in a body not originally mine, I was sure the phrase actually came because of other beings who possessed humans. Would our two souls battle for control, cause the body to react violently, tear the flesh apart like an earthquake? I felt conflicted—I wanted to see if Lanie truly could match the strength of my soul, but I also wanted no one to know I was here, or I might not be able to get back into my home. We would have to compromise, for now.

No one can hear you but me, Lanie.

An image of Lanie pounding on metal bars filled my head; she shook them, a silent scream contorting her face. I wondered if she imagined the bars as symbolism for her new prison. Would insanity take over? Would we have an epic battle now for her soul?

And I won't leave, yet. You are my ticket home, like in the Wizard of Oz. *You are my ruby slippers.*

Who are you? What's wrong with me?!

I hadn't intended to disclose my presence, because I felt I should stay hidden. But I am always up for a good battle of wits. I am Bartholomew and it seems you inadvertently shared your body with me.

How? she thought. *Does this mean I'm possessed or am I really schizophrenic?*

Oh my dear, you are most certainly possessed.

"What are you thinking?" Olivia interrupted our conversation.

Lanie still fought to take up space within our body, shouting as much as a thought could shout. She was weak and I would keep her that way. "Nothing."

"That's funny," Olivia said, looking concerned. "Your eyes are flickering back and forth like you're watching a movie."

"Well, I was remembering the movie we watched at Stephanie's sleepover, *Poltergeist*. Do you believe in ghosts?" I said.

"Hmm...do I believe in ghosts? I don't know. I've never seen one, but I dream of seeing your dad a lot. Maybe our memories create ghosts."

"Do you think Dad is in Hell?"

Olivia's eyes widened. I wanted to know how she felt. She didn't go to church, and I'd never witnessed her praying. So her husband had to also be a heathen.

"I hope he's in Heaven. He was a good man—kind, loving. But you know that. He wouldn't have been such a good dad if he wasn't."

"Did he sin?"

Olivia laughed again and shook her head. "I suppose it depends on your idea of sin. He swore, he drank occasionally, and I know you probably don't want to hear this, but your dad and I slept together before we were married."

I don't want to hear any more, Lanie thought. *I don't want to know these things. My dad is in Heaven. I know he is and when it's my turn to die, he'll be there waiting for me. Please don't ask her any more.*

I'll make you a deal, stop your screaming and yammering and I won't ask her any more awkward questions, I thought.

155

She stopped the screaming and her ridiculous banter in my head. Once I got what I wanted, I'd honor her wish to see her father. For now, I had to figure out how to shut her mother up.

"Your dad helped everyone he could. He always stopped to help change a flat tire, no matter if we were expected somewhere or not. He never hesitated to give a homeless person money."

"He enabled their lack of work ethic and desire to spend money on drink."

"Lanie, not everyone is homeless because they don't have a work ethic or because they are alcoholics. Some have mental illness. Some are just down on their luck."

"Maybe if he hadn't spent his money on strangers, we wouldn't be living in a shack."

"Lanie!"

I shrugged and stood to clear the empty plates and glasses. I even washed the dishes while Olivia sat at the table. I'd show her we didn't need to be put in any facility...

We went to our room after dinner and turned on the boombox. I put in several different cassettes until I found one I could tolerate. It had a red and blue cover, *Making Movies* by Dire Straits.

It was my dad's favorite, Lanie thought. *He had it on an 8-track and we'd listen to it when he took me for dessert.*

The organ on the first track was lovely, soothing almost. It made me feel like I was back in church for a moment. I could live without the banging, twanging though.

That's a guitar, she said.

Guitar.

The name sounded familiar, but I didn't quite know what it meant. I'd heard similar-sounding music coming from the annoying tenants, including Samantha, but I never knew the name of the instrument.

A sensation of calm came over me; I wasn't sure if the music caused it or if it was Lanie's emotions. As soon as the music started playing, I felt her resistance fade. I opened the bottle of pills to see what we had left.

Are you going to kill me? Lanie asked.

I'm not quite sure. You are the first person I've possessed.

Why did you choose me? Lanie thought.

I didn't answer. I wasn't sure how much I wanted her to know about our predicament and the lack of control I had over leaving her body.

Are you a demon?

I am simply a man without a body, because…

Because you hanged yourself after you murdered your wife, she thought.

Murder is such a harsh word. I simply gave her punishment she deserved.

So she could now see my memories as I could see hers. Interesting our roles had become reversed. No matter, her body was mine to control. I felt anxious, wanting to do something with my hands, build, create. Did I still have the ability to turn wood into art? We went outside, past Olivia who had fallen asleep to some sitcom on television. She started when we opened the door.

"Where are you going?"

"To collect some sticks. There were kids in school whittling today. It looked…cool," I said and continued out the door.

In the fading light I found a pair of clippers hanging from a hook on the outside of the house. For trimming the bushes, I assumed. We found a two-inch-diameter branch on the crabapple tree. Perfect. We cut it into six-inch lengths and returned to our room where I whittled a small fox. The wood shavings tumbled into the trash bin.

I've never made anything with my hands like this before, Lanie thought.

You didn't make it, I did, I replied. *Idiot girl.*

I swallowed another half a pill to shut her up. It had only been a few hours since I'd taken the last one. I would definitely need to visit Mark.

SAMANTHA

Since Maggie's middle son, Shane, had been a small child, he had a fascination with my dad's Roadmaster. When I lived in California I would take him out on backroads and let him sit on my lap while I drove. So, when they moved to Colorado, I promised him I would take him out for a drive. His eleventh birthday seemed the perfect opportunity.

Alex hadn't arrived home from work yet, so I moved my Nova to the street, then I removed the dusty cover and my heart dipped. I hadn't driven it in months. I felt like I had neglected my dad, not just the car.

When I opened the car door I saw the key hung on its rabbit foot chain in the ignition. I usually hid it in the ashtray. I felt instant panic. I needed to be more careful.

The car started with a rumble and I smiled, remembering the adventures my parents and I would go on. I stepped on the gas and the powerful car lurched forward.

I pulled up as Maggie ushered her boys into the house. They all had light blond hair, were tall and gangly. Dillon and Shane were in awkward growth stages where their pants were either too long in the legs, or too wide in the waist. Maggie often complained about finding clothes to fit them. Both Maggie and Russ had blond hair, darker now they were older.

Maggie smiled and waved me inside. "Shane has a little bit of homework to finish up, then you guys can go."

"Really, Mom? It's my birthday. Can't I do it later?" he whined.

"We both know you won't do it later, so hop to it. Auntie doesn't want to wait all night."

He huffed off to the kitchen, the other two boys following. I looked in and saw he pulled out his pack to get to work.

"It won't take him long. He's smart, but he's a procrastinator."

"Hmm...like his mom," I said, smiling.

"I have no idea where he gets it," she said, smirking. We both knew exactly where he got it. "Let's sit on the back porch while Shane does his homework," she said, leading me out the back door. The other two boys ran out behind us and picked up a ball to throw back and forth.

We sat in new folding lawn chairs.

"What are you smiling for?" Maggie asked me.

"Just remembering Alex and me sitting out here smoking pot after Brian died."

"I can't imagine Alex ever smoking pot," she said, laughing.

"Thanks for the other night," I said. "I'll try not to make it a habit to take you away from your family twice in one week."

"It was fun! Especially watching you squirm when Joel came to the table."

I shook my head and rolled my eyes.

"Did my advice work? You and Alex okay again?"

"Yeah, it worked. We're as okay as we'll ever be."

"I hope one day you can be honest with him."

"Maybe on my deathbed," I said.

"You are so fucking morbid!"

Shane hollered, "Hey, Mom! I finished. Can we go now?"

We turned to see Shane standing in the doorway with his homework spread flat against the screen door.

"Let me look it over, then you can go," Maggie said. To me she said, "I told you it wouldn't take him long." She gave my hand a squeeze, then went to her son.

I sat on the porch for a few minutes. When Brian was alive, we never came out here. We gathered in the kitchen. The yard was neat, with a six-foot privacy fence, lined with flower beds and a large patch of grass in the center. A swing set and trampoline took up most of the space now. I hoped Brian was at peace and felt good about having a family occupy his home, the opposite of Bartholomew.

"Auntie! I'm ready." Shane shot out of the back door full of excitement. "Can I drive?"

I laughed, "I'm afraid you are too big to sit on my lap these days. But I'll tell you what, when you get your driver's permit, I'll take you out in the Roadmaster and help teach you to drive."

I dug the seatbelt out from beneath the passenger seat, thankful my dad had the foresight to order his car with them, then Shane buckled in.

Our first stop was ice cream, then I promised him a game of putt-putt golf.

We sat at the counter in Menagerie Ice Cream deciding between flavors such as strawberry pistachio, peach mint, or lemon chocolate. They didn't have the typical flavors, one of the reasons I loved the place. Shane didn't seem to mind the uniqueness either and wanted to sample everything. I settled on the strawberry pistachio in a dish and he went for the PB & grape jelly cone.

"So, how's school going? Making friends?" I asked between bites.

"It's okay. I have a couple of friends, but I miss my old friends in California," he said, licking drips off his cone.

"Moving is hard. I was pretty lonely when I moved here, but I made some really great friends, including your Uncle Alex."

"Yeah, he's cool."

I smiled, glad he thought so.

"My best friend is a girl. Her name's Lisa. Some of the other kids make fun of me for it," he said.

"Kids can be dumb. It doesn't matter if she's a girl," I replied.

"She has a Black dad and a white mom, so she gets teased about that, too."

"That must be really hard for her. I was teased in elementary school a lot because my parents were so much older than the other parents. It's different than what your friend is going through, but hopefully it'll get better when the kids mature a bit. It got easier for me, at least."

"I had dinner with Lisa and her family last night. Stephanie, her sister, was sad because someone she thought was her friend said a really bad thing to her. I didn't understand what she said, but it hurt Stephanie. Why do people have to be so mean?"

"Stephanie? Is Lisa's last name Hatch?" I asked.

He nodded. Ice cream dripped down his hand, so I reached across the counter and grabbed a few napkins. Stephanie had always been such a friendly girl. I didn't understand why someone would be cruel to her.

"I wish I knew why people were mean. But sometimes it's because they're afraid. Sometimes it's because they're jealous," I said.

"Lisa's not scary, so I don't know why anyone would be afraid of her. She's nice and so are her mom and dad. Stephanie won't let us play with her though, so I'm a little afraid of her. But, I won't ever be mean!"

I hadn't had to have this conversation with my young students, so I felt completely inept. How could I possibly explain to Shane that people were afraid of the concept of two people of different races falling in love, and some people were afraid of people with a skin color not like their own? It had nothing to do with anyone being scary. Maggie surely had to have had this conversation.

"Does your mom know about Lisa getting picked on?"

"Yeah, she says to just keep being her friend and ignore the other kids. Lisa's not scared of anyone. She tells them to shut up when they're mean."

"That's great advice," I said.

We finished our ice cream and drove to the mini-golf course. I wondered about the friend who'd been hurtful to Stephanie.

I asked Shane and he said, "I don't remember her name, but Stephanie said she was her best friend."

Could it have been Lanie? I thought. *What would cause her to turn on her friend? It's none of your business, Sam. Stay out of it.*

Shane beat me at two rounds of putt-putt, then it started getting chilly, so we called it a night.

161

"Thank you, Aunt Sam! That was the best," Shane said as we walked up to the house. He gave me a hug, then ran inside. I was sure he would boast about how he beat me at golf.

BARTHOLOMEW

Tuesday evenings we had our standing appointment with the therapist. I especially looked forward to speaking with Sara today. Would she be able to tell the difference between Lanie and me? It would be great fun to toy with the therapist.

On the walk home from school, I swallowed another half of a pill. I'd taken one only two hours earlier, but I wanted to ensure Lanie would not interrupt me while I spoke to Sara. I would need to make a visit to Mark's house tonight, as I was running a bit low on the ludes.

Ludes. Ludicrous. Lewd.

The words bounced around my brain, catching Lanie's attention. She drifted away. In a few moments, I would no longer even feel her.

I could see Lanie's disgusting friend walking ahead of us, her devilish red hair gleaming in the sun. I'd been tempted to throw a rock at her, but if I missed she might notice us and then we'd have to deal with her again. As it was, she mostly ignored us throughout the day, only sending us occasional glances ranging between a glare and a look of sadness. I returned unkind smiles, making sure she knew we hadn't changed our mind about her. Well, *I* hadn't anyway, the only mind that mattered now.

As I turned down the alley to our house, I could see the backend of Olivia's car. I'd been the model child since her threat of sending us to a facility, even made her breakfast this morning. She beamed at the positive change taking place within her daughter. Maybe I could stay living in this body as long as Lanie was out of the picture. And I didn't ever have to have sex with a man again.

The Possessions of Bartholomew Ka

"Hi Mom," I said as I stepped into the living room. I'd rehearsed dumbing down my language all day, finding the biggest morons at school to practice on, so I could speak like Lanie. It felt humiliating and...demeaning. But I could not risk being caught.

Olivia was on the phone and held up her finger. I walked past her to dump our backpack in our bedroom, used the facilities—a very awkward and uncomfortable activity—and then went back to the living room to wait for Olivia to finish her phone conversation. She looked distressed. Not my problem, but if she didn't hurry, we'd be late and I wanted to play.

"I really do appreciate you calling me. Uh huh, you, too," Olivia said, then hung up.

"Ready?" I asked brightly.

"We have a few minutes. Sit down, Lanie. I'd like to talk to you."

I did as she asked, she seemed genuinely distraught. Had someone else died?

"That was Natalie."

"Who?" I asked.

Olivia stared at me and I realized I must have made a very big misstep. For the life of me, I could not recall the name. Lanie remained buried deep in our unconsciousness, so I received no help from her.

"I'm really worried about you, Lanie."

"Why, because I don't know who you are talking about? I don't know all the random people in your life."

"Lanie, I'm talking about Stephanie's mom. You've known her your whole life."

Oh! Yes, it was a misstep. I quickly recovered.

"I thought you were talking about someone at work. I didn't realize you were talking about *that* Natalie."

She frowned, but continued, "She's also very worried about you. She said you called Stephanie an 'irritating half-breed' in school yesterday?"

"That's not what I said."

"Oh, thank God..."

"I said she was a bothersome half-breed."

"Lanie Jo!"

Interesting, our middle name was Jo. I had no idea. Two new pieces of information to store for the future.

"Why would you say something so horrific to your best friend?" Her voice rose and grew higher in pitch.

"I don't understand. Isn't she? And she annoyed me. I simply wanted some space from her. The girl is smothering."

Olivia closed her eyes and took several deep breaths. "What's happened to you?" she said.

"Mom, I don't know what you mean. Nothing has happened. I'm just being the normal old me. I'm doing well in school, doing what you ask. I'm trying to be better."

"The Hatches have been in our lives since before you were born. They are very close friends, like family. I don't understand *why* you're being racist to our family! Your father would be appalled. *I'm* appalled."

Darn. We've disappointed Mother.

"I'm only stating the obvious. I cannot help it if they don't like the truth."

Olivia looked at her watch, sighed, then said, "We have to go. Maybe Sara can make sense of this."

I shrugged and stood. I couldn't understand why she got so upset. Olivia immediately turned her back and walked out of the house, leaving me to trail after her.

Lanie's mother remained silent as we drove, which I found acceptable as I wanted to plan what I would say to Sara. How would she react if I revealed myself? Would she believe me? If so, would she push for the facility Olivia mentioned? Best not to go there, even though it would be the most entertaining.

I could reveal all of Lanie's deepest, darkest secrets. She would eat that up. Of course we would surely land in a facility then. The girl was practically a prostitute.

When we arrived, Olivia didn't wait in the lobby. She went into Sara's office with us. Last time, she allowed us to go in alone. What was she up to?

"Lanie, Olivia. Welcome," Sara said as she opened the door.

"Hi Sara," Olivia said, sitting in the chair instead of on the couch next to me. "I'm feeling angry and frustrated, so I wanted to see if you could maybe help mediate. Maybe help me understand the hatefulness spewing out of my daughter's mouth lately."

I did not see that coming. But this could be fun…

"Okay, tell me what's been happening?"

"Her best friend, Stephanie, has a Black father and white mother. Our families have been very close for years. Lately, Lanie has been using very vulgar, racist language. I don't know what's come over her."

"Mom, I don't understand why you're freaking out. I said…" I hesitated, thinking of the word the principal used. "…the N-word in class once because the teacher was being a jerk and he wouldn't listen to me. I tried to point out Lincoln was as horrible as the rest of the people in power and he wouldn't listen. Then on Monday, Stephanie kept hounding me, trying to get me to ditch with her because she didn't study for a test," I lied. "I probably shouldn't have said what I did, but she stopped pressuring me."

Olivia stared at me, her eyes wide. "Before we left the house today, you said you didn't understand what you did wrong. You said you were telling the truth."

"You get so worked up over everything I do anymore. You overreact. On Monday you trashed my room because you thought I was hiding drugs," I said.

"What has happened to you?" Olivia said, her voice cracking. "You used to be my sweet girl, kind. These past few weeks you've…you've turned into someone I don't recognize."

"*You* happened to me," I said. "There are lipstick stains on my carpet that

166

look like blood. I scrubbed them, but they won't come out. Every time I see them, I think of Dad. Did he hit his head? Was there blood? I have nightmares where the car is filled with blood now, pouring from his eyes, his nose, his ears. I've told you over and over, I don't have any drugs. I've smoked pot. Only. But I don't buy it. You don't believe me. I was hurt because I saw you kissing a man who wasn't Dad. Of course I was upset. You never even told me you wanted to date. I thought you were still grieving and I wasn't ready to witness something like that. You hid it from me. And you accuse me of lying? You're the liar. You lie every day."

She stared at me. Sara furiously scribbled notes.

"I...I didn't think about the lipstick stains," she said.

Success. The conversation shifted away from me, I thought.

"That's what you have to say to me? Not, 'I'm sorry I trashed your room. I'm sorry for lying to you'? Maybe *you* are the one who needs therapy, not me." I sat back in typical Lanie style and crossed my arms in front of my chest, then glared at her. She couldn't hold my gaze. Her eyes moved to the window where I watched with pure satisfaction as tears pooled in her eyes.

"I wish you had died instead of Dad," I said.

Olivia crumbled, sobbing. Her face turned bright red, her nose ran. She covered her face with her hands, but we could still hear her pathetic cries. Sara stood and handed her a box of tissues, then turned to me. I fought to keep the smile from spreading across my face.

"I can tell you're angry, understandably so. Is there a better way to express yourself, a healthier way?"

"Than telling her the truth? No. She keeps asking me to be honest, so I'm giving her what she wants. It's not my fault she can't handle me telling her she's a terrible mother."

Fresh sobs wracked Olivia's body. I broke her. I actually broke her! I'd never done that before, even when I killed Abigail; she remained strong until the end. Fighting me. Samantha did the same. This woman before me...I was sure I could kill her with only my words.

"Lanie, would you mind waiting in the lobby so I can talk to your mother alone?"

"No problem. I hate these sessions anyway," I said, then stomped out of the room, the smile finally free to spread across my face.

I didn't wait in the lobby. I walked out of the office to the bus stop in front of the building and hopped on the first bus. It headed north, but I didn't care. I'd get directions back to Stafford as soon as I was far enough away from Lanie's sniveling mother.

Getting back to Stafford proved to be a little more difficult, as I had to interact with the bus drivers to figure out how to transfer from bus to bus. It took three different buses to get back to Stafford, but after detailed instructions from the drivers, we were able to disembark the bus directly in front of the high school. From there, I found my way easy enough to get to Mark's. It was dusk, the shadows long as we walked to his house.

Mark's door was open and I could see him sitting on the couch watching television in the sparsely furnished room. Did the living not have anything else better to do? No wonder they were dull and lifeless.

We knocked and he looked up, a sly smile across his face.

"I didn't expect to see you so soon," he said after he opened the door. As we stepped inside, he tried to pull me into a kiss, but I stopped him.

"Sorry, Mark. We don't have time tonight. But we have money," I said.

"Fine, Lanie. Whatever, but this is getting old. What do you need?"

"Twenty of the little pills and four of the marijuana cigarettes, please," I said.

"I think I only have ten pills left. I'll get some more on Friday," he said, walking down the hallway.

"Fine, fine. We'll take what you have," I said.

"What's this 'we' business? Develop a split personality or something?" he hollered.

"Or something," I whispered under my breath.

He sauntered out of his room and across the dingy brown carpet. I looked down at where we stood and noticed clumps of mud in the fibers.

"That's why houses should only have hardwood floors. Disgusting."

"Gee, thanks for the decorating tip," he said, shaking his head.

We handed him the money, he handed us a small baggie. I counted the pills.

"Thanks! We'll be back soon."

"Not that soon, I hope."

"Don't go getting a conscience on *me* now," I said and walked out the door.

As we walked through the dark, I wondered how Olivia had fared after our little appointment. She was asleep when I walked into the dark house; blankets covered her head. She did not acknowledge me. I felt great satisfaction at seeing her curled up and hiding. I won.

The light blinked on the answering machine. There were fourteen messages. I pressed play.

"Olivia—"

Delete.

There were thirteen more for her, and I deleted them all. The last one, the most recent, was for Lanie.

"Lanie, it's Mrs. Morris, from Aspen Care. I just wanted to call and tell you Ms. Valencia passed this morning—"

Delete.

An orange bottle of pills sat on the counter next to the sink. The label said Lithium and had been prescribed by a Dr. Hertz. These were the pills Lanie said her mother had taken previously that turned her into a zombie. I wondered what they would do to Lanie, so I dropped a pill into my pocket.

In the bedroom, it looked as though Olivia had tried to clean the lipstick stains, but they only faded and spread. Exactly like I imagined a bloodstain would look if someone tried to cover it up.

SAMANTHA

I hadn't let the disagreement between Alex and me bother me again. I could forget he thought women who had abortions were murderers as long as I kept pretending nothing was wrong with my body. When Alex realized I couldn't get pregnant, I'd go see my doctor, and I'd be very grateful then for patient confidentiality. People with different beliefs were married all over the world. And they were happy. So I could be happy, too. I loved Alex, with all of my being. Nothing would change how I felt.

The Wednesday before my birthday party, I sat on the porch finishing the trail of insects crawling up our front porch stairs. I created quite the infestation—spiders, ants, centipedes, scorpions. I briefly wondered how difficult it would be to remove them. But, I decided the effect was too cool not to continue with. Besides, I was married to a carpenter. If I really messed anything up, he could help me fix it.

Lanie walked by alone a little after four. A chill crept down my spine. She walked with confidence. Her hair was clean and brushed away from her face. Her shoulders were back and her jeans didn't have holes in the knees. Instead of a T-shirt, she wore a green blouse beneath a light jacket.

"Hi Lanie, you look really good," I said, walking toward the fence.

"I know," she replied. I smiled, not expecting her confidence. "I got tired of looking ratty all the time."

I didn't know what to say. Agree she looked ratty or say she never looked bad? Before I could reply she said, "I think I'd like a friend. Does the offer still stand?"

"Sure. Yeah. I have plans tonight, but why don't you stop by after school tomorrow? I'll get some snacks and we can talk."

"Perfect. I'll see you then," she said and bounded down the sidewalk. Her transformation happened so fast. I wondered what changed.

Tonight, Alex and I made plans to deliver gifts to our friends for the party this weekend. I'd been collecting amethyst and black tourmaline jewelry for them over the weeks. They knew to expect us. Max's parents would join us for the party as well, so he was our first stop since he lived so close. We didn't have to worry about Maggie and Russ, as they already wore theirs.

Max and his parents lived on the same block as Maggie and her family. Maggie said Sandra, Max's mother, brought over a casserole when they moved in. The difference between Sandra and Rosemary, though, was Sandra did not insert herself into Maggie's life in an unwelcome manner.

"Good evening, Sandy and Gary," I said as they opened the door.

"Come in! Come in," Sandy said, pulling me into a hug. "Max is out back, let me get him."

"Howdy," Gary said, reaching out to shake Alex's hand, then mine. He gestured to the living room. "Won't you sit down?"

"Oh, we can't stay long. We just wanted to drop these gifts by." I held out the two boxes wrapped in purple paper with black bows.

"Sandy wants to tell you something. Are you in a terrible hurry?"

I looked at Alex and he shook his head no.

"Okay, but don't get us talking! You know how that goes," I said, laughing.

The Kowalskis' living room was painted a pale peach, with sea green furniture surrounding a wicker coffee table with a glass top. Pictures of Max over the years were everywhere. They even had a picture of him standing in my garden, with my house in the background. It had been taken shortly after we finished the outside. I felt honored to be included in their memories.

Max and Sandy joined us in the living room.

"So, Max has some exciting news he wants to share with you," Sandy said, beaming.

"I'm moving into my own house!" he said and clapped his hands together.

Emotion welled up inside me and I couldn't respond. I felt ecstatic. I stood and went to him to give him a hug while the lump in my throat receded. He stood to greet me. Alex joined us; he shook Max's hand and slapped him on the back. I noticed tears in his eyes as well.

"House? So not an apartment like you talked about before?"

He gave a little nod of certainty. "House."

"Have you noticed the carriage houses with some of the bigger Victorians around the neighborhood?" Gary said.

"I have," I said.

"Well, Max didn't want an apartment because he couldn't have a garden of his own, so we've been keeping watch and we kept asking the neighbors until one opened up. It's about a block away from you, between Madison and Monroe. The owners are having a hard time keeping up as they are getting on in age, so for a reduced rent, Max will help them with their yard."

"Max, that's the best news I've heard in a long time!" I said, giving him another squeeze.

He beamed. "You can come to my house for dinner," he said.

"I think you'll need to have a housewarming dinner. Say when. Alex and I will be there."

"Oh my! What are these cute little boxes?" Sandy said, motioning to the gifts on the glass-top coffee table.

"They aren't nearly as exciting as your news," I said and handed each of them a box.

They unwrapped the boxes and pulled away the cotton batting.

"Oh, Sam. It's beautiful," Sandy said.

"These are to protect us from the demon haunting you, aren't they?" Gary said.

I knew Gary and Sandy were aware of Bartholomew, but he said it so matter-of-fact, like it was no big deal. I shouldn't have been surprised, because Max was their son after all. But it still felt weird to have it seem so normal.

"Yes. They match our theme and we don't want to take any risks."

"Well, Max has beat you to it," Gary said, smiling as he tugged a simple pendant strung with black rope from beneath his shirt. "But I'm happy to wear yours as well."

"We are excited to celebrate with you," Sandy said. "You have a lot to be celebrating this year and I hope your good fortune continues."

"Thank you," I said.

"I have a favor to ask you, Sam and Alex," Max said, going somber.

"Sure, anything," I said.

He looked at his parents and they nodded, smiling.

"The state says I can't take care of myself—they say I need a guardian—and if something were to happen to my parents, I would be appointed one. It would be someone from the state or someone I don't know very well. I would like my parents to put it in their wills, if anything happens to them, you two will be my guardians."

I sat stunned for a moment, unsure of what to say. Why did Max need a guardian?

Alex asked the question, "Wait, Max is perfectly capable of taking care of himself. Why does he need a guardian?"

Sandy and Gary glanced at each other, then Gary said, "We've been put through the ringer over the years. At one point the state wanted to get involved and take Max away from us because they believed Max's autism was caused because Sandy was a 'refrigerator mother.' They said she was incapable of showing love."

"What?!" I said.

Gary held up his hand. "I know, ridiculous. But they were going off of archaic studies. It's gotten better, but if someone happens to get a wild hair up their ass—pardon my French—they could decide Max can't take care of himself. We'd rather pre-empt them by designating you as guardians. Max is perfectly capable. We've made sure he has a checking account, pays bills like rent and utilities, talked finances, emergencies, et cetera. We don't want his rights taken away by someone who would abuse him or take advantage."

"You won't take advantage of me," Max said, interrupting his dad. "I trust you."

"I...I don't know what to say," I said. "This is a huge thing you are trusting us with."

"Of course we'll do it," Alex said. "Should the time come."

"There's a condition. Max loves it here; he's developed a community, he has a routine. His own business. He doesn't want to move. Ever. So you have to promise us you'll stay in Stafford. I know this puts you in a bit of a predicament with that demon, if it's still around."

Max nodded. Alex and I looked at each other. We'd talked about running away, leaving, if Bartholomew was still around. Could we make this commitment to Max?

"Okay," I said. "Max is family to us. We promise and I'll sign whatever it is you need me to."

"Me, too," Alex said.

I felt honored Max trusted us with something that could impact his life so extensively. We said our goodbyes, gave hugs all around, and went on our way to the next three houses on our list—Kimber and Colin, Thea and Tim, and Jillian and Anthony. They were all excited for the party and loved their gifts. Of course, they didn't know the real reason we gave them gifts, we just said the jewelry matched our theme. I hoped they'd wear them.

Alex and I were mostly quiet on the trip. I was lost in my own thoughts, so I felt happy not to have a conversation. I couldn't quite express what I was feeling about everything. At one point Alex said he'd like to ask Max to be the godfather to our children. I simply smiled at him and nodded.

BAR T H O L O M E W

Olivia remained under the blankets Thursday morning; only her toes were uncovered. I watched the lump beneath the blankets rise and fall, so I knew she lived. I wasn't sure how she breathed. The curtains were pulled closed, not letting in the early morning sun. I wondered if she planned to go to work. But I really didn't care enough to ask her.

I went about my morning routine. When I left for school, she remained in the same position. I stared at the mound wondering if I had imagined the blanket moving. Was she really there or did she stuff pillows beneath the blanket? Then she snored and I turned and left the house.

Mom... Lanie thought.

I felt her desolation, her worry. She wanted to go to her, to shake her awake. So I swallowed another half a pill as I walked down the alley. I had to take more and more pills to silence Lanie. I was up to half a tablet every two hours or so. At this rate, ten pills would not last very long. I would have to supplement. Maybe with Lanie's mother's current condition, she wouldn't notice if our eyes were a little glassy, a little bloodshot.

We did very well in school, but it seemed to drag as I felt excited to finally spend quality time with Samantha. I went through the morning distracted, making it difficult to stay focused on the lectures. During English, I shifted in the chair while everyone read a Dickens short story, causing it to squeak. The noise made me jump. Me! Other students turned to look at me and laughed, so I stilled. A flush came over my cheeks. Embarrassment? Was I now feeling embarrassed? No, it couldn't be.

In between classes, I made a detour to the girls' bathroom. After thoroughly washing my hands, I turned to leave. Stephanie stood between me and the doorway. I should have paid more attention, as normally I avoided this restroom—it was too close to her locker. I had been successful in eluding her since Monday.

I cocked my head, squinted my eyes, and sneered at her. She stormed across the tile floor, her arm flew back as she made a fist. I tried to dodge the punch, but it landed on Lanie's cheek. Our hand flew to the dull throb. Lanie's eyes watered.

"I could see *that* word in your eyes and I told you, never use it again! Don't even think it," she screamed, then turned and ran out of the bathroom.

The pain spread across our cheek and up into our eyes. Tears streamed down our face.

I thought back—never in my life had a female struck me. The only person who ever laid their hand on me was my father.

I could not control Lanie's body as the liquid seeped from her eyes. I didn't feel her, so it could not be her emotions I felt. I shook my head, soaked a paper towel in cold water, then hid in the stall. Hopefully the swelling would go down.

As I sat there, contemplating the little brat who hit Lanie, my thoughts drifted toward my date with Sam. Excitement filled my body as I thought about how I would use Lanie to get back into my home. I could gain Sam's trust by sharing some of Lanie's deep dark secrets, like Sam and I had done all those years ago. That's how trust is built. I'd share Lanie's, Sam would share hers and then I'd be back in Sam's good graces. Then what? What did I want?

I thought of sticking Lanie's head in a noose in the third floor loft, like I had done myself. Realization dawned on me then: I wouldn't taste food again, smell. Oh how I yearned to smell the spring time daffodils, lilies, lilacs. Did I want to go back to floating through this world aimlessly and missing out on all the pleasures of living?

I think not.

What would Sam say if she knew I possessed Lanie? She would think me clever, sly. Oh, the look on her face when I revealed myself! I closed my eyes, imagining the look of shock, the fear on Sam's face. She would scream, run from me, fear me again.

Although, maybe I shouldn't tell Sam. Instead, I needed to figure out a way to possess her, get out of this unworthy body. The things I could do to Sam then...

After another bell rang, and the bathroom grew quiet, I checked Lanie's face in the mirror. Her cheek was still pink, but the bright redness had gone away.

Well, this weakling body could certainly do nothing about it. I would have to figure out another way to get back at the half-breed.

We went through the rest of the day watching the clock tick the seconds by without further incident. Stephanie was not in any of our afternoon classes, so I wondered if she had run home, afraid of me.

When the end-of-the-day bell finally rang, we hurried to my house.

Samantha stood on the porch, among fake skeletons, purple feathers and plastic insects. She strung white cotton along the banister. She stretched up to reach the ceiling, elongating her body. She looked so beautiful and lithe. At that moment, I desperately wanted to make love to her again, to feel her silky skin beneath my fingers, to hear her angelic gasps of pleasure as they escaped her lips.

Something happened to the girl's body then and I wasn't sure it felt entirely appropriate. I had to get control of my thoughts.

I smiled and waved as I walked through the gate, I loved that feeling. The feeling of being able to stroll past her guards, the wards supposed to keep me out. Her face lit up when she saw me, there was no awkwardness or discomfort. No fear. Did I want her to be afraid? A little—just enough for her heart to race, for her face to flush.

Samantha invited me inside the foyer. I desperately wanted her to see me, to know who possessed Lanie. Once the time was right. Would she find me ingenious for figuring out a way to get past her barriers?

SAMANTHA

At lunch I called Kimber to get some advice on how to talk to Lanie. I felt ill-equipped. I'd asked Alex the night before and he said, "Just be yourself." He was no help at all.

"Well, remember you are her teacher, so don't go spilling your guts like you do. You gotta keep it professional."

"I don't spill my guts," I replied.

She laughed. "You are the most open person I know—do I need to remind you about dinner last week?"

"I had a few glasses of wine. No wine today."

She laughed again. "You know what I'm talking about. She's a kid, an impressionable kid, who probably wants an adult to tell her how everything she's doing is okay and cool. She wants validation. So, give her validation on positive things."

"I don't want to shame her. I don't want her to feel like I'm accusing her."

"Then don't. And don't go into your past. That will just reinforce that pot is okay, drinking and partying is okay. Promiscuity—"

"Hey! Now who's shaming?" I laughed. Kimber's past wasn't all that different from mine and she damn well knew it.

"Well, no sharing secrets, okay? You certainly don't know what a teenage girl has been up to. Especially one who is struggling with the death of her father and who you know is already smoking pot. Don't go there."

"Shit, Kimber. I'm going to mess this up."

"You won't. Just be yourself, but not yourself. You'll be fine!"

Just like Alex, she was no help at all.

BARTHOLOMEW

We stood in the foyer, I stared up at the stairs and wished I could run my hand along the smooth, polished banister. I wanted to feel the wood beneath my fingers. It had taken me weeks to find the perfect piece of pine, then several more weeks to carve the intricate scrolls and details. It was by far my most proud accomplishment in the house. At least Alex and Sam did that right.

"I'm so glad you came," she said, interrupting my thoughts. "I've been worried about you."

I turned to face her. As I looked at her, I felt conflicted. Loathing. Adoration. If I were to find a solution to this predicament I was in, I had to figure out how I felt about the woman.

"Thank you, Ms. Blaine. But you don't need to worry. I am very capable, even if the adults in my life are incompetent."

"You've grown up so much. I imagine you've had to. I lost both my parents within a few months of each other, but I was older and I had my life together."

Together? Not only a whore, but a lying whore. When she first came to live in my house, she wallowed in self-pity, she was friendless and hid behind false bravado and humor. There was nothing "together" about her. We cocked our head to the side, assessing her. She shifted under our gaze, almost uncomfortably so. Could she feel the truth I knew about her, hiding beneath the flesh of this fifteen-year-old girl?

I dropped my hands and hid both behind my back. As my fingers curled and uncurled, this time I remembered what it felt like to squeeze her throat through the yellow plastic shower curtain. To feel her breath stop. Even now, falsities and betrayal still lived behind her eyes. She learned nothing from her time with me, of how to be honest, of how to be faithful, of how to be loving. I wanted to teach her, using this new innocent body, what it meant to betray me.

She stared at us, waiting for something. For us to speak? She was so sure of herself, so positive she could save a fifteen year-old girl she barely knew, confident she'd get us to talk to her, to open up. Why would we?

"He's coming for you!" Lanie screamed.

We lunged forward and grabbed Sam's arms. Fear flashed in her eyes as she jerked her arms free from our grasp.

Lanie had regained consciousness.

Sam took a step back, her eyes wide with shock, hands up in defensiveness. I clapped a hand over our mouth. I struggled in The Darkness, forcing her soul deeper, trying to contain her, to diminish the little strength she gained. When had I taken a pill last? In my rush to get here, I must have forgotten.

You little devil, I thought, pushing her into the back of our mind. *I won't let you ruin this!*

"Bathroom?" I managed to squeak out and turned away from Sam. Then remembered, Lanie should not know her way around. I swiveled my head, like I was looking for direction.

Sam gestured to the little hallway next to the stairs and we hurried away from her. Once inside with the door locked, we breathed a little slower. Our hands were sweating, itching to squeeze. To hurt. We popped one of the pills into our mouth and swallowed it dry.

The fear in Sam's eyes when we touched her thrilled me. I wanted her to fear me and I wanted to see it, to smell her sweat.

SAMANTHA

The fear I felt around Lanie intensified. I did not want to be alone with her. She seemed odd even before she yelled and grabbed me. She was not the girl who had confronted me about talking to Stephanie. She had a nervousness about her, skittishness. Her eyes were clear and focused, but I could see the muscles in her arms contract even though her hands were hidden behind her back. I felt edgy, unsure what I would say.

Feeling self-conscious about standing so close to the bathroom, I moved to the living room and sat on the couch, facing the foyer. My heart beat quickly. I felt afraid. I changed my mind about sitting in the living room. The front porch felt safer. I moved the pitcher of lemonade, glasses, and plate of cookies to the table between the two rockers. Then laid the feather boa-adorned skeletons in the corner of the porch.

After about ten minutes of waiting for Lanie to return from the bathroom, I started to get worried. Should I go check on her? What if something was really wrong? I stood and started toward the stairs when I heard the bathroom door open. She came out, looking bright eyed.

"Let's sit outside," I said, motioning to the door.

"Sure." She followed me outside.

The hairs on the back of my neck stood up and I instantly regretted walking in front of her. My fear felt irrational. I pushed the fear down and sat in the farthest chair from the door.

I had no idea how to start a conversation with the person sitting next to me. She seemed so strange, so awkward. Her eyes kept shifting back and forth like she heard a conversation inside her head. I couldn't keep eye contact with her.

"I really am glad you extended an invitation to talk," Lanie said after a few moments of silence. "It's been hard without my dad. I miss him so much and my mom—well, she doesn't get it. She's moved on with her life. I saw her kissing another man last week."

"Oh," I said. Unsure how to respond. Of course Lanie's mom wanted to move past her husband's death, to continue living. But I didn't feel I could express that to Lanie. I needed her to trust me. "I heard what happened at school a few weeks ago in history class."

"Yeah, I'm on this weird medication since my dad died and I think it makes me say things, like just now when I said 'he's coming for you.' I don't even know why I said it." She laughed, a weird, forced, high-pitched titter.

"That's odd." I'd never heard of medication making people suddenly shout, but maybe there was something new for depression or something. I poured us both a glass of lemonade for something to do, then put a cookie on a plate and handed it to Lanie. She suddenly looked amused and I was taken aback. I didn't understand why lemonade and sugar cookies were funny.

"My mom and dad used to make vodka and lemonades, but they'd make me a *virgin* lemonade. When I was little I had no idea what it meant."

"Oh!" I said, feeling awkward. What was I thinking, believing I could have a conversation with this girl? This felt very different than teaching six-year-olds.

We crunched our cookies in silence for a few more minutes.

"So, what would you like to discuss with me?" Lanie said.

"I...I wasn't sure exactly. I wanted you to know you aren't alone out there. I can relate to how you are feeling. After my parents died, I kind of went off the rails a bit. It's hard to cope sometimes."

"But only my father died, my mom just gave up and stopped paying attention. She chose to abandon me." She tilted her head and stared at me; her eyes finally stopped moving as they focused on my face.

"I understand why you'd feel like she stopped paying attention, but she was

183

grieving the loss of her husband. I don't know much about their relationship, but I'm sure she loved him. When I saw you all, which admittedly wasn't a lot, you seemed happy."

Lanie never did take her eyes off me, not even when she took a bite of cookie or sip of lemonade. I felt disconcerted for someone so young to look at me like she did, but maybe she was an old soul.

"I suppose we were happy. I have good memories at least. But I don't know how much she loved him. Otherwise, why wouldn't we have gone with him on the trip? Why would she be whoring around with another man?"

Fear crept into my belly again. The hairs on my arm rose. For me, the word *whore* meant Bartholomew; he had been the only person in my recent history to use the word. But that wasn't possible. We'd gone through the house multiple times with Max looking for him. He hadn't been here for weeks.

I heard a truck rumble down the road. *Alex*. I looked at my watch. It said almost five thirty. Moments later his truck pulled into the driveway.

Lanie tensed. "I should be going. Mother will worry if I'm home late."

She stood and left without acknowledging Alex.

"Hey, I didn't mean to interrupt," Alex said, throwing his tool belt over his shoulder and walking across the yard.

"I'm not sure you interrupted anything. I think you rescued me from a very awkward situation. I don't know what I was thinking inviting her over."

"Shower?" he said, waggling his eyebrows. I laughed at what had become his normal greeting when he arrived home.

"No. Not today. I need to meditate or go for a walk or something to clear my head. That was...well, that was awful and terrifying for some reason." A chill went through my body. "I'd like Max to come over to walk through the house with us again. I'll see if he's available tonight. I'm just really creeped out."

Alex helped me carry the dishes into the house, then I put on a jacket.

"I'm going for a walk," I said.

He raised his eyebrows and nodded.

I didn't get far. Rosemary stopped me at the fence, an envelope in her hand.

"Here! This is for you and Alex," she said, shoving it at me. A smile bigger than I'd ever seen on her spread across her face.

"Oh, I can't wait for you to open it, so I'll tell you what it is. It's my wedding invitation! We're having a small gathering at our house on October 20. It would mean the world to us if you came."

I stood there, stunned. Why on earth would these two invite us to their wedding?! They were truly insane!

"Um, okay. Thanks, Rosemary," I said.

"I don't have a lot of friends anymore, just you...well, and Jim. Jim's kids refuse to talk to him since he and I moved in together, so it will be small."

Oh God...

"Okay, I'll talk to Alex and see if we're available."

She hugged me, then scurried back across the street. I stood there, staring at the invitation before turning to walk back inside the house.

"It's time to sell the house, Alex," I shouted after I closed the door and hung up my jacket. "Rosemary said I'm her friend!"

I heard hysterical laughter coming from upstairs.

"We've been invited to their wedding!"

He appeared at the top of the stairs then, partially undressed. "No. We're busy. Definitely busy."

"But Alex, I'm her only goddamn friend!"

He doubled over with more laughter.

"It's not funny. We have to move. Tomorrow."

"*That* makes you want to move? Not a psychotic ghost with an unhealthy obsession for you! Sam, I think you might need help. Serious help."

He turned and walked into the bathroom, leaving me standing at the bottom of the stairs. Dumbfounded.

Shit! Shit, shit, shit.

BARTHOLOMEW

I arrived home to find Olivia in the same position on the couch I'd left her in, except a partial glass of water sat on the floor next to where her head must have been. The curtains were still closed.

Ignoring her, I went to our bedroom. Large patches of carpet were missing from the bedroom floor; the only thing left in the holes were small tufts of pink carpet fluff. It had scuffed hardwood beneath. Well, it was proof Olivia moved. Her guilt must have eaten at her while she wallowed in what I hoped was self-loathing.

I closed the bedroom door, then pulled the small cigarettes and their paraphernalia from inside the box spring and smoked until I felt something, a lightening of my burdens. When I finished, there was nothing left of the cigarette except for what Lanie called a "tiny roach." My stomach grumbled, so I ventured out of the bedroom first to flush the remnant, then to find some dinner.

The phone rang as I came out of the bathroom. I stared at it for a moment, wondering if I should answer it.

"Leave it" came a muffled reply beneath the blankets.

The answering machine clicked on. "Olivia, this is Charles again. I am really worried about you. It's unlike you to not call to let us know you aren't coming in. If you don't call me back in the next few minutes, I'm sending someone over to check on you." Charles hung up.

"What do you want me to do?" I asked the lump.

It sighed. "Call him back. Tell him I'm sick with the flu and I won't be in for a few days."

I didn't know the number, but Lanie should have known.

"Um, I'm, uh, blanking on the number," I said, hoping the lump would believe me.

She rattled off the number and I called her boss.

"Hey, um, this is Lanie. Sorry, I was in the bathroom when you called. Um, my mom is sick. She has the flu. She said to tell you she'll be out for a few days."

"I hate to say I'm relieved she's sick, but I am. I was worried something awful happened," he said. "Thanks for calling."

I hung up.

"Um, are you hungry?" I wasn't sure why I asked. Maybe I was still afraid she'd think I needed to be committed.

No response.

So I cooked boxed macaroni and cheese. While I waited for the noodles to soften, I ate an entire bag of BBQ potato chips and three slices of cheese. I sat at the kitchen table and watched the lump. It did not move. Olivia's condition would simplify my predicament. I wondered how long it would last...

SAMANTHA

I felt nervous. Even though we hadn't seen Bartholomew in weeks, he could still be lurking, biding his time. We took a risk having our friends over, but I wanted to live my life without hiding. The restoration of our home had been complete for several years and it was a shame we hadn't gotten to use it as a gathering place for the people we loved.

Alex's mom agreed to watch the boys for Maggie. Since Daniel had died, she went to social gatherings with her friends and actually went on vacations. It was nice to see her experiencing life.

This was the first celebration we had in the house since our very small wedding, so I may have gone over the top. I went into full decorating mode. Alex and I both even took the day before the party off work. We switched out the white bulbs in the living room with black light bulbs, draped purple Halloween lights from one end of the room to the other, and hung clear glass teardrops from fishing line. We'd moved all the furniture to the back porch and set up two banquet tables covered in purple linens, with black lace overlays. I'd cleaned out the thrift store's selection of mismatched silverware and bought mismatched china plates. One candelabra with dripping candles and crystals on silver trays sat at each table and we'd rented silver cane chairs. Tattered lace curtains hung sporadically from the ceiling. The only open flames came from the candles in the centerpieces and the fireplace, crackling softly. No roaring fire with all those fluttering tatters.

I dressed a few hours before the party, choosing a black floor-length gown with a plunging neckline, long sleeves, and a side slit going almost to my waist. The mask I wore had a purple base, with silver filigree details sweeping and twirling up away from my face. Crystals lined the tops of the eyes. My hair hung down my back in loose curls.

Alex went the opposite with a purple tailored suit, complete with three-button vest, paisley tie, and a silver dress shirt. He wore a delicate laser-cut black wolf mask. His green eyes shone brightly through the mask. It did nothing to disguise the hunger in his face when he saw me. I was sure he saw the exact same expression.

"Wow, Sam," he said. "How long do we have until the guests get here?"

"Not enough time for me to get undressed, then dressed again," I laughed.

He wrapped me in his arms and kissed me.

"Well then there's a preview of what I'll do after they leave," he said, pulling away from me.

He left me breathless.

Clanging pots and pans drifted up the stairs as the caterers finished their preparations. Butterflies danced in my belly as I hoped our guests would be thrilled with our efforts.

Everyone began arriving at seven o'clock, looking splendid. Max and his father wore purple pirate hats and coordinating masks with a black suit, and his mother a wench's costume, something I never thought I would see.

"You don't strike me as the wench type," I whispered as I greeted her with a hug.

"Oh, honey. I'm as wenchy as they come!" she laughed.

Maggie and Russ were decked out completely in purple, from their masks to their shoes. Her gothic dress was tea length, with black lace covering the bodice. Russ had found a velvet suit, complete with a purple pimp hat. A black feather tucked into the band.

"Wow, Sam! You really went all out," Kimber said as she and Colin arrived. Their mouths were agape as they looked around the foyer and living room. We'd put up a black room divider in front of the doorway to the kitchen.

I was delighted with everyone's willingness to participate in the theme. They even wore their jewelry, Colin included—he wore a purple smoking jacket and simple black mask. Granted, he draped the jacket over his chair soon after he arrived and removed the mask, but it was something.

Dinner conversation was lovely and jumbled with so many people talking at the same time. My heart swelled at having our home full of the people we loved at last. Everyone laughed, sipped their wine or witchy cocktails. I hoped the imprints of their happiness would imbed in the walls and stay forever.

"Oh, a grown-up party! Aren't you all splendid looking in your fancy purple clothes and jewels," Lanie said as she walked into our house, uninvited. Silence dropped like a bomb. "I've never crashed one of these, only the keg parties the high schoolers throw. I guess I should have done laundry. This was all I had clean," she said, looking down at her T-shirt and jeans.

I stood quickly and ushered her past the divider and into the kitchen, disrupting the caterers while they washed dishes. *Better the caterers than my guests*, I thought. "This isn't an appropriate time. Is something wrong?"

"No, I just wanted to thank you for the awkward conversation. It really helped," she said as she rolled her glazed eyes.

She was high. My heart sank.

"Look, I'm happy to talk to you, anytime when I don't have company. Tonight isn't a good night."

"I saw gifts. Whose birthday?"

"Mine, but I really should get—"

"Well, happy birthday!" she shouted, interrupting me.

"I should get back to my guests. I'll be home all day tomorrow. Come by, we can sit on the porch and talk."

"Yeah, I think I'm busy tomorrow. Not sure what I'm doing yet, but I'm definitely busy," she said and plopped down at the kitchen table.

"Is everything okay?" Alex asked from the doorway.

"Yes, Lanie needs someone to talk to. I was telling her—"

"The kitchen is really hideous, you know. I feel like I'm in one of the stupid black and white movies my mother watches. Can I have a glass of water?"

I took a deep breath and closed my eyes, trying to find my patience. One of the waitstaff appeared with a glass. "Thank you," I said.

Lanie sipped the water, watching the hubbub of the kitchen.

I pulled the phone book out from the metal rack beneath the phone.

"Hey, whatcha doing?" she asked.

"I don't have time for this tonight. I'm calling your mother."

"Okay! Okay! I can see when I'm unwanted. All you had to do was ask." She stood and stormed out of the house, slamming the door behind her as she went.

"That was odd," Alex said.

"I have no idea what she was thinking. I'll try to talk to her this week. Let's get back to our guests," I said.

The mood had shifted. I felt an awkwardness. No one quite knew what to say to me.

"She was a past student who is having some problems," I said, returning to the table.

Kimber caught my eye and mouthed, "Talk?"

I shook my head.

"Was she high?" Colin asked. "She smelled high."

"I'm not sure," I lied.

"Well, she definitely looked like the druggies I've had to deal with at the high school. No class, with their ripped clothes and heavy eye makeup. I think it's the heavy metal they're all listening to these days."

I rolled my eyes. "Yes, it's the heavy metal music making kids do drugs. So what was the excuse before 1980?"

"It wasn't nearly as bad as it is now," he said.

No one else said a word. Colin and I had gotten into numerous debates about the cause of drug use over the years. We didn't agree on any of it.

The caterer chose that moment to bring out my birthday cake—a Godiva chocolate cake with white and dark chocolate shavings decorating the top. A masquerade mask white chocolate medallion said Happy Birthday, Sam! My guests broke out into song. Lanie's interruption had been pushed to the back of everyone's mind.

BARTHOLOMEW

Since I was unwelcome at Sam's fancy party, I walked to Mark's house. I was running low on pills. It took more and more to keep Lanie in check.

His house was surprisingly quiet for a Saturday night. I knocked on the screen door and he walked out of the kitchen wiping his hands on his pants.

"Hey, Lanie. Back so soon?"

"Yeah, um. I lost some pills. They must have fallen out of my bag," I lied.

"Okay..."

His hesitation made me think he didn't believe me, but the man could *not* be smart enough to know whether we told the truth or not.

"No time to dilly dally. I'd like an ounce of marijuana and twenty of the little pills."

"That seems like a lot."

"Why does it matter to you?"

"I don't know, I suppose it doesn't. I'll see if I have enough."

He walked back to his room and I rolled my eyes. Now he found his conscience?

He's not the brightest apple in the bunch, is he? I thought.

I wondered if he'd always been this way or if the drugs addled his brain. His idiocy could be the reason he did drugs. Would the drugs I took to control Lanie's body damage our brain? I hoped I wouldn't be around long enough to find out. I looked down at the floor and noticed the carpet no longer had chunks of mud adhered to it. Maybe the man cared what Lanie thought.

Mark came back naked. I guess he had gotten tired of my rejections. His naked body with his pecker sticking straight out below his paunch looked hilarious. I burst out laughing, and Lanie joined the laughter in my head. Her laughter caught me off guard for a moment. I hadn't expected her to become conscious yet, but then I realized it had been several hours since I took the last pill. I'd have to fix that soon. Very soon. The nude man who stood in front of me had what I needed. Blush slid up over his neck into his face as I doubled over with laughter. Would his whole body blush? I looked up through the tears in my eyes.

Nope, just the neck up.

What do you see in him? I thought.

I thought he loved me, Lanie replied.

I felt her sadness, her remorse. She should repent for what she's done with him.

He stood, fuming. One hand held up the bag of marijuana and pills, one hand covered his now-flaccid penis. "You want this, stop being a bitch and suck my dick."

My laughter ceased. The situation no longer amused me. The man suddenly seemed violent, intimidating. I was in the body of a young girl who weighed less than a hundred pounds. She had no strength. If he chose to hurt us, he would cause us grievous harm. I froze, afraid of what he would do next.

I've never seen him angry, Lanie thought.

He shook the drugs at us. "What's it going to be?"

I stared defiantly at him, angry at the control he had over me. I was the one in charge, not him! A flash of a memory crossed our mind, of times before when Lanie performed the sexual act.

I will not do this! I thought.

"Fine," he said and turned to walk back to the bedroom.

Do something, Lanie! I said.

She remained quiet, her soul surrounded by The Darkness. Then I felt her joy, her amusement and The Darkness began shrinking away from her Light.

Pulling away from the muscles I now moved. The angrier I became, the more frustrated, the brighter she burned. Our mind was still under the influence of the last quaalude, but for how long? What would happen when the girl regained control?

She would never let go now she knew I possessed her. I had no choice.

"I'm sorry I laughed!" I blurted out. I rushed after him down the narrow hallway, the carpet silencing our steps. I still gripped the money in my hand.

Who's the prostitute now? she thought.

You will pay for this, I replied.

I already am. In so many ways, she thought.

Visions of the people she loved filled my mind. Her mother crumpled and sobbing in Lanie's bedroom, then in Sara's office. The hurt on the faces of the Hatches at Stephanie's party. The memory of Stephanie yelling at us as we walked down the hallway at school, Stephanie punching her. All these memories followed me to the man's room. She would not take control, she would not allow me the decency to do what the man wanted herself. But the images kept bombarding my brain, showing the hurt I caused the people she loved the most.

Once the deed had been completed and we received the drugs I needed, we hurried from the room. Nauseous. It was dark outside. I felt numb with shame at what had transpired. We didn't get very far out his door when I retched; the contents of my stomach splattered across his driveway.

Lanie's laughter bounced around my head, her soul growing brighter and stronger as time passed. The man had not given us any drugs until we did what he wanted and then we ran out as soon as we could. I dry swallowed a pill to shut her up, to prevent her soul from expanding, but after we walked a few more feet I vomited again. The pills would not stay down.

Ready to let go of my body, yet? Lanie asked. *I can do worse.*

So can I, I replied.

I did not allow Lanie to even *think* after what she forced me to do the night before. I didn't sleep; instead I sat and whittled animal figures to keep my mind and my hands busy. I moved the drugs to a hole I dug in the yard, beneath a medium-sized stone. Just in case Lanie somehow regained control. I took half a pill every two hours. I smoked the rolled-up cigarettes, as Olivia certainly was in no condition to notice. I had hoped the lithium pill of Olivia's would do something, but I felt no different after taking it. I grew tired of this body! It did nothing to get me closer to living in my own house. These hands were not strong enough to strangle Samantha. And now...now the situation with Mark was grave. I would not go back to him.

I still did not know if killing the girl would end me. Being confined to Earth felt preferrable to blinking out of existence. Or being sent to purgatory. I didn't believe I belonged in Hell, but God seemed to have given up on me, otherwise why would I be STUCK INSIDE THIS UNWORTHY CHILD?! Maybe the imbecile Sam was friends with could assist me. He sure knew how to purge me from my house. If they knew what was at stake, they would help me. Otherwise, I would kill the girl before I put another...

I hurried to the bathroom where I vomited once again.

Olivia barely moved off the couch over the past several days. Her stench grew riper by the minute. I never saw her eat, but she piled her dishes in the sink for me to deal with. Again, I feared she would lock us up in a facility if I did not behave like a dutiful daughter.

"I'm going out for a walk. Maybe you should think about showering. Your stench is unbearable," I said to the lump that was now Olivia. Then I walked out the door.

It was late on Sunday afternoon. It would have been a lovely day for a stroll—the autumn crisp from the morning had burned away—if only I could stop thinking about the disgusting, vile thing I had been forced to do the night before. I could not shake the memory, no matter how hard I tried.

Sam and Alex sat on the front porch with Max. Perfect.

I opened the gate and walked toward them. Sam stood and waved, a nervous smile on her face.

The idiot looked at me in an odd way. Could he see me through the shell I was in?

"I can take no more," I said, walking up the steps. I stumbled on the top step, but caught myself on the railing.

"Hi, Lanie," the whore said.

"Something's wrong with her," Max hissed.

Sam turned and looked at him, her eyebrows creased at his comment. Then she returned her attention to me, scrutinizing and skeptic. "Are you okay?"

"I really wish you had let me stay and celebrate with you last night. You would have spared me a most unpleasant encounter."

Sam stepped closer to me and her skepticism was replaced with disappointment. "You don't look okay. I should call your mom."

"I'd wait to hear what I have to say before calling her," I said, grabbing her arm. I had the intention of shoving her in ahead of me, but she did not move. Proof this body was thoroughly useless to me.

Instead, I turned and stormed into my house.

The memory of Sam spinning in the foyer greeted me. The hate I felt now surpassed what I felt then. Her betrayals. Her rejections. The hurt and emotional stress she caused me! It was my turn to do the same to her. Now, she had a choice. She would give me what I wanted or she would suffer the consequences.

SAMANTHA

Shocked and confused, I stood staring after Lanie as she disappeared inside my house.

"Let me talk to her alone for a minute. See if I can find out what's going on. She knows me," I said to Alex and Max.

"Something is wrong with her. I need to go home." Max walked past me and out the gate, clearly agitated.

"Go on, I'll give you some time. It's beautiful out anyway," Alex said. He was leaning against the porch railing looking out over our yard and the neighborhood. I gave him a kiss on the cheek, then went inside.

Lanie stomped up the stairs, her hand sliding up the banister. The screen door slammed behind me and she turned. The noise didn't seem to startle her.

"He did a nice job. I'm impressed. It would be lovely to live here again."

"I don't feel comfortable with you walking through my house. Can you come back down here?"

"It isn't your house. It never has been. You've been borrowing it and I'm here to take it back."

What was she talking about? Lanie didn't walk back down the stairs, so I hurried after her. At the top of the stairs she went right as if she knew exactly where to go. Hairs on the back of my neck stood up. Max was right—something felt wrong.

"Lanie, stop. If you don't tell me what's going on right now, I'm calling your mother and if she doesn't answer, I'll call the police."

"And tell them what? The police never stopped me before." Lanie walked to my bed and sat down, running her hands over the satin comforter. "This is different than you had before. It used to be teal. Do you—what was the word you liked to use so much?—*fuck* him here?"

She looked up at me and I knew. Her eyes were clear, focused. Sitting on my bed, she looked totally and completely sober.

"How'd you do it?" I asked Bartholomew.

"How did I do what?" The face smirked. It wasn't Lanie, though. I knew that now. "Oh, you mean how did I acquire a physical body? I honestly don't know. I was minding my own business, hating you as I so often do these days, and she bumped into me. The drugs she takes make everything so easy. It's not so bad, being alive again. But she isn't who I'd prefer."

I stayed close to the door in case I needed to run, even though I wasn't sure my feet would move. Fear coursed through me, paralyzed me. How in God's name was this possible?

It wasn't all that difficult for him, Sam. He just never stopped when he passed through you, remember?

"She's only a little girl, Barty," I whispered.

"Don't call me that! You don't have the right! And you think she's a sweet innocent little girl—if only you knew! If only you *knew* what I know, you wouldn't care if I possessed her. But, I'll make you a deal. I'll trade her for you. I'm not sure exactly how to get out, but maybe your idiot friend Max can figure it out. I'll leave willingly as long as we're here, in this room and as long as you are right here next to me."

"Why would I ever agree to allow you to possess me? You'll kill me as soon as you can."

"No. I don't think I will. I rather like being alive. The food, the smells, the…sensations."

"What have you done?!"

"I didn't do anything. She's been doing things *all* by herself. I don't prefer her methods or choices. I'm sure you'll make a much more pliant host."

"I won't do it. I don't even know how to get you out."

"*I* know how to get out... It won't end well for sweet Lanie."

"She's just a little girl. She hasn't done anything to you."

"Oh, she has! She is a whore and I will *not* suffer her adulterous behavior with her man friend any longer."

I couldn't help it. I laughed. I laughed until tears streamed down my cheeks. It was so very rewarding to know Bartholomew had sex with a man. The sexist, homophobic ghost got what he had coming to him.

"I'll kill her. I swear. It won't be hard. I could make her jump out of the window right now if I wanted," he said. Calmly. Quietly. There was no shouting now. I knew he spoke the truth.

His threat grounded me. I knew what he was capable of and I knew not to trust him. He stood and rushed to the bay window. Panic gripped me. He had no regard for her life. He had no regard for anyone. I needed to buy some time.

"Okay!" I yelled as he climbed onto the window seat and slid the window open. "I'll work on it. It'll take me some time. You'll need to be patient."

"You have a week," he said, moving closer to me. "It's all I can stand. In the meantime, Lanie's mother has become...inept at caring for her daughter. I might be a little more patient if you let me sleep, here, in my room." He motioned to my bedroom.

He stood within a foot of me. If he wanted, he could reach out and touch me. My feet would not move. If I ran, would he chase me? Jump out the window?

I shook my head.

He ran his finger up my arm. "Soft, like the petals of a peony."

I tried to move, tried to step away from him. Fear paralyzed me. He smiled then, contorting Lanie's face into something monstrous.

I smacked his hand away from me and stepped back. I didn't want to hurt Lanie; I knew she was in there. Somewhere. I had to help her.

"You can't stay. Lanie's mother needs to know where she is. I'll call her."

I turned and left him standing in my room.

Alex sat in the living room watching television when I got downstairs.

"Lanie had a fight with her mother."

Should I tell Alex about Bartholomew?

"Why did she come here? Doesn't she have other friends?"

"I'll explain later. I'm going to call her mom."

"So, you just left her upstairs? How well do you know this girl?" He stood and turned off the television, then went up to find Lanie.

"Alex, wait," I said. "Just give me a minute to call her mom and I'll explain."

"It's fine. I can watch a teenager," he said and continued up the stairs. I couldn't just blurt out what was happening. I still worried about Alex judging me.

Bartholomew better behave himself.

Lanie's number was in the phone book, as I hoped it would be. But the phone was busy. I called several times with no success. She couldn't stay here. But I couldn't leave her alone. What if Bartholomew decided he had enough and killed her? Panic filled my throat. She'd have to stay until I got ahold of her mother.

Feet stomped down the stairs. I stepped out of the kitchen to see Alex with his hand on Lanie's upper arm, forcing her down the stairs.

"She was looking through our dresser. How could you leave her alone up there?"

Lanie had a sickening smirk on her face. Or was it Bartholomew? I don't think Lanie was conscious of anything happening to her at the moment.

"You're so strong. Do you handle Sam so rough? In bed?"

"I'll take her home," I said.

As soon as the words were out of my mouth I regretted them. Alone in a car with Bartholomew, or alone walking down the street? Walking seemed to be the safer option, but the terror of what happened last time I was alone with him shook me. I couldn't do it.

But I couldn't put Alex in danger either. Weren't we both in danger if he stayed here?

"You didn't tell him, did you? Still worried he'll think you're crazy?"

I rolled my eyes to the ceiling. Would this devil ever be out of my life?

"Tell me what?"

I stared at them both, not saying anything. What could I say?

"This is sweet. How long have you been married? I would think after all this time you would have trusted him with *all* your dirty little secrets."

"Bartholomew has figured out how to possess people and he's currently in control of Lanie."

Alex dropped Lanie's arm and stared at me, mouth agape, eyes wide in disbelief. Or in judgment? Again. I felt like a fool standing there, waiting for him to respond.

"That's...that's impossible," Alex said.

"Need me to prove it? The first time you defiled Samantha was right there at the top of the stairs."

"But, the crystals. The herbs. He shouldn't be here."

"I know, Alex."

Bartholomew stood with her—his?—arms crossed. This was so weird.

"So, am I staying or am I going? I've missed car rides with you," he said, looking at me.

He enjoyed this, the tormenting. Enjoyed my fear. I had to get my emotions under control, stop allowing them to show.

I looked at Alex.

"I'll drive. You watch her until we get her home," he said.

The smile widened on Lanie's face.

Alex moved his truck, then I slid into the back seat of my Nova next to Lanie. It was the safer place. This way, I could keep an eye on her and make sure Bartholomew didn't make her do anything dangerous.

"Do you know what we need to do to get you out?" Alex asked, glancing in the rear-view mirror.

"I figured you two knew all about it, since you were so successful in removing me from my home."

"We wouldn't have had to if you hadn't tried to kill Samantha. Three different times."

"Oh come on, I was just having a little bit of fun."

Lanie reached over and stroked my cheek. I cringed, then slapped at her hand. The memory of the day she came to my house popped into my head.

"When Lanie came into my house and was acting so strange..."

"I so want to hate you," Lanie whispered. Chills crept up my arms. *Eerie* was the best word to describe hearing her speak, a child, with the soul of a man inside her, the soul of *that* man, who manipulated me, raped me, and terrified me to the point of being a prisoner in my home. Did Bartholomew's spirit in any way change Lanie's appearance or physical make-up? Her voice, was it deeper? Did he change who she was?

"We'll figure out how to get you out," I said.

What I didn't say was we'd figure out a way to get him out, but there was no way in hell I'd give him my body. We needed to find a way to remove him from our lives permanently.

"You don't have to be afraid, Sam. I'll be gentle. Lanie didn't feel a thing. At first."

His words horrified me as though he'd just given me a dire warning about what life would be like if I allowed him to possess my body.

"She only just learned I'm even here," he continued. "It's a simple insertion, me into you. And who knows, you might even find it pleasurable."

"What's he saying, Sam? I can't hear over the tire noise."

"Just hurry, Alex," I said, not taking my eyes off of Bartholomew. How would Alex react if he heard Bartholomew or if he knew what he said?

Bartholomew would be an even more formidable foe now an innocent girl was involved. This was my fault. If I'd have just left the house and left him in peace, none of this would be happening now. I didn't think through the consequences of what would happen if we got him out of the house. Never in my wildest dreams did I think he'd resort to possession. I didn't think he'd hurt anyone who wasn't associated with me.

"This is me," Lanie said, cheery and light, pointing to her house as if this was the most normal thing in the world. A car was in the driveway.

Lanie leaned over and kissed me on my cheek, then climbed out of the car. I watched her bound up to the door.

What the fuck? This was a delightful game to him. We were all here for his entertainment, for his whims. This had to end.

I climbed out of the back seat and stood next to the car for a few minutes. Lanie was inside and I could see her and her mother framed in the living room window. Her mother hugged her, Lanie's arms were limp at her sides. What would Bartholomew do to Lanie's mom? Would he harm her through Lanie or would he let her be?

I had to warn her. She would think I was crazy, but I didn't care. I walked to the door and knocked. A moment later, Alex joined me.

"Are you going to tell her?" he asked.

I nodded.

Olivia opened the door.

"Hi, I'm Samantha Blaine. Lanie was a student helper for my class when she was in sixth grade. Do you have a minute to talk?" I saw Lanie glaring at me over Olivia's shoulder, so I added, "Alone."

"Um, yes, um. Let me grab my jacket."

She closed the door. I looked at Alex and he nodded.

BARTHOLOMEW

Olivia's embrace was not in the least bit welcome. I had expected to return home to her still lying on the couch, buried in blankets. Instead, I was accosted and assaulted.

"I just want you to know, I'm sorry. About everything," she said, pulling away from me to look in my face.

"You're forgiven. Can you just let me be?"

She looked defeated again. "Look, I know I've been down in the dumps this past week. Sometimes things hit me harder than on other days. I think the lithium has started working. I'm unsure how I feel about it, but I felt motivated today."

Well, that much was obvious.

A knock at the door interrupted us. Olivia stepped away from me and opened the door. There stood Sam and Alex. What would they say? *The truth, of course*, but Alex hadn't believed Sam at first, and he knew all about me. Would Olivia believe them? I could not risk it.

"She's a liar," I said as soon as she closed the door to grab her jacket.

"Okay, honey."

"You have to believe me."

"Okay. I'm just going to hear what they have to say. I'll be right back."

"I should be allowed to defend myself. If you trust me, you'll let me hear what they say."

"Fine," she said, reaching for her coat, then pausing. She turned to open the door.

I noticed then, the couch had been stripped of linens. Naked pillows were strewn across the seats. The curtains had been removed from the windows. Knickknacks, books, and framed photographs were stacked in neat piles on the floor. The shelves were dust free.

The house was a wreck. What had Olivia been up to?

There wasn't time to ask, so I smiled as Olivia pushed open the screen door. "Come in."

Sam looked at me, then hesitated. I would never tire of seeing the fear in her eyes.

"I wanted to talk to you alone," she said.

"If you have something to say concerning Lanie, I prefer she is present." Olivia looked around. "We can sit... Well, um." She hurried to remove her pillows from the couch and the linens from the chair. She placed them all on the floor.

"It's okay. I'd rather stand," Sam said. Alex stepped next to her, putting an arm around her.

So chivalrous. Does he still think he can protect her from me?

"So, this is going to sound crazy. But for Lanie's sake, I need you to believe me," Sam said, glancing at me, then quickly looking away. Alex glared at me. I stuck out my tongue.

I couldn't see Olivia's face, but I watched as she crossed her arms. The same defensive pose Lanie took.

"Lanie came to me tonight and said she's possessed by a man named Bartholomew. He's using drugs to control her."

Olivia laughed.

I breathed a sigh of relief.

Lanie shouted in my head, *She's telling the truth, Mom!*

They can't hear you.

I needed a pill.

"I know it's hard to believe, but he's evil. Show her your back, Sam."

Sam twisted her head to look at Alex, her eyes wide, and gave him a little shake.

206

"Show her what he's done to you. What he could do to her daughter."

Oh, this was fun!

I slid a pill out of my pocket, then sat on the couch. They were tiny, easy to slip into my mouth. As I swallowed, Olivia, Mom, turned to look at me and raised her eyebrows. I shrugged.

Yes, Mom, they are the crazy ones.

I didn't have to say a thing, just sit there and look like the innocent daughter she wanted.

"Look..." Sam started.

"You can stop, just stop. This is ridiculous. Lanie's had some problems lately, but..." She laughed again. "That is just so far-fetched. I don't even know what to say."

Olivia walked into the kitchen and came back holding a card.

"Here." She handed it to Sam. "This is the number for a very good psychiatrist. It sounds like you both could benefit from his services. If you've got your husband convinced of a little girl who's possessed, I don't... I don't even know what to say."

I smiled at Sam; the fear returned to her eyes. She took the card and walked out the door.

For the first time since all of this started, I felt proud of Olivia. She redeemed herself. Of course, she was wrong and it might have been wise for her to listen to the whore and the carpenter, but she didn't need to know what I believed.

Olivia locked the door and turned to me, her hands on her hips.

"You're right. I thought she was going to tell me something about you and drugs. I never expected her to come in here with some cockamamie story about you being possessed!" She laughed again and I stood to hug her. Because that's what Lanie would have done.

"I did some cleaning while you were out. I'm sorry about the carpet in your room. I'll call someone tomorrow to get a quote to replace it."

"We can't afford for you to replace it," I said, because it sounded like something Lanie would say.

"I'll have to use our vacation money."

"I don't need carpet," I quickly said. "Just rip it out. I bet the floor underneath is fine."

I couldn't have her finding the missing money, not yet.

"And you don't mind cold floors? Without carpet it will be very chilly in your room."

"Nope, don't mind at all. I can get a rug or something."

I inched my way toward my room, but she moved with me. Why couldn't she have stayed depressed?!

"Okay, well if you're sure. I took tomorrow off, just one more day to recover and to clean. Since you don't have school tomorrow, I bet you and I could rip out the carpet in no time."

I bet we could, I thought.

She looked around the living room and frowned. "I don't know where I'm going to sleep in all this mess."

"I'll help you put it back together," I said quickly.

There was no way she could share Lanie's room with me. She would know then, I rarely slept. I had to remain in control and if Lanie should wake when I wasn't prepared to swallow another pill, she would ruin everything.

"One more thing. The phone was off the hook. I appreciate you not wanting me to be disturbed, but I'd rather listen to it ring. Let whoever it is leave a message and I can decide if I want to call them back. There could have been an emergency."

"Okay, Mom. I won't leave the phone off the hook again."

I paused. She was acting weird. It could be the lithium, but she had said last time it made her feel like a zombie. There was no zombie-like person now.

"Are you okay? I thought the lithium made you feel weird?" I asked, turning back around to face her. Was this new Olivia going to be a problem for me?

"Mhmm. Dr. Hertz thought maybe my dose was too high last time. When I saw him last week, after...well, after you got so upset with me at Sara's office, he put me on a lower dose. He still thinks it's the best option. I'm really trying,"

I nodded. We would have to see what new problems arose.

SAMANTHA

I t was a long shot," Alex said on the ride home.

"I know."

"You tried, though. And we'll figure something out."

I nodded. "Can we just not talk right now? I need to think."

He reached over and squeezed my leg in response.

Since I knew where Bartholomew was, I could at least keep him contained for a short time while he believed we'd help him. Neither one of us had a track record for trust. Bartholomew had betrayed me so many times, I knew I had to be careful and tread lightly. I also knew he would only go along with this scheme until it no longer suited him, then I could only imagine what he'd do.

Monday was a teacher in-service day. I called in sick. We had to figure out what to do about Bartholomew. Alex and I invited Max to spend the day with us, hoping he would have a solution. He said he'd come over after his chores. It wouldn't be as leisurely as other times. Often we'd spend the time outside in the gardens or we'd go hiking in the foothills just west of Denver. Today we'd be figuring out how to perform an exorcism.

I made French toast with strawberry butter and sausage for a late breakfast. It was ready when Max arrived. I wished cooking took my mind off the problems I was dealing with, but all it did was give my mind idle time to wander. Bartholomew terrified me, because I knew he would lose patience quickly and Lanie was in serious danger when he did. I wasn't scared of a teenager, because as long as I was vigilant, she couldn't hurt me.

The clinking of silverware caught my attention. Alex was setting the table. Usually we just pulled utensils out of the drawer as we grabbed our meal, but maybe he needed something to keep his mind busy, too. This wouldn't be easy for him. Not that it would be easy for any of us. I'd battled Bartholomew so many times before, it seemed I would be fighting him until I died.

Max had similar experiences. Since he was a child, Bartholomew tormented him, taunting him from behind the fence. Once we unleashed the monster, Max had to be more vigilant. His family's yard and home had the same protections as ours—juniper, sage, chamomile and lemon balm, as well as purple amethyst and black tourmaline in the corners of the yard. We didn't take any more risks than necessary.

During breakfast, Alex and I relayed the previous night's event. Max didn't seem surprised.

"I could see something was wrong with the girl, she had the same brown aura he did. You were right, Sam, he is too stubborn to leave," Max said. The news didn't have an effect on his appetite, which was good for me as in my distracted state, I made too many pieces of toast.

"I wish I had been wrong. Max, you said an exorcism could get him out. How do we perform one? I don't know anything about exorcisms," I said.

"A priest could do it," Max said.

I hadn't stepped foot in a church with the exception of Brian's funeral since I was a little kid. But if going to church meant getting rid of Bartholomew, I'd do it.

"I'll call Father Thomas. My mom still talks about him. He might be able to help," Alex said, moving away from the table.

He pulled the phone book out, found the number, and dialed. Max and I sat and waited.

"Hello. Hi. Is Father Thomas available?" Alex paused.

"Oh, okay. Well, I am having a bit of a crisis, when will he be back? Two weeks? Okay." He paused for a moment then laughed awkwardly. "Well, maybe you won't think I'm crazy, but there's someone I know who needs an exorcism."

The Possessions of Bartholomew Ka

Alex's face fell. He looked me in the eye and shook his head, then gave the person his name and number, then hung up the phone.

"He's gone on a mission." He shook his head again. "Apparently only certain priests can perform them. He's the only one on the Front Range. He said he'd have Father Thomas call when he returned."

Now what?

BARTHOLOMEW

I was quite surprised to learn I still enjoyed manual labor. Olivia and I spent all of Monday morning moving furniture out of Lanie's room, then we pulled up the carpet and padding, cutting it into sections so it was easier to move. It was disgusting work. Unrecognizable stains seeped clear through to the floor. Black and sticky. Almost like blood.

Once the carpet was out, we went to work on the tack strips, the difficult part. We had to borrow tools from our landlord to pry up the carpet tacks. The wood splintered. The tacks bent. It was tedious.

I was in the process of sweeping the room when the phone rang. Olivia had been filling a mop bucket in the kitchen. I'd scooped up the last of the pieces of wood and dust when she came into the room.

"That was the diner. Two waitresses called in sick. They need me to come in. I told them I could be there by four o'clock. It's one now. Think we can get the room at least ready for you to sleep in by then?"

"Sure. We don't have a sander or anything anyway, so the best we can do is scrub and oil it."

"Well...I don't think I have any wood oil. So I guess I'll see if the Burns have some when I return their tools."

"I'll pretend I'm Cinderella and keep scrubbing then..." I said.

She laughed. "Okay, Cindy, I'll be back in a jiff."

We worked well together. Which was odd, because Lanie hated doing projects with her mother. Hard work didn't bother me. It was Olivia's coddling. The babying. The suddenly-too-agreeable-to-everything-we-said part. I briefly wondered what it would be like to possess Olivia. She was equally broken, so it wouldn't be too difficult. If only I could get out of this current body.

The room was scrubbed, but the Burns said we would have to oil the floors then let them dry and air out the room. So we moved my bed back into the room and decided to oil the floors another day. I suppose I could have told Olivia about the oil requiring time to air out the room. But then she might wonder how Lanie knew...

Olivia left for work and I made myself dinner, then did what other modern-day humans did—turned on the television.

I must have fallen asleep, because I woke when my body moved. We stood, motionless, in the middle of the living room. It was still light outside, so I could not have been sleeping for more than a few minutes.

Lanie had full control. I had forgotten to take a pill. The day had been hectic and I exhausted myself.

Lanie felt confused. Our vision blurred, then cleared. She had no idea what day it was.

"Mom!" she screamed. "Mom!"

No answer. She had snippets of memory seeing her mother lay motionless on the couch. Then she remembered her mother kissing that man, the man who wasn't her dad.

She picked up the phone and dialed.

What are you doing?! I thought. *I'm trying to find a way out. I need more time!*

You're going to kill me.

"Hello."

"Stephanie, I'm in trouble."

The line went dead. She called again.

"Hello."

"Mrs. Hatch, this is Lanie. Can I speak with Stephanie?"

"She doesn't want to talk to you. Don't call here again."

"I'm sorry. I'm scared and I need help. There's a voice—"

"Call your mother, Lanie. We won't help you anymore."

The line went dead again.

No one wants anything to do with you, Lanie. You're a spoiled brat.

"You're lying!" she screamed.

Her brain felt foggy. She could not remember much over the past week while I had been in control.

"Week? I've lost a week?! Why did you say that to Stephanie? She's my best friend!"

Slaves can't be friends! They burn. Or we burn.

Lanie slipped on a pair of shoes. She did not think. She just ran out the door.

You cannot run from me, you stupid girl.

Think, Lanie, think.

Mark would not help her. She remembered asking him for little white pills the night… She laughed at the memory. Anger surged through me at what she made me do. *Where were the drugs? I have to get rid of them.* She turned and went back into the house. She'd throw the drugs out, never touch them again.

She pulled back the box spring lining. The only remnants were the toilet paper roll and dryer sheets.

This time I laughed in her head. *You can't beat me.*

She ran back outside, pulled the door closed behind her, and hurried down the alley. The sun was low on the horizon. The air still felt warm, but not for long. It would be dark soon.

Fifteen minutes later, she stood in the parking lot of the diner.

Where is her car? It's not here. Shit! Maybe it's parked around the corner.

She pressed her face as close to the window as she could get without leaving a smudge. Three waitresses moved about inside the harsh lights, all in light blue identical outfits. They drifted among the booths, carrying trays piled with bloated cheeseburgers, crusted chicken fingers, and limp French fries.

Lanie searched for her mother. There! She caught a glimpse of black hair, hope flamed within her and she started toward the door. The woman turned.

Not her mom.

A sting pierced Lanie's heart. She searched the faces, panicked. Maybe she sat in one of the booths. Maybe she was on the picnic bench.

With him.

Scott.

She started around the back of the building, then froze. Afraid to see if her mom was on the picnic bench. Terrified to see if she wasn't.

She rounded the side of the building, expecting to see her mother in some lurid pose, tangled up with the man between her legs.

The table sat empty, illuminated by a lone floodlight. Lanie stood so long looking at the space, the light blinked out.

No one wants you, Lanie. I'm all you have now.

I don't want you! I want my mom, Stephanie. Anyone but you.

I laughed.

She refused to go inside to have someone say the words, "She's not here." What would she do if she couldn't find her mother? Where else could she go?

I felt Lanie's fear, her utter desolation. It was only a matter of time now...

She waited. Outside and alone. She would not step inside to talk to the waitresses. Last time she'd discovered something she couldn't unsee. Her mom loving someone else, instead of loving her. Customers came and went, smiling families. Content couples. Mothers and sons. Fathers and daughters. The smell of cooking grease drifted out the door every time someone walked through them. Her mother never appeared.

Lanie knew her mother wasn't on break. She simply wasn't there.

A waitress came outside, someone Lanie recognized, but she couldn't remember her name. "Are you waiting for your mom?"

She nodded.

"Honey, she doesn't work here anymore. She quit."

Lanie just stared, unable to speak. A lump formed in her throat. She fought back tears and hurried away from the woman before they spilled down her face.

She lied to you, Lanie. She said the diner needed her tonight. So, if the diner isn't more important than you, what is?

She sat on the dark, gritty curb of an empty parking lot a block away. Her small body shook with the oncoming chill of the October night. She wrapped her arms around herself—not quite a woman's body, but not a child anymore either. Of course her mother found someone else. *I didn't want her anymore, I said I didn't need her.*

She knew then where her mother was. She was with him. And Lanie had no idea where he lived, or even his last name.

She lied to me. She lied because I wasn't good to her. If I'd been good like Ms. Valencia said to be, she wouldn't have left me today. I'm so scared. You're going to kill me, I know it and I'm so afraid to die. Please, let me stay here with her.

You said it, she doesn't want you anymore, I thought.

Her soul shattered. It flickered and dulled.

The Darkness spread through the center of her body, taking me with it. I felt more alive than I did the first day I possessed her. It was then I knew I'd beaten Lanie. Or maybe life had. Either way, it was my gain. She no longer had anyone to fight for her, no one who needed her, no one who wanted her. I won.

I don't want you to win!

She stood, picked up a rock the size of her fist. She turned and saw an office window painted with orange pumpkins. She cocked her hand back.

I laughed. What could she do with a rock?

I can throw it. And keep throwing more. They'll come and take me to jail and I won't be able to get high anymore. And someone will help me.

They'll lock you up in a home. For the insane. Go ahead. I'm sure they have really good drugs there...

Ms. Valencia, Lanie thought. Her soul brightened. She dropped the rock, looked around. The nursing home was only a few blocks away.

Should I tell her she's dead? That the nursing home called and left a callous message? Or see what happens to her soul when she realizes there is no one left on Earth who cares about Lanie Schnell. Will *she* blink out this time?

The sun dipped lower on the horizon. We shivered as we walked to the nursing home, Lanie rubbed our arms wishing she had a jacket. She picked up the pace, almost running to try to keep warm. The exterior lights created shadows on the building.

A man sat at the desk and looked up as we entered. How he heard us was anyone's guess. The doors were silent. Our shoes made no sound.

It was overly warm inside; a gas fireplace glowed in the waiting lounge. A digital clock outside the reception window read 6:20.

"Can I help you?"

We stopped at the desk, where Lanie drummed her fingers excitedly on the counter.

"Um, yeah. I need to see Ms. Valencia. Tell her Lanie's here. I know it's after visiting hours, but I need her help."

He shook his head. "I'm sorry, Ms. Valencia passed away a few days ago. Are you family?"

Lanie shook her head.

The news of her last hope being dead broke her voice, I was sure of it. I laughed and laughed as her soul grew dim once again.

Lanie turned and walked across the silent floor, absent of color, of life, back out into the cold.

She felt numb.

What would you have done if she'd been alive? Tell her you were possessed?

She stopped then. Just outside the light of the building. I felt our face smile and she turned and ran.

Give up already, I yelled.

It took less than five minutes for Lanie to get to my house. Alex's truck was gone. Was Samantha home alone? We hesitated outside the gate for a moment, then we hurried to the porch. The sconce next to the door glowed softly in the dying light.

Lanie pounded on the door, but there was no answer.

"Hello!" she yelled. "Hello! Ms. Blaine!"

She ran around to the back of the house, banged on the door again, tried the handle. It was locked. She collapsed on the porch, shivering from cold. From disappointment. She wrapped her arms around herself, rubbing, shaking. She dropped our head to our knees. Defeated. Her soul was now the size of one of the crabapples we smashed underfoot. The Darkness filled *my* body. Lanie's soul had grown weak from the agony of the past hour. I no longer needed the drugs, but she didn't know that.

I bet it's warm inside, I thought. *If you really think she will listen and she will help, go inside. Wait for her.*

How much could I toy with the girl now, make her do my bidding? Punish her for attempting to take back control.

Are you really the only one left who wants me? she thought.

Of course. I've grown...fond of you. I don't want to hurt you, I simply don't want to possess you anymore. Samantha said she'd help. Go on, break the window. But hurry and be quiet about it.

Lanie looked around the porch. Alex's toolbelt lay next to the couch.

Use the screwdriver and hammer. Just a little tap, though!

She did as I instructed and shattered the bottom corner pane of the window. Then she reached through the opening and unlocked the door.

I stepped into my house. It was just the way I wanted it, empty. And dark. The only light came from the hood of the stove.

I'm all you have left, I said.

Her soul crumpled. *I don't want you...* she thought. *I don't want you to win. There has been nothing you could do to stop me.*

I reached my hand into our pocket, fingered one of the little pills Lanie knew nothing about next to a small hand-carved carnation I'd made especially for Samantha. I didn't swallow the pill, instead I stood.

Wait. What are you doing?

It's my turn now.

219

I ventured through my house, reveling in the peace. In the beauty of its restoration. Lanie continued to cry, and beg me to leave her be, to let her return to her mother. Her incessant whining would be the death of me! I swallowed the pill to shut her up.

I want my mom, she pleaded.

"She doesn't want you!" I yelled aloud, rolling my eyes to the heavens.

I climbed the stairs to my room and lay on the whore's bed. It smelled of lavender.

Hate filled me. I wanted to kill her, crush her throat. But these hands were weak! They would not do!

As I lay there, Lanie's protests dimmed until they stopped completely. I was left in peaceful bliss while I wondered what it would be like to possess Samantha's body as I did this girl, Samantha belonged to me after all. Even if she refused to admit it. What could I make her do? Nothing to cause myself pain, of course, as Lanie's period proved pain was amplified for me. But I could force her to cut Alex, flay him alive, then burn him. Listening to his screams and feeling Samantha's despair would be my ultimate revenge. It would be nothing like my father had done. Alex would be deserving of his fate. Then she would just have me. She would be powerless and have no choice but to surrender to me. I could touch her petal-soft skin anytime I desired, because it would also be my own.

But what if I possessed Alex instead? Then, I could inflict as much pain as I desired, both physically and emotionally, using the love she felt for the carpenter against her. She would not deny me. I could feel the sins of the flesh once again and experience the release. Life would be thrilling again!

I reveled in the possibilities and decided, yes, Alex would be a much better possessee. He would be easier to break than Samantha. After all, I was the cause of his uncle's death and I knew *his* beloved's deepest, darkest secrets. Had she told him yet? Told him about her broken and barren body?

After some time, the urge to urinate came over me and I smiled, remembering the time when Alex marked his territory while Samantha was away. Well,

I didn't actually witness it, but I was sure he'd done it. The thought crossed my mind to pee right there on their pillows. But they would discover what I'd done quickly. I wanted them to live in my stink, to smell me as they made love and wonder why.

Where? I looked around the room. The floors were hardwood, so a puddle would be noticeable. Then I spied a small, round, hand-crocheted rug below the padded window seat.

I moved off the bed, pulled the girl's pants down, and urinated on the seat. It dripped down onto the floor, soaking into the rug. I moved my feet wider to avoid my shoes. I then used one of the velvet pillows propped against the window to wipe between my legs.

I returned downstairs. And waited. I wanted to see the fear on Sam's face again, wanted her to know she would never be free of me.

SAMANTHA

Alex took me to the restaurant where we had our first date for a birthday dinner. We'd talked longer than usual, so it was late by the time we pulled into the driveway. I was exhausted, emotionally and physically, from the weekend. I just wanted to collapse on my bed.

We opened the door and something felt off. We weren't alone.

I flicked on the light. My heart jumped. I screamed. Alex shoved me behind him.

Bartholomew sat on the bottom step in Lanie's body, head cocked to the side. A cruel smile on his lips. Except it wasn't Bartholomew, it was Lanie's teenage voice. Lanie's sweet face. Lanie's young body. Bartholomew's desecration of Lanie devastated me.

"I brought you a gift," he said.

"What the fuck are you doing in our house?!"

"This is MY house!" he roared.

"Call the police," Alex said.

"I wouldn't if I were you."

It was then I saw the steak knife, held to her wrist at first, then he moved it to her neck.

Alex and I froze.

"All I want to know is if you made any progress?" he laughed. "Everyone is so very dramatic tonight! Look," he said, spreading her hand, "let's sit and talk. I want to hear all of your plans. I'm thirsty... Maybe get me something to drink?"

"Get out," Alex replied.

"You grew some balls, as the kids say these days. Did Samantha teach the little man how to stand up for himself?"

Alex took a step toward Lanie, fists clenched. Lanie's eyes glinted as Bartholomew wiggled the knife. Alex stopped mid-step. "If you want us to help you, we have to know how you did it. How you're controlling her. We're working on finding a priest," Alex said.

"No priest!" he screamed, momentarily distracted.

Alex rushed forward, knocking Lanie to the ground. The knife skittered across the wood floor and I kicked it farther into the kitchen, away from us so it could do no harm.

"She's just a kid, Alex!"

He had Lanie pinned to the ground, his fist drawn back. Anger flared in Lanie's eyes.

"She's an innocent kid and she's still in there somewhere!"

He dropped his arm, but still held her in place.

"Call the police, Sam," Alex said again.

"Go ahead. I'll tell them I'm possessing her. They'll lock her up and I'll make sure she never gets out."

"What do you want us to do? We don't know how to get you out. Only a priest—"

"I said NO PRIEST!" he roared.

"You're scared," I said. "Scared they'll send you to Hell for everything you've done."

"I've done no worse than you, Sam. We've both taken a life."

I froze. I felt the blood drain from my face. Suddenly I was lightheaded, dizzy. I needed to sit down. Bartholomew knew what I'd done. I'd told him all those years ago when I thought he and I were friends. When I thought my secret was safe with him.

Alex looked at me, confusion clear in his eyes. Lanie shifted beneath him.

"You haven't told him," Lanie said. The anger in her face at my mention of a priest was now gone. Humor, delight lit up her face, reminding me of the twelve-year old girl I had in my class. Young. Innocent. I had to be careful. Bartholomew could hurt me. And he could hurt her.

"What could you possibly know? You're nothing. You wasted life and now you're pissed because we're living the life you wanted. We love each other. You wish you had a wife as devoted to you as Sam is to me. Instead, your wife was so disgusted with you she found solace in the arms of someone else. Who could blame her? You're repulsive," Alex spat.

"Let me up, you buffoon."

Alex didn't move.

"Well, fair is fair, Samantha. It seems you've shared all my dirty little secrets with Alex. It's only fitting I return the favor."

"Please. Please don't," I said. My plea felt weak. I never imagined he would find a voice and use that voice to betray me.

"Oh Samantha, don't beg. It's unbecoming."

"Don't what, Sam?" Alex looked at me. I didn't return his gaze. I stayed focused on the girl on the floor.

"I'll do anything you want."

"You will anyway, my dear. Or I'll kill the girl. Alex, tsk, tsk, tsk. You're a fool if you think she's devoted to you. After all these years, she must have been lying to you. Otherwise, why would you have stayed? Lean in closer and I'll whisper it in your ear if you like."

Alex continued to stare at me.

Now's the time, Sam. Now's your chance to come clean.

"Alex...I...I can't have kids."

Alex released Lanie and sat down with a thud on the bottom step.

Lanie jumped up, clapped her hands together, and squealed. "Oh this is fun! My turn! She got knocked up at eighteen, had an abortion and the doctor destroyed her uterus. I can't believe after all this time she never told you. You've been together, what, six years? And she never told you?" Lanie laughed a bitter, soul-destroying laugh. It sounded unnatural, fake.

"What's going on, Sam?" Alex asked.

I grabbed Lanie by the arms and shook. Her head flopped back and forth, but Bartholomew continued laughing. "I don't know how you did it, but you need to leave this little girl alone! She's innocent. Lanie, Lanie can you hear me? You need to fight!"

Alex grabbed me, pulling me away from Lanie.

"Lanie! You have to fight him!"

As Alex restrained me, Lanie ran for the door.

"I'll burn it down. I swear to God, I'll burn it," I said through gritted teeth.

He turned. "You wouldn't dare. Not now. Not after all this," Bartholomew said. Raising Lanie's arms, he gestured to the foyer. "What are you going to do, Sam? I only know one way out. So you better find me another one before I become tired of waiting."

He turned and walked out the door. He'd left his gift on the step next to Alex. I picked it up.

A carnation flower delicately carved out of wood, like the one I'd wanted to give to Alex all those years ago. The one I'd had in my hand when he passed through me to hug me.

Oh God, if he did anything to hurt her I'd never forgive myself. I unleashed the devil.

We moved to the darkened living room. Alex wouldn't look at me. I sat in front of him on the floor and tried to put my arms around his legs, but he removed them.

"Alex, I'm sorry, okay? I didn't mean to keep it from you. I meant to tell you so many times, but it just never seemed to be the right time."

"Six years, Sam. You've had six years to tell me what happened. After everything we've been through together, you couldn't tell me this? Do you know how ridiculous you sound? You told me about a ghost, something I couldn't see, couldn't understand, but telling me you are barren was harder?"

"I know! I know, I'm so sorry. I was—"

"What? Embarrassed? Afraid? Chicken shit?"

"No. Yes. I wanted to tell you. But then you said women who have abortions are murderers."

"That was a week ago! What happened to the previous six years?"

A chill went through me and I wrapped my arms around myself. "Would you have wanted to marry me knowing I could never have children? That I aborted the only baby I would ever make?"

He didn't answer and yet he did. I knew he wanted children before we got married, before I said yes. And still, I didn't tell him.

"I'm an asshole, Alex. I know."

"Were you ever going to tell me?"

I just stared at him then, because I made the decision never to tell him.

Alex looked up and for the first time I saw the hurt in his face. I hated knowing I caused his pain.

"I can't believe you'd tell Bartholomew over me. I need to think," he said and walked upstairs. I heard drawers open, a thud on the floor. Then he came back downstairs with a suitcase and walked out our door.

Would this end my marriage? The thought hit me right in the stomach and I couldn't breathe. I wouldn't let it end us.

He was patient and insistent when he needed to be. I could be the same.

I shoved the heavy kitchen bench against the back door and slept on the couch Monday night with a knife under the couch cushion. Two things kept me from sleeping—Lanie and my marriage. When I did dream, Brian was there; his mouth moved, but no words came out. I woke up even more frustrated.

I had no idea where Alex was. I called out sick for the rest of the week, afraid to leave my home. I kept the curtains drawn, the doors locked. I moved all of Alex's tools inside and had the back window boarded up instead of having it replaced in case Bartholomew decided to try to break in again. He could break glass, not plywood.

I called every Catholic church in town, even though Bartholomew said no priest. I didn't know what else to do. They all kept referring me to Father Thomas.

Alex finally called Thursday afternoon. I'd been staring at the wall, trying to figure out what to do. Praying.

"Where are you? Are you okay? I've been fucking worried sick," I said before he could say anything more than "Hello."

"I'm in Glenwood Springs."

"Oh."

"I'm not fine, but I'm here."

"I miss you," I said.

Silence.

"Look, why don't you come up for the weekend? We can talk," he suggested.

"What about Lanie? I can't leave her."

"Find her. Tell her Father Thomas will be back next week."

"Okay. I'll come up for one night. I don't want to leave her any longer." I twisted the phone cord around my finger, looping, unlooping with nervous energy.

"You're always putting other things before our marriage, Sam."

"Don't, Alex. You know that's not true. This is important."

"Fine. One night. I'll be at the Hotel Colorado," he said and hung up.

Shit. Shit. Shit. Shit.

I banged the phone against the cradle, then regretted it when part of the earpiece popped off. I pushed it back together and thankfully heard a dial tone. But it didn't stay put. I went to find the duct tape. He didn't ask me if I was okay, if I was safe. There was no worried tone in his voice.

BARTHOLOMEW

Although Lanie's soul remained engulfed in The Darkness, and I had complete control over my body, I could not abide her whimpering. However, I would not endure any more sexual acts, so I consumed the pills as little as possible. I smoked when Olivia wasn't home. Which was quite frequently. Her absences helped me keep Lanie in check; they proved my point, Olivia cared so very little about her daughter. I never asked Olivia where she went at night, and I didn't care. As long as she left me alone.

Mark called on Wednesday to apologize for his behavior, but said he wouldn't sell me any more pills. Pot only. He invited us to a costume party, so I wondered if maybe I'd find someone else who would supply them for a short while.

Lanie had not attempted to resist me since Monday night.

You are no longer amusing. Where's the fight? I asked her on Friday morning while we were getting ready for school.

There's no point, she thought.

We should hear from Samantha any day now. Her week is coming to a close, I thought.

We sat at the vanity in our bedroom, combing through our hair.

"Tut, tut, looks like hell," I said, repeating the phrase she'd said the first day I possessed her.

There was no reaction.

Her mother came in after she was dressed for work and stood behind us. She pulled our hair away from our face.

"I'm sorry," she whispered. "I've been gone a lot this week. Let's do something tomorrow. I have big news."

Olivia leaned down, pressing her cheek to ours, and wrapped her arms around us. We relaxed and let her hug us. "You know, you are beautiful and you look so much like your father. I love looking at your face." She smiled at us in the mirror, then said, "I'm really proud of you, honey. You've worked so hard these past few weeks to stay sober, to not get in trouble. Your grades are up. You help me around the house. I think the counseling sessions really made a difference."

Tears slid down our cheeks.

You're right, Lanie thought. *I'm a waste.*

"What is going on with you?"

"I'm just really tired," I said.

"Maybe you should stay home today. I think you've earned one of your free days."

"But there's a party at a friend's house tonight I want to go to. Can I still go, if I stay home?"

"I think I could allow that," she said, putting her hand on our head. "How about a spa day tomorrow? We haven't had one since you were little. It would be good for both of us. We'll get the works—massage, pedicures, and manicures. And facials."

I nodded. But I wasn't so sure about a pampering day. It sounded more like torture than relaxation. Olivia stood for a few moments longer, looking at our reflection in the mirror.

"I love you, honey. More than anything in the world."

I love you, Mom, Lanie thought.

I just smiled. A flash of sadness passed through me—Lanie's emotion.

She left for work and called later to say she made the appointments beginning at ten o'clock the next morning, so not to stay out too late. She said she'd be going from the office to the diner after work, so not to plan on her for dinner.

The diner! Ha! The lying whore, I thought.

We spent the day watching television and whittling animals. There were wood shavings all over the couch, stuck to the crocheted blankets. We smoked, then slept, then watched more television.

Once school let out, we went for a walk. We passed my house, where Samantha was buzzing around like one of the bees in her garden. She had two soft-sided bags she flung into the back seat of her Nova. Then she caught sight of us. She walked down the driveway to where we stood on the sidewalk outside of the fence.

"You! You made a real mess. I can't believe you told Alex. Now he's run off and I have to meet him."

"What about our predicament?" I said.

"We don't know what to do besides getting a priest. I called every church in town. The only one who can help will be back next weekend. Please, give us more time."

"I said no priest," I said, glaring at her.

"There's no other way," she said. "I have to go talk to Alex. Please. Please don't hurt her. I'll be back tomorrow. We can talk again then."

Why don't you want a priest? Don't you want help to get out? Lanie thought. I ignored her.

We walked downtown to the diner as I wasn't ready to go home. There was a new Help Wanted sign in the window.

We sat at one of the booths and ordered a strawberry milkshake.

"Hey Lanie," one of the waitresses said as she took our order. "How's your mom? I haven't seen her since she quit last week. We sure do miss her."

"Um, she's good," we said.

"Well tell her I said hi," she said.

We finished our milkshake, left a couple of dollars on the table, and left.

Lanie felt angry again, thinking about her mother lying to her. *Every fucking day. She's probably off with that guy.*

We walked past a department store window where they had costumes on display, so we went inside. Mark had said to come in costume. It took me only a few minutes to decide—a nun. The costume made me laugh. Lanie was definitely no nun. It would be fitting for tonight.

SAMANTHA

On the drive to Glenwood Springs to meet Alex, I felt edgy, panicked. Did he invite me away for the weekend to end it? No, if he wanted a divorce, he wouldn't invite me to a romantic getaway. Of course, he could want to be uninterrupted while he did it. Given what we know about Bartholomew, we could be interrupted at any moment. For two and a half hours, I went over every single scenario while I drove. Of course, I knew it was useless to stress over it. I could do nothing until I heard what Alex had to say. So, I turned up the music loud enough to drown out the voice in my head and sang along.

I arrived at the Hotel Colorado. It looked haunted, so I was glad I wore my crystals. I wouldn't be able to hear any of the spirits if they were around.

Alex booked us a suite—I felt this was a good sign—and the hotel clerk said he waited for me in the bar. I opened the door to the suite and was taken aback. It was complete with a living room with wingback chairs and a view looking over the hot springs. Why didn't he wait here for me? There was much more privacy. The anxiety came back.

I freshened up, adding mascara and lip gloss, and put on his favorite shirt, a flowing dark blue peasant shirt that tied above my breasts. I wore an acid-washed jean skirt and sandals.

Alex was seated in the corner of the bar, away from the crowd. It was an odd little table, with booth seats meeting in the middle of the corner. Half a glass of beer sat in front of him, along with a glass of white wine. I presumed the wine was for me. The beer made me uneasy. As I got close, I could see his face was flushed and his smile was lazy. It was only four o'clock in the afternoon.

Did I really expect he would take the news I'd been keeping a very big secret from him like a champ without any kind of consequences?

"Hey babe," he said, sliding over and patting the seat next to him.

'Babe?' He must be drunk.

"Looks like you've been here for a bit," I said, sitting next to him. I moved close so our legs touched, he didn't move away. Another good sign.

"A bit. I ordered you a glass of chardonnay," he said, then kissed me on the cheek.

I relaxed and took a sip of wine.

"You know, the good thing about the bastard possessing the girl is we know right where he's at. I know he couldn't have followed you, unless you dragged her along. Which I assume you didn't."

"No. I didn't. You're right, at least we know where he is. I don't want to talk about him though, Alex. I want to talk about us."

"He *is* us. There's always been you and him, and then me. I've made room for you in my life, but I also had to make room for him. He rules over us. And it makes me fucking angry." His voice rose at this last part. We were separate from the other guests, but not far enough they didn't notice. They glanced at us briefly, then turned away.

"Alex, do you think we should have this conversation somewhere private? People are staring."

Anger flashed in his eyes, something I rarely saw, and for a moment, I was terrified.

"I'll whisper, so I don't embarrass you. But you don't want to be alone with me right now." He moved closer to me, put an arm around me, and dropped his voice. I could smell the beer on his breath.

"I'm a very angry person, Sam. Do you know that?" he whispered in my ear.

Anyone looking at us would think he was whispering sweet nothings to me. I took another sip of my wine.

"That's *my* big secret. All those times when I left, I had to, or I would have said things I might regret. I might have *done* things I'd regret. I've figured out how to control my anger, but it's there. You can thank my father for that trait."

"Alex, it's okay to get angry. Everyone gets angry,"

"Not like this. Why did you lie to me, Sam? Angels don't lie," he spat.

Angel, the nickname Brian had given me, stung. He scared me. Maybe I was glad we were in the bar and not upstairs alone. I'd never in my life been scared of Alex. He was so patient, so kind, so loving. Angry? I never would have used angry to describe him. It seemed we both had secrets.

"I'm sorry, Alex. I should have told you. I know. I told you I wanted to tell you so many times. I was afraid. Afraid you'd respond, honestly like you are responding now. Afraid you'd call me a murderer. Afraid you would hate me, wouldn't want anything to do with me. I don't think we should be having this conversation now. I think we should wait until you...calm down."

Sober up, I thought.

"I wanted a family with you, Sam."

"Wanted? Past tense?"

"Yeah, past tense. I don't know what I want now." He was quiet for a minute, staring at the doorway I'd entered through. "You know, I really thought I wanted to see you, to talk to you. As soon as you walked through the door, the anger came back. I worried it would. My rational side said *meet her in the bar, you really don't want to hurt her*. The irrational side wanted to be alone with you. But..."

He turned and looked at me. I could see the anger, but I could also see the hurt.

"I love you, Alex. If you need time before we can talk about this, I'll give you time. Just don't walk away, don't leave until we can." My breath hitched, like I'd been crying, but I hadn't. Not yet.

"I got two rooms. The suite for you, in case this conversation went better than I thought, and a smaller room for me. Again, you can thank Sober Alex for being rational."

"I trust you. Let's go upstairs and talk."

"You have a habit of trusting people when you shouldn't," he said.

He had a point, but as angry as Alex got with me, I didn't feel he would hurt me, physically at least. Even if he'd had a few drinks.

"Alex, we've been together for almost six years. I trust you."

"*Now* you do."

"I deserved that. And it wasn't that I didn't trust you. Or maybe it was. But really what I didn't trust was that I was enough for you to love, to not walk away from us if I couldn't give you a family. And to be completely honest, Alex, you were raised Catholic, with pretty traditional beliefs. Your faith says I am a murderer. *You* said I was a murderer."

"I never—"

"In a roundabout way, you did."

"In the six years we've been together, when have I ever gone to church? Just because I was raised Catholic doesn't mean I believe everything the church preaches. I watched my mother stay in an abusive relationship because the Bible said divorce was a sin. She's as devout as they come, and look where her faith got her." He stared out the window into the courtyard for a few minutes, then turned to me and said, "I don't think you are a murderer. I think you are a liar."

His words felt like a knife pierced my lungs; I couldn't breathe. I sat there holding my wine glass, twirling the stem between my fingers. What could I do to change how he felt about me? We'd worked so hard to build trust, to ensure we could be honest. I touted its importance. And he believed every word, trusted me completely. I knew about his first love, while I rarely talked about mine. Alex knew he existed and knew the breakup was ugly, but I never could tell him the truth.

"Let's talk tomorrow morning, when you're sober."

I slid out of the booth then and walked upstairs to my suite. Alone.

BARTHOLOMEW

We walked back to our house to change. But we had plenty of time, so we sat on the couch in the living room and smoked a joint. Right there in the open, where the smell might linger, where Olivia might catch us.

Who fucking cares? Lanie thought.

We pulled the nun costume out of the bag. Then I saw the words sexy nun on the bag. What on God's green earth?

Lanie laughed. She'd show Mark. She'd show everyone. After tonight, no one would ever shun her again.

But why am I so excited to see him? she thought.

Because you are an idiot, I thought.

She laughed. She actually laughed at me. The situation was even more serious than I thought. She should be afraid, not find me amusing.

The dress barely covered our derrière. And it came with stockings with giant holes.

Fishnets, Lanie thought.

We didn't have proper shoes, so she wore her combat boots. We would be the laughingstock of the party.

On the walk to Mark's, Lanie thought back to how she'd ever gotten involved with him. She'd met him at a party and he'd given her a joint to smoke, along with his phone number. Her mom had been busy then, too. Mark kept her company, showed her attention. Made her feel wanted and loved again. One thing led to another. She never told him no.

Is he my boyfriend? Does he see other girls? Does he sleep with other girls?

The memory of the woman she'd seen at his last party came back to her. The one Mark had his arm around. Lanie was sure he slept with her.

The music and people laughing were loud enough for us to hear a block away. When we turned the corner to Mark's house, we saw about twenty people standing around outside in various costumes. It was one heck of a party and it wasn't even nine o'clock yet.

We wound our way through the crowd, only getting a few strange looks. Everyone was older than us. Lanie decided tonight, she was eighteen. I couldn't care less.

Mark sat on the couch, a giant floor-sized bong between his legs. It reminded Lanie of a penis. She laughed. *Boys and their fascination with penises.* He looked up through a cloud of smoke and waved us over. Two women sat to one side of him. *Look at that wannabe poofer.* I assumed she meant the woman with the rats nest of bleach blonde hair, not the one next to her with dyed black hair. They looked up when we approached the couch. The blonde one smiled. She had no front teeth.

Lanie sat on Mark's lap farthest from the woman and whispered in his ear, "I'm eighteen, okay?"

"Of course you are!"

Close up, we could see his bloodshot eyes. The man was higher than a kite on who knew what. He kissed Lanie, which surprised her. And repulsed me. The memory of the last time I was here made me gag.

Then he offered us the bong. We took a small hit, because Lanie worried she'd cough and make a fool of herself. The thing was huge! Smoke filled our lungs and our head felt instantly light. The women sitting next to Mark were doing lines of coke. The blonde woman offered it to us from her pinky.

"I don't know how," Lanie said.

The woman laughed; spit flew out of her mouth. Our stomach turned.

"Watch," she said and held her pinky to her nose and inhaled.

We copied the woman. Our nose burned, making our eyes water. We decided we didn't like the feeling. We continued smoking.

The Darkness hadn't changed since Lanie's breakdown on Monday; it still wrapped around what little of her soul was left.

At some point we realized Mark had left the living room. We sat in a cloud of marijuana smoke. Our head rested on the arm of the couch as we took in the room. We needed to go. I tried to stand. Lanie resisted me. The Darkness became thick, like the time she first had sex with the man. Somehow she still kept control, unlike when we used the quaaludes. She refused to move; instead she watched something in the kitchen. The blonde woman slid her hand up and down Mark's arm in a rather seductive way. He paid her no attention as he was caught up in a conversation with a man to his right. Pangs of jealousy filled Lanie's stomach. The feeling confused her.

A new person sat next to us; they passed us a pipe and Lanie took a hit.

The woman next to Mark whispered in his ear.

Lanie took another hit.

Mark let the woman lead him away from his friend and they disappeared down the hall.

Lanie took another hit.

Something strange happened to our vision. None of the other drugs we tried felt this way. I tried to focus, but couldn't. People morphed into and out of animal shapes. We stood and went down the hall after Mark, squinting to focus on the shifting tunnel in front of us. Stopping outside a door made out of steel bars, we waited and listened. Muffled voices came from behind the door. We couldn't see a handle to turn, only a lock. But we didn't need a key. Lanie pushed on the door and it creaked open. It wasn't as heavy as it looked. Sitting on the bed was Mark; in between his legs was a strange-looking bird with white and yellow feathers. We stared, confused at what we saw. Mark's face changed to a horse and a whinny escaped its lips. The horse wore Mark's shirt, but no pants.

Horror filled Lanie's mind. The bird was eating Mark's dick! Oh my God! We saw blood everywhere. And he just sat there and did nothing! Lanie picked up a book off the dresser and smacked the bird woman upside the head. The book melted. The bird woman shrieked. Horseface Mark whinnied and Lanie ran away from the animal house. Our feet didn't even touch the ground.

We staggered down the sidewalk. Lanie couldn't figure out why the street lights bent down to curtsy at her, but she curtsied back. Until one of them opened its mouth to bite. She ran away from the street lights.

We found my home, dark and inviting. No cars were parked in the driveway. We tried the doors—all locked. Wood covered the back door window, so we could not get in. We shook the doors until they rattled, but they would not budge. *She thinks she can lock me out of my home!*

Hurt filled Lanie's heart—her mother's lies, Mark's rejection, Stephanie's hurt. Revenge filled mine. I was tired of being trapped here! Trapped in a world where fifteen-year-old girls hid from life because it was too miserable to bear, where they wished for death, even though they didn't understand what it meant.

And where was Sam? Off with her lover on a romantic weekend making up instead of trying to help me out of my dilemma.

Lanie still tried to grasp what she saw in the bedroom. The image of the beak wrapped around Mark's penis wouldn't leave her. We collapsed on the grass and pounded our hands against the ground, screaming and beating our fists against life, love, and constant pain.

"Keep it down!" a male voice yelled from across the street, disrupting our angst. It came from Rosemary's house.

We stood and went to the garage. Unlike the house, we found it unlocked. The garage doors scraped open. We threw back the car cover, and the door clicked open. As we slid behind the wheel, I expected to feel the keys jingle against our knee like last time. There was no jingle. I opened the box in front of the passenger seat—nothing. I dropped the flaps above the steering wheel. No keys there either. A small metal box glinted at us from beneath the stereo.

We slid it open and there, connected to a furry foot, was the key. There were no cars in front of us tonight. No obstacles in our way.

It wasn't hard to figure out how to turn on the car. The ignition ground to a start and the Roadmaster rumbled beneath our bottom. Making it go would be more difficult.

I've never driven a car before, Lanie thought.

Me either. It'll be an adventure.

We fumbled around, trying to figure out how to make the thing move. The lights flicked on. We pulled on the lever near the dash, but it wouldn't budge. Then, we pulled the lever toward us and down, the car jerked backward. Reverse. We dropped the lever down a notch, stepped on one of the pedals at our feet and the engine roared. Gas.

What are we doing?

Going for a ride.

We dropped the lever down once more and pressed the gas to the floor. The car lurched forward and we crashed through the decrepit garage doors, splintering wood. We hadn't opened them wide enough for the behemoth car.

The headlights illuminated the wooden gate. I crashed through it and mashed on the gas with one goal in mind—death.

I don't want to die! Lanie screamed, trying to wrest control. Her soul was weak, faint.

However this ends, it ends in death. *I'll be with you, Lanie, and you'll take me to Heaven.*

I don't want to! she screamed inside my head.

The car gained speed, heading straight for Rosemary's rose garden and beyond the garden, Rosemary's darkened living room. The needle on one of the gauges pointed to 50. Was the car heavy enough to penetrate the house?

Our headlights framed a face in the window as we crashed through. Rosemary flew up and over Sam's beloved Roadmaster, her body crashing into the rear windshield. An explosion filled our head. The car slammed into a post and we hit the windshield.

Lanie screamed.

But she didn't die. We were stuck in the broken body. Lanie was unconscious.

I screamed. In frustration and in pain.

The Darkness swelled and grew, then began to retract, withdrawing from the fingers, the toes, the legs. As it did, the pain lessened. Lanie's soul became a tiny pinpoint of light.

Our impact had been slowed just enough by the rose bushes and the front porch to prevent the instant death I wanted. Sirens filled the night, and then blue and red flashing lights. I kept our eyes open so I could see. I needed to watch for her departure so I could go with her.

Men loaded us into an ambulance, kept our heart beating and our lungs breathing. Lanie's light continued to fade. I was on my way out of this body. Out of this horrible existence.

The ambulance pulled to a stop and we were rushed into a brightly lit hospital. I looked down at Lanie's body, broken and bloody. The nun's costume didn't save her from the devil. I could feel the tethers loosen, but still she clung to life.

All you have to do is let go and we can go to Heaven, you stupid girl!

I don't want to go to Heaven, she thought, then said aloud, "I want my mom."

"She'll be here, honey. Hang on."

Her heart hurt. Her head hurt. Her breath caught in her chest; she wanted to cry, but the pain restricted her. Silent tears slid down her bloodied face. The nurse squeezed our hand.

"Hold on, honey. Just a little longer, okay?" the nurse said.

The doctors will save me and I'll go with Mom tomorrow and get manicures and pedicures and everything will be alright.

But I knew something Lanie didn't. Her heart slowed. There was nothing the doctors could do. Lanie would take me with her. I would finally get to go home!

I started praying, knowing I was close. So close!

I believe in God the Father Almighty, maker of heaven and earth. And in Jesus Christ, His only Son, our Lord; Who was conceived by the Holy Spirit, Born of the virgin Mary, Suffered under Pontius Pilate, Was crucified, dead and buried. On the third day, He rose again from the dead. He ascended to heaven, And sits at the right hand of God the Father Almighty; From thence He will come to judge the living and the dead. I believe in the Holy Spirit, The holy universal church, The communion of saints, The forgiveness of sins, The resurrection of the body, And the life everlasting. Amen.

Then I saw them, my guiding angels. Two men. Their appearance surprised me. No wings, no halos, no white robes, no ephemeral image, just average men. One wore green hospital scrubs; the other wore a red flannel, jeans and a... leather toolbelt! God sent His only Son!

My prayers have been answered!

"Dad," Lanie said aloud.

'Dad?'

"*I'm here, my princess. Right here. I won't leave you again,*" he said, moving toward us he stroked our cheek, kissed our crushed and bloodied forehead. Nothing hurt anymore. Our eyes closed, yet still Lanie resisted.

"*I don't want to leave Mom alone.*"

"*She'll never be alone. We'll be there, princess. Always.*"

"*Why are you wearing clothes like the doctors?*" she asked him.

"*Because this is what I wore the day you were born, the happiest day of my life,*" he replied, keeping his arms wrapped around our broken body.

The doctors and nurses buzzed around, pumping on our chest, sticking needles in our arms. They paid no attention to the two beings who now joined us in the emergency room.

Lanie's heart beat one last time. We left our body. Her soul glowed with pure innocence, which astonished me. As we rose, she gazed at me with misery. There was no fear, or anger. Just sorrow. She should be grateful!

She turned away from me, a hand in her father's, and moved into the hallway. Where they stopped as though they waited for something.

I moved to follow, afraid to let them out of my sight for fear they would leave me behind. Jesus blocked my way. Then more figures appeared. I held out my arms to them and dropped to my knees; gratitude filled my soul for the first time since I could remember. My angels had arrived!

Jesus stepped aside and the next three figures who emerged stunned me. I couldn't understand why God would have sent *them*! Doctors and nurses passed through these new arrivals to get to Lanie, still trying to revive her broken body.

The Jensen's stood before me, dressed in fine clothes from their wedding day—he wore a dark gray peacoat, she wore a white floor-length veil, bridal dress, and satin white slippers. I couldn't understand why these tenants from my home now stood before me. They were insignificant, nothings in my life. Rosemary, their daughter, stood next to them, young and vibrant. Her hair was tied back in ponytails and she wore a green poodle skirt, a revolting smile smeared across her smug face. Other faces, bodies appeared. One by one they materialized. Dozens of them obstructed my view of the girl and her father. None I recognized.

And then the crowd parted and she appeared.

My beloved Abigail! Her blonde hair hung loose and flowed down over her shoulders, across her brow. She had truly become an angel in a pale pink dress, a dress I'd never seen before. It allowed more of her neck and shoulders to show than was proper. But I could forgive her, because she came for me! She finally came.

I stood to follow the girl and her father. Jesus barred my way.

"Not you, you son of a bitch."

Jesus would not speak this way! Who *was* this man? I tried to push past him to reach the girl. He would not budge. My angels surrounded me, moving me out of the emergency room, into the corridor in the opposite direction from Lanie. They parted slightly so I could watch Olivia race down the hallway, shrieking for her daughter.

Still the angels shoved me away from the girl.

I saw the girl and her father surround the mother as she collapsed on the floor outside the room, all three of them encased in God's Light. They stayed with her as I was ushered off. The hallway darkened; the only light came from my angels.

"*I told you I would send you to Hell,*" the black-haired man said. "*I'm here to make good on my promise.*"

"*Hell? No, no sir. You are mistaken. These are my angels, to take me to Heaven.*"

Abigail shook her head. "*You know your scripture, Barty. Why would you ever think there would be a place for you?*" she said. "*The Lord preserveth all them that love him: but all the wicked will he destroy—Psalms 145:20.*"

"*No! He sent you to me! He sent my angels to carry me home at last.*"

Abigail shook her head.

"*I prayed!*" I screamed, dropping to my knees once again, my hands clasped together, pleading. Begging for salvation.

Abigail shook her head. If she didn't stop, I would rip it off her neck!

"*She did no such thing,*" Abigail said.

She? She?! No. Absolutely not. God was a man, not a filthy woman.

I lunged for her. Bob Jensen stepped in my path. "*It's judgement day, for you sir,*" he said.

His wife and daughter sneered at me.

"*I don't understand. What have I done?! I've been waiting for God to save me, to show me the way!*"

"*She did. All of us, among so many others, were put in your path to show you love, for you to learn to love. Lanie was the last soul you will ever harm. You had a hundred and thirty seven years, more than those of us you murdered, hurt and betrayed. You squandered it,*" Abigail said.

She stepped aside and a small Black child robed in a pale blue dressing gown moved forward, a face that haunted my memories no matter how hard I repressed it. Andre.

"*We all loved you, you know. All you had to do was love us in return,*" he said.

"*I do not know how!*" I screamed.

244

He lifted his arms and gestured to the souls surrounding me. *"We all showed you."*

Abigail raised her arm, made a fist, then pointed her finger. *"The soul that sinneth, it shall die. The son shall not bear the iniquity of the father, neither shall the father bear the iniquity of the son: the righteousness of the righteous shall be upon him, and the wickedness of the wicked shall be upon him—Ezekiel 18:20."*

"No! No! No! This is not supposed to be the way! I should have redemption!"

They shifted then, circling me, surrounding my soul. I looked down at myself. I saw only The Darkness.

"Please! Please! Make it stop! I repent. I repent!"

"Stop begging, Barty. It's unbecoming," Abigail said, repeating the words I'd said so many times.

At her words, I felt a sharp pain. A hand grasped my soul and ripped. I screamed and twisted to find the culprit.

Rosemary, Bob, and his wife surrounded me; their hands seized pieces of me and yanked. The Darkness clung to their fingertips for a moment before disappearing completely as if it had never existed. *"For destroying our family,"* Bob said.

Jesus stepped before me.

"Please! I beg you, Son of God, show mercy."

A smile crossed his face, then he shifted, his hair turned snow white, his face and body plumped, wrinkles deepened across his face. Not Jesus. Brian. How did I make such a horrendous mistake?!

I recoiled, but did not escape. He reached into the depths of my center, his fingers turning to claws, and he sliced. A thousand times worse than Lanie's period. Wisps of Darkness dissolved; my soul resembled the inside of Lanie's body—except there was an absence, no Light.

"For the pain you caused Sam, for murdering me and taking me away from Alex."

Andre stepped forward with dozens of slaves, all dressed in brightly colored robes—I recognized none of their faces.

"*For knowing what he would do, but befriending me anyway. For not embracing compassion and love in that moment. And for all the innocents you murdered thereafter,*" he said. Hands pulled, tore, slashed. I had no reprieve from the constant torment. They ripped my soul to shreds.

I screamed in agony.

"*For not ever loving anyone but yourself and all the harm you did in the world. Behold, all souls are mine; as the soul of the father, so also the soul of the son is mine: the soul that sinneth, it shall die—Ezekiel 18:4,*" Abigail said, reaching for where my heart should have been.

And then I—

SAMANTHA

I woke the next morning to knocking on my door. Stress dreams haunted me until early morning when I received a visit from Brian, in his typical red flannel. He tried to tell me something, but no words left his mouth. He reached for me and stroked my hair. Love radiated from him. Light spread from his fingers to the top of my head, down to my toes, healing my soul. I slowly came to, overcome with a sense of peace. And immense loss.

The knocking continued. Then I heard Alex's voice. "Sam."

I climbed out of bed. The room was chilly, so I threw on a robe over my pajamas.

Alex stood in the doorway, holding two cups of coffee and a bag. I presumed they were blueberry muffins. "I'm ready to listen," he said.

I turned my back and walked away, sitting in the wingback chair. Alex stood for a moment, looking at me, looking at the couch. He set the bag and one of the coffees on the table, then sat in the middle of the couch.

The distance between us felt immense.

I opened the bag. Yep, blueberry. "One of these is yours, right?" I said, holding up a muffin.

"Not right now. My stomach... They didn't have blueberry downstairs. Only poppyseed and banana nut. I had to go to a shop on Main Street."

Did he want a medal for finding me a blueberry muffin? Anger flashed. I drove over two hours to find a drunk, *angry* Alex and he wants a fucking medal for going six blocks?

If I wanted to save my marriage I would have to figure out how to get through this, how to forgive him. And he would have to find a way to forgive me.

I sipped my coffee and ate in silence, avoiding his gaze.

"Do you want to start?" he said.

"I don't know how, Alex. I can't tell you what happened and see hate in your eyes, your condemnation. You're blaming me one hundred percent for this, but it's not all me. You have some responsibility here, too. You can't let go of your judgement."

"I'm trying, Sam. And I really want to. Please."

He leaned forward. I thought for a moment he would stand, to come near so I didn't feel so alone. He remained sitting.

I sighed. "What do you want to know?"

"Everything."

I brushed the crumbs off my lap onto the floor, then felt guilty and bent down to pick them up. I focused on the soft bits, trying to get each one off the carpet. I knew I was being ridiculous, I was stalling, but the process allowed me to breathe. To think. He wanted to know everything?

I stood and dumped the crumbs in the small trash can in the bedroom and returned to sit in the chair. I avoided looking at Alex.

"Okay," I said, taking a deep breath. "You know I've only ever been in love twice. I've told you this part."

He nodded. I kept his gaze now, I needed to see his reaction, even though I desperately wanted to talk to the wall, or the window or the lamp.

"What I didn't tell you was I got pregnant. We found out before graduation. He was my first everything. We used protection, but you know condoms aren't a hundred percent foolproof. I walked across the stage to get my diploma, six weeks pregnant and unsure of my future. I wasn't ready to have a child. I wanted to go to school. I had planned to be a writer."

"You never told me you wanted to write," he said, sipping his coffee. He kept my gaze, didn't look away. His leg bounced. Good, he was nervous, too.

"It was too close to the truth of what happened. My decision changed because of the abortion. I knew they were illegal, so I didn't know what other choice I had besides becoming a mother. Paul was adamant he didn't want a child. The week after graduation, he asked me to go for a drive with him. Nothing unusual. In the car he told me he'd found a doctor, about three hours away, who would perform an abortion. He told me it was perfectly safe. He said he'd stay with me the whole time, he said he loved me and wanted to have a family with me, but he wasn't ready yet and he knew I had plans. A baby would prevent me from going to college, from having a career. I trusted him and agreed to go.

"I didn't realize he'd meant right then, but we were on our way. I'm not sure he would have given me a choice. I think back and wonder what would I have done, what would he have done, if I had said no, I wanted to keep it. Would he have made up some kind of story claiming it wasn't his? Now, sixteen years later, I know he would have. He was the only one I'd ever slept with up until then.

"We walked into the house—not a clinic, but a house—and there was a 'surgical' room. In actuality it was an oversized pantry with a surgical *table*. There was one lightbulb. I remember because I stared at it above me as it swayed back and forth, trying to breathe through the pain and not scream. The doctor told me not to scream or the neighbors might hear. He gave me some nitrous oxide, but that was all. If you've ever had it at the dentist, you know it doesn't do shit for real pain.

"I'd always had a high tolerance for pain, but the experience was something else altogether. The pain alternated between sharp stabbing pains and a dull throb, coursing through my entire abdomen, like a piece of myself was being amputated. At the time I felt like it was my punishment for ending a life. When he was done, he placed all the tissue—which didn't seem like much—on the cart next to me. 'Remember this, next time,' he said, then left the room. The callousness of the doctor still surprises me. I don't know why he agreed to help me if he was just going to shame me. Paul helped me get dressed, but there was so much blood. I hadn't brought any pads or anything, so he got me some paper towels from the kitchen. The doctor said it was normal to bleed after the procedure.

"We left and the bleeding got worse. I soaked through the paper towels and bled on Paul's car seat. He was pissed. He kept looking over at me, glaring at me. At one point he said something about ruining his car. I started feeling faint, so after about an hour of driving, he dropped me off at the emergency entrance to the hospital and said he'd park the car then be right in. He told me not to give them my real name and put a couple hundred dollars in my hand.

"He never came back. The doctors said my uterus had been torn and one ovary had been severed. I begged them to save my uterus, even though it would scar. They had to remove one damaged ovary. I stayed in the hospital for a week. The doctors said I was lucky and smart to seek medical care. Many women bled out or got severe infections. Some died. I just wouldn't ever have children. I counted myself lucky, even though I was devastated. I did want to be a mother one day..." I paused, took a sip of my coffee, then said, "I didn't tell anyone until I met your uncle. I'd been running from it for ten years, believing if I didn't think about it, or talk about it, I would heal from it. You remember the night you found me on the floor?" I asked Alex.

"I do. It was the first time I was really angry with you. You scared me, because I thought you were dead. When you weren't, I wanted to hit you, to shake you. I'm glad you made me leave, because I don't want to know what I would have done if I had stayed."

"You wanted to hit me?" I shook my head. "I guess it's time for both of us to finally be honest, then."

He nodded.

"Well, I told Bartholomew that night. I was tired of running from it. Tired of closing myself off to happiness and the possibility of a relationship. Joel told me the night before he was in love with me. I felt nothing for him. But you, you were different. I think I loved you from the moment you walked in my door. You took my breath away and I was so nervous. I was afraid of what you'd think of me. I'd never felt that way before. You know, I don't give a shit what anyone thinks about me. But I cared what you thought. I know it was cowardly of me not to tell you, I know it was deceitful and wrong and so many things. But I love you so much, Alex. I was afraid you'd leave me if you knew. I was afraid you wouldn't love me because I was damaged and couldn't give you what you wanted most."

His eyes never left mine, the whole time I spoke. I hoped it was a good sign.

Tears pooled in my eyes, but didn't fall. I wouldn't let them fall. I'd cried too many times over this. I had to forgive myself. My life changed and morphed so much since then. Who knows what I would have missed out on? I know I would have missed out on meeting Brian and Alex and Max and all the friends I now had in Stafford. I wouldn't have helped restore a beautiful old Victorian. I would have most likely been a single mother, struggling to make ends meet.

"I love you, Sam," Alex said, interrupting my thoughts. He stood and moved toward me. Kneeling on the floor in front of me, he placed his hands on my knees and looked up into my face. My heart skipped a beat. I felt nervous, because this was it, right? This was the moment when he and I decided if we could get past this. If we could move on.

"I wish you would have told me sooner," he said, gently squeezing my knees. "I wish you could have trusted me with this. It hurts so damn much that you trusted Bartholomew, but you couldn't trust me. I don't know what it will take for me to trust you again. But as you talked, I felt less angry. So, maybe this is a start."

I leaned forward until our foreheads touched.

"I thought I'd lost you, Alex. You are my world. Know that. You are my whole world. I'm sorry I didn't tell you," I said.

"I'm sorry you didn't feel you could," he replied.

"What do we do now?" I asked.

"Keep talking," he said.

He raised up and kissed me with such tenderness, my heart broke right open and released the fears and tension I'd held inside for so many years. Tears flowed down my cheeks. I opened my eyes to see Alex crying. He pulled me down into his lap and we held each other.

"Alex, I'm worried. We need to go." I shifted away and held his face in my hands so I could look into his eyes. I needed him to know I wasn't running away, I wasn't abandoning us.

"You're right, there's a girl who needs us."

We finished our coffees, then he left to pack. Everything I brought still lay in my suitcase.

I arrived home Saturday afternoon to find police tape across my driveway. The gate and garage doors—or what was left of them anyway—were in splinters. There was an empty place in the garage where my father's car used to be parked. Rosemary's house had a gaping hole with police tape across the front. A note taped to my front door asked me to contact the police department.

Someone had obviously stolen my father's car.

I sat in the rocking chair on the porch and stared at the ruined house across the street. Alex would be home any minute. He got stopped at a light a few miles back. I'd make the call when he sat next to me. I was afraid to go inside, afraid to move off the porch.

My hands throbbed and I realized I was gripping the arms of the rocking chair too tight, cutting off the circulation. The rumble of Alex's truck came up the street; he parked and jumped out, running to the house.

"Oh my God, Sam! What the hell happened?" His hands were on his head, clenched in his hair.

"I don't know. I'm afraid to find out," I said, just as a police car slowed to a stop in front of our house.

Colin climbed out of the car. "Alex, Sam," he said, nodding at each of us as he sauntered up the sidewalk, his hands clasped in front of him instead of on his hips.

"It seems there was some excitement while we were gone," Alex said, trying to be more nonchalant than he actually was.

"Can we go inside?" Colin said.

"Sure, sure."

I was grateful Alex was doing the talking.

Alex unlocked the door and we went inside. "Would you like some water?"

"No, no I'm fine. Thank you, Alex. There's no easy way to say this. The Roadmaster registered to you, Sam, was stolen last night. The perpetrator didn't get far, as you can see." He gestured toward the house across the street, visible through the screen door. "I'm sorry to tell you this—it was your student, the one who came to your party last week, Lanie Schnell."

Please, God, let her be okay.

He stopped talking and stared at me. I knew what he would say next. I dropped to the floor and covered my ears. Alex bent down next to me.

"I'm sorry, Sam. She didn't make it. Rosemary Jensen also died in the crash."

I failed her. I fucking failed her.

"No! No! Don't tell me anymore. Please. I don't want to know," I sobbed.

I shook my head. It was all I could do. The son of a bitch killed her and Rosemary. I didn't stop him.

"We'll have some more questions for you. They need to know if you gave her permission to drive the car."

I shook my head.

"I'm sorry," he said, bending down to put his hand on my shoulder. I looked into his face and saw sincerity. He shared my grief. "Kimber's pretty shaken up about it, too. I'm so sorry."

Colin stood, "Look, I know you know how to find me, but here's my card so you can reach me at the precinct." He handed me his card and I stuck it in my jeans pocket. Then Alex followed him to the door and watched him until he left.

"I thought I'd find a way to get him out," I said. "Oh, God!" I rocked back and forth. "This hurts. This hurts so fucking much! She was just a kid. Her whole life was ahead of her and he took it!"

I threw my head back and screamed into the hollowness of the foyer. It echoed back, swirling around me. I screamed until I had no breath left, until my lungs burned, until my throat ached. I failed her. And I couldn't undo it. My body shook with the grief of that bastard murdering another person I cared about. Alex held me until my screams abated, until silent tears slid down my swollen face.

I looked up through puffy eyes around the foyer where I first heard him speak. I'd felt so much hate coming from him then, I should have known. I should have packed up and left this place—they would have bulldozed it and maybe then he would have moved on. I kept him here. My breath hitched.

"Sam, we can't stay here."

"I know," I whispered. "He won't stop."

"I can let the renters in my house know they'll have to move when their lease is up. We can move there. Until then, we find somewhere else to stay. I don't fucking care where."

"What about this house? What do we do? I can't sell it knowing he's out there and could come back to terrorize the next people."

"We burn it," Alex said.

Burn the house? I'd thought about it before, threatened Bartholomew with it, but now the thought of it created an ache deep in my belly. This was my home. I'd renovated it with my blood and sweat. Bartholomew had taken so much from me. Could I let him take this?

Early the next morning, I dreamt of Lanie. It was the in-between time, when you could remember the sweetness of dreams. Nightmares never came during this time for me; those happened when the night was deepest.

Lanie was surrounded by peace, but I also felt immense sadness. We sat on the schoolyard swings, outside of my classroom, swaying gently. Her father stood beside her. Along with Brian. In his red flannel shirt and jeans. He smiled at me, but I still could not hear him. It was a comfort to know Lanie wasn't alone.

"Tell my mom what happened, even if she doesn't believe you. Please?"

"Why me?" I asked her.

"Because you listen. And you'll remember."

She paused and looked around the playground. "So she'll believe you, tell her to look in the inside pocket of my backpack. There's a locket. I didn't wear it, but I carried it with me. Tell her I love her. I didn't say it enough before."

"I'm so sorry, Lanie. I should have protected you," I said.

"Bartholomew did this," she said. Grief crossed her serene face. "Not you. Let go of him, let go of your guilt."

She looked at Brian for a moment. I watched his lips move, but I heard nothing of what he said. My heart hurt, because I desperately wanted to hear his voice again.

Lanie turned back to me. "Brian wants me to tell you Bartholomew's gone. As long as you let go of him, he'll never hurt you, or anyone else, again." She put her hand on my arm and peace radiated through me.

I woke then, slowly opening my eyes so the feeling of serenity continued to flow through my body, healing the hurts Bartholomew caused. It would take time, I was sure. But now I had time. The sun turned my room orange. The color of hope? Of new beginnings?

I turned and wrapped my body around Alex's, kissing his bare shoulder. He stirred.

"I have to go see Olivia," I whispered.

He shifted and turned onto his back. "Honey, it's early," he said, his voice still heavy with sleep.

"I dreamed about Lanie. Brian was there, too. I need to tell her what happened, so she knows it wasn't Lanie. Brian said Bartholomew is gone."

I looked at the digital clock on the nightstand. It was almost seven o'clock.

"I'll make coffee, then we can go. Eight can't be all that unreasonable an hour, right?"

He sighed, but turned to climb out of bed. "Let me wake up. I'll go with you," he said, resting his head in his hands. "Do you really think he's gone?"

I sat for a moment in the quiet of my home and listened. I felt overwhelming peace, a calmness I hadn't felt in years. I didn't know for sure if Bartholomew was truly gone, but I sure as hell felt *something* different.

Sadness. Guilt. Anger. All flooded through my body since Colin had told us the news. Why did he have to take Lanie with him?

Because I didn't stop him, I thought.

Now I felt guilt over feeling relief, relief at the idea he could finally be gone. But at such a terrible price.

"*Let go of your guilt*," Lanie had said in the dream.

I took several deep, cleansing breaths.

"I hope so," I said, responding to Alex. I tossed the comforter off me. "Do you remember where she lives?" I asked. I hadn't been paying much attention the night we took Lanie home.

"I remember. Well if he's gone, I can stop figuring out how to burn down the house without getting caught." He looked around our bedroom and said, "I do like what we've built here, together."

"It's pretty great."

We dressed, had a cup of coffee each, then Alex drove. The ride was mostly silent. We had a lot to process and like I had done with my parents' death, I wanted to deal with my grief alone. Without talking. At least for now. I didn't know what I felt, what I wanted to say. My hands shook—from nervousness or anger, I wasn't sure. I wished there was a way to confirm what Lanie had said — Bartholomew truly could never hurt us again.

Max.

"Alex, drop me off and go to Max. He needs to know."

"Okay, I'll hurry and then come back for you."

Alex turned down the alley. As we approached, I saw Stephanie standing with her father beneath the crabapple tree, the orange leaves lit up by the morning sun. Her face was buried in her father's chest, his arms wrapped around her while she shook. An image of great sadness. And great comfort.

"You can do this, Sam," Alex said, reaching over to squeeze my hand. "For Lanie."

I stepped out of the car and Stephanie looked up, surprised. Tear imprints streaked down her cheeks below her puffy eyes.

"Is Olivia inside?" I asked.

"She is," Mr. Hatch replied.

"I'm so sorry, Stephanie." Tears filled my eyes. I felt like I should show her strength, resolve that everything would be okay. But I couldn't.

She tucked her head back into her father and sobbed. He pulled her to him, kissing the top of her head. I left them in their embrace and I felt comforted, just a little, that Lanie also had her dad.

The interior door stood open, but the screen door was closed. I could see Olivia and Mrs. Hatch sitting on the couch. Olivia nodded at something she said, but stared off into space. I knocked, startling the two women.

"I'm sorry to interrupt. I know this is a bad time, but could I talk to you? It's very important."

Olivia looked up at me standing in the door and said, "You. You came to me with that ridiculous story."

"I know," I said. "I'm so sorry about Lanie, but I need to talk to you."

"And it was your car she used...to..." She shook her head. "I don't want to talk to you."

"She came to me in a dream this morning. She said to tell you she loves you and she wants me to tell you what happened."

"You're crazy!" she screamed. Tears filled her eyes.

"Look in the inside pocket of her backpack. She said there's a locket. Please."

A hand touched my shoulder and I turned to see Stephanie's dad standing there. "Maybe now's not a good time," he said.

I nodded and walked down the driveway. I heard the screen door creak open, then slam close. Alex wasn't back with the car yet. So I stood there and waited. It was cold. I could smell snow in the air. Would we get our first snowfall?

Stephanie sat propped against the fence, her head on her knees. I felt awkward; I knew I didn't belong there. My grief would never match Stephanie's, or her parents. Certainly not Lanie's mother's. I felt helpless. And responsible.

Something occurred to me then. Stephanie probably knew a whole lot about Lanie, especially who she got her pot from.

"Stephanie. What was the name of her drug dealer?" I said. Maybe Colin could check into the guy. Hope bloomed as a leaf flitted to the ground like a bird's feather. I stuck my hand in my jeans pocket and found Colin's card.

She looked up at me, her face red and swollen. "Mark. I know where he lives," she said.

"This is the officer helping to investigate what happened. He's Mrs. Jones' husband," I said, handing Stephanie the card. She took it and tucked it into her coat pocket.

"Okay," she said, then we slipped back into silence. A moment later, she went inside the house.

A few minutes later I heard the screen door open. I turned to see Olivia, her face red and puffy, holding a silver locket in her hand.

"Come inside," she said.

Stephanie, her mother and father sat on the couch. The only other place to sit was the overstuffed chair. I stood near the door, my arms limp at my side. Helpless.

"It's the locket I gave Lanie for her fifteenth birthday so she could put a picture of her and Stephanie inside it," she said as she handed it to me. The outside said Best Friends with two intertwined hearts. Inside were two pictures, one of Stephanie, the other of Olivia.

"Tell me what happened to my daughter." She choked on the words.

Olivia did not sit; she wrapped her arms around herself. I told her what I believed to have happened starting with Stephanie and Lanie coming into my house and telling her what Bartholomew had hinted at, given me pieces of.

Olivia glanced over at the table. There were dozens of carved animals and flowers strewn across the surface. I moved then, without seeming to realize, and went to the table. The carvings were detailed with little eyes, perfect noses.

The carnation he'd give me for my birthday.

"Bartholomew carved these. He was a woodworker when he was alive. He built the house I live in." I picked up a miniature fox with a bushy tail, rubbing my finger over the texture. I set it down and returned to the living room.

"I know this doesn't change anything. But you have to know none of this was your daughter's fault. She wasn't cruel."

Olivia stared at the wall. I couldn't tell if she believed me. I knew it was ridiculous, so unbelievable.

"On Monday, Lanie called the house," Mrs. Hatch said. "She'd been so mean to Stephanie. I was protecting my daughter. I didn't know." She paused as her breath hitched. "I...didn't know. But she said something before I told her to talk to you, she said, 'There's a voice.'"

Olivia closed her eyes. Tears slipped down past her dark eyelashes.

"I was in class that night," she whispered. "I didn't tell Lanie I'd gone back to school to get my Real Estate license. I didn't want her to get her hopes up. She hated this house. I wanted to give her something better."

"In the dream last night, she wasn't alone—her father stood by her. She's not alone."

Olivia fell to her knees, wrapped her arms around herself. Her voice was muffled, quiet. "These past few years...all she wanted was her father. I couldn't do anything right. I couldn't help her. I couldn't save my baby girl."

She hammered the floor. A scream burst from her and I swore it carried the pain and heartache only a grieving mother could experience. I went to her then, needing to provide comfort, solace. I held her and Mrs. Hatch joined me. One friend, one stranger. Forever linked by a devil.

"Is he gone? Is the son of a bitch who took my daughter from me gone?" She looked up, pleading with her eyes.

"I...I think so," I said.

She dropped her head to the carpet.

"She loves you," I said. "And she's at peace, but she's sad she's not here with you."

"How am I going to live without her? It hurts. It hurts so goddamn much, right here." She pounded on her chest. I wished I could take away her pain, comfort her more than this.

A knock on the door interrupted us. I looked up to see Alex and Max.

"Do something for me?" Olivia said, grabbing my arm. "Take those disgusting things off my table. Burn them. Please."

She turned away from me then. I motioned for Alex and Max to come in so they could help me carry the figures.

"I'm sorry for your loss, Mrs. Schnell," Alex said.

"She's not gone," Max said.

Olivia snapped her head up, hope, then anger rippled across her face. "What?" she said.

"She's right there, next to you. With your husband. They won't be here forever, but they're here now."

Olivia looked around, confused and hurt.

"Why are you doing this to me?" she screamed.

Max didn't bat an eye at the harshness in her words; his face remained kind, like always.

"It's okay to be angry. Harry and Lanie will stay with you until it subsides. Lanie said to tell you she wishes you and her could have gone for a spa day, but she hopes you'll go with Natalie and Stephanie," he said.

Olivia looked at Natalie, confused, then asked, "I don't understand. Do you know each other?" Natalie shook her head and lifted her shoulders.

"I'm sorry you are hurting," Max continued. "The evil man is gone now, though. Lanie did that. Because of her, he can't ever harm anyone else."

"No one matters but my daughter," she said. But she said it with much less fury.

Max nodded, then stepped outside.

"If you need anything, even just someone to talk to, let me know," I said, then Alex and I followed Max.

I hoped he had been able to give Olivia some peace, some solace knowing her daughter was still with her, even though she couldn't see or feel or hear her.

"That was a kind thing you did, Max," Alex said as we walked down the driveway.

Max shrugged. "It was the truth."

I climbed into the front seat of the car; Max sat behind me. He put his hand on my shoulder and it stayed there during the entire drive home. I reached up and held on, grateful for my friend. Alex said Max had insisted on coming. Brian and Lanie had also made a visit to him, just not in his dreams.

"How often does Brian visit you, Max?" I asked as houses blurred past us.

"Only today. He's at peace. Lanie will be soon, but she'll stick around a little while longer. I hope she comes to visit me sometimes. She's nice. Can I come over?"

"Sure. We should celebrate," Alex said.

I didn't respond, but celebrating was not what I had in mind. Honoring Lanie in some way felt truer. I didn't know her well enough to know how to do so appropriately. And all at once I was sad again, because I didn't know her. Somehow I felt like she saved my life, Alex's life and I didn't even know her.

I wasn't sure what tomorrow would look like, what challenges life would throw at me, whether Alex and I would be able to forgive, to move on. But Lanie made my future possible. She gave me a future without fear, without imprisonment. A future without Bartholomew.

The Possessions of Bartholomew Ka

THE BEGINNING

AUTHOR'S NOTE

Depression is a lonely disease, whether you are an adult or a teenager. Please know, if you are struggling, tomorrow WILL be better. I speak from experience. If you are having thoughts of suicide or self-harm, please reach out to a friend, family member or call the Suicide Hotline 988. There is always someone willing to help and you are NOT alone.

The Possessions of Bartholomew Ka

ACKNOWLEDGMENTS

They say it takes a village to raise a child, well as the mother of three young men, I can say the same is true for writing a novel. I could not have done this without the help and encouragement of so many people. First, a huge thank you to my husband, Steve - my beta reader, my biggest fan, the person who believed in me most, who supported me during the many breakdowns and breakthroughs of this book. I could not have done this without you.

Jay "MORE!" Barry, Brandy Mustoe, Felicia Sabartinelli, and Marne Kirstatter you are my writing tribe and you all make me a better writer. A special thank you to my editor, Kristen Hamilton, who kept telling me to "give yourself more credit." – the words are as flawless as they can get because of your diligent work. Thank you to Victoria Wolf who made the inside and outside beautiful. Thank you to my personal librarian, Leah Morris for helping me with research, teaching me how libraries work and for just being awesome! Thank you to my beta readers – Teresa Daly, Misti Sanders, Lara Nance, and Brennan McGee for reading the "shitty first draft" and giving me your honest feedback. Thank you to Clémie Bouton for letting me use the name of your dream restaurant in my novel. I thanked my sensitivity readers at the beginning, but I'll say it again – THANK YOU to Veronica Calisto, Mariah Evans, Merrily Talbott, Kelsey Kuehn, Carter Keegan, and Moosey.

I have the best family in the whole world (just ask them!), they support me and love me – even though I have ugly days. Without my son, Tristen, telling me exactly what I was doing wrong, then explaining exactly how to correct it, the transitions between Lanie's thoughts and Bartholomew's thoughts would have been a jumbled mess! My son, Chris, did another incredible, albeit terrifying, job on the *hand drawn* cover art. I am grateful for my son Zack and my DIL, Chelsea for supporting me. Mom and Dad continue to encourage me to follow my dreams and show up to every book signing they can, even though they are the first to get copies of my book.

Without all my family, friends and readers who believed in me, The Possessions would not have happened. I have so much gratitude for my North Fork community who were so excited for this second installment that they stopped me in the grocery store or on the street to ask about it.

You all kept me writing, kept me living. Remember that always.

ABOUT THE AUTHOR

To get this question out of the way so we can be friends - yes, Sunshine Knight is my real name and I love that I'm an oxymoron. I thank my parents now...cursed them when I was little. Anne Rice and Stephen King are huge influences, as well as so many others. I have a degree in Creative Writing from Colorado Mesa University and have  taken dozens of continuous writing education classes over the years.

I live in a small, rural town on the Western Slope of Colorado with my amazing husband, (whose only flaw is he thinks he's The Brain and I'm Pinky) and our three psychotic cats. You know the types - the ones you aren't sure whether they'll smother you while you sleep? I'm talking cats, not husbands... When I'm not writing, I spend time reading different genres of fiction and non-fiction, camping in the solitude of the Grand Mesa and West Elk mountains, tending to my numerous flower, vegetable and herb gardens - some years with success, others not so much. And most important, spending precious time with my three sons, daughter in law, grandson and family and friends.

Made in the USA
Middletown, DE
04 April 2023

27648130R00165